the
species crown

the species crown

a novella and stories

Press 53
Lewisville, North Carolina

Press 53
Suite 202
6610 Shallowford Road
Lewisville, NC 27023

First Edition

Cover design by Curtis Smith & Kevin Watson
Cover art by Michele & Curtis Smith

Grateful acknowledgment is made to the following
publications in which these stories first appeared:

"Murder" *CutBank 60*, Fall 2003 (Best American Mystery Stories
Distinguished Stories List)
"My Totally Awesome Funeral" *Hobart*, Issue 6, Summer 2006
(Pushcart Prize nominee)
"Vacation in Ten Parts" *American Literary Review*, Volume XIV,
Number 1, Spring 2004
"Three Teeth" *West Branch*, Number 53, Fall 2003
"The Real, True-Life Story of Godzilla!" *Greensboro Review*,
Number 71, Spring 2002
"The Cuckold" *Parting Gifts*, Volume 20, Number 1, January 2007
"Killer" *West Branch*, Number 53, Fall 2003
"The Baby Cries" *Night Train*, Issue III, Fall 2004 (Pushcart Prize
nominee)
"Beneath the Net" *Night Train*, Issue VII, 2007
"Professor Asher's Magnificent Party Hat" *South Dakota Review*,
Winter 2002
"Amelia Imagines Herself in Terms of a Circle" *Hobart*, Issue 7,
Spring 2007

Printed on acid-free paper

ISBN 978-0-9793049-0-3

To the families kind enough to
count me as one of their own

I do not know what I may appear to the world, but to myself I seem to have been only like a boy playing on the seashore, and diverting myself in now and then finding a smoother pebble or a prettier shell than ordinary, whilst the great ocean of truth lay undiscovered before me.

—Sir Isaac Newton, shortly before his death

contents

murder

● ● ● you notice the forms far up the road, a pickup truck on the shoulder, hazards blinking, the exhaust coughing dirty clouds, and the fields on either side of you ripple with snowy, wind-sculpted dunes, and the morning sun, swelled and heavy, shines brilliantly on the white expanse, and you squint against the glare and stab your cigarette into an ashtray already brimming with crumpled butts, then you cough and cough and cough, deep, dredging spasms that end when you spit blood into your waiting handkerchief...

A two-foot length of galvanized pipe. When you were done, there were stringy blond hairs stuck to the metal. Pink strips of flesh embedded in the grooved threads.

... wipe the blood from your lips and stuff the handkerchief back into your pocket, and your vision isn't what it used to be (the letters at the bottom half of your ophthalmologist's chart squirm like minnows in muddy water), and there are no other cars on the road, the cows penned up in the distant barns, a barren vista populated by just you, the blurry figures behind the idling pickup, and a knot of circling crows, and you crack your window

11

and the numbing air whistles in your ear—closer now—and the twitching minnows arrange themselves into a strange focus, a man and a boy struggling to hoist a weighted tarp onto the pickup's open gate—closer—the two of them wearing hats and gloves, stained winter jackets, and over their mouths and noses, they've tied bandanas whose triangled ends twitter in the breeze, and as you pass, you spot the stiff-limbed doe peeking from the tarp's covering, and in a speed-blurred glimpse, you see the other carcasses lining the truck's bed, a snout-speckled heap of rigid paws and hooves...

Stutterers shouldn't tell jokes, but Gill did, and his hiccupping rhythms swelled as he neared his soon-to-be butchered punch lines. "Be-be-because she's my sis-sis-sis-sister!" At the bar, you'd seen more than one man bail out in mid-joke, poor Gill abandoned in a socially mortifying freefall, his stutter left to fizzle itself out in the vacated, smoky space. But you always stuck out his jokes, even the long ones with endings you already knew. Maybe you were a sucker; maybe you were something else, but there you'd be, half-listening, then not listening at all, your eyes drawn to the way his uneasy hands bothered with his cigarette, a toothpick, the collar-smothering mane of his sandy mullet. You met Gill at the Wednesday night dart league ("Con-con-concentrate, Gill!" the opposing team would chide when he stepped to the line in a tight game), and in the dark alley behind the bar, he'd pop his trunk and glance fretfully about as you and the other players surveyed the still-boxed electronics (or shoes, power tools, sewing machines...) he offered for half of what the department stores charged. Once, you bought a winter coat for your daughter; another time, a bracelet for your wife—but most nights you said no, thanks anyway, and then felt like a sucker every time you opened your wallet at the mall.

… study the dwindling scene in your rearview, and you've heard the local department of transportation pays by the pound for roadkill, but since you've never known anyone who's actually bothered with the stench and mess, you'd assumed the story was bullshit (after all, you know men who've done seriously fucked-up things for money—the monthly plasma sellers, the ones who pen bad checks on their invalid mothers' accounts, the mail frauders and welfare scammers), and far behind you, the pickup, its hazards still blinking, lurches onto the road…

The first time Gill brought up the loading docks where you worked you laughed off his daydreamer's math of how much the two of you could make on a skid of Levis or a crate of Lucky Strikes. To you, these things were simply boxes in a day filled with boxes, transient burdens waiting to be piled onto the next eighteen-wheeler, but when you received a mistyped invoice for spools of copper wiring, you called Gill. In the dark of an early December night, your only company the warehouse rats and the lone security guard drunk again in the heated office, you and Gill wrestled the uncounted spools into a panel truck. Gill stammered excitedly about your coming windfall as you drove through town, his bubble-snapping wad of gum exacerbating his stutter, his gloved hands attacking the truck's vibrating gearshift with a spastic rhythm that had you stalling at every stop sign. Your thoughts drifted back to your wife and daughter asleep in your tiny apartment, and you wished you were with them, dreaming this predawn scene of empty streets and blinking traffic lights. The heavy spools rolled with each turn, and you feared the truck was one steering-wheel jerk away from tipping over, your dream crumbling into a nightmare of bloody police strobes, questions asked, nonexistent papers requested. With morning's first purplish hint breaking over the hills, you dropped the spools at a deserted construction site across the river, your getaway delayed when you lost a boot in the ankle-deep mud.

...near the river, the pastures give way to steep wooded hills, and the sun flinches behind the ridge's skeletal branches, the valleys shadowed and the road spotted with black ice, and you check your watch and figure you should reach the hospital in twenty minutes, a trip made because your daughter has just given birth to a seven-pound boy, your first grandchild, and she called last night from the delivery room, her voice fatigued and ecstatic, and asked if you'd like to visit this morning, a timetable you suspect has been arranged to keep you from crossing paths with your ex-wife, and you say, "Sure, honey, I'll be there," hanging up before asking the baby's name, and alone in your trailer, the windows' plastic coverings twitching with the night's frigid gusts, the air polluted by cigarette smoke and the kerosene heater's gassy stink, you swallowed some pills and drank until you passed out...

With your two thousand split, you covered three months of rent and car payments, and then used the rest to splurge on Christmas gifts. For days, you discovered curls of ribbon between the sofa cushions, crinkled tissue paper wads beneath the tables and chairs. New Year's Eve, the tree lights glimmering in a nearly emptied bottle of French wine, your wife asleep with her head on your lap and the floor strewn with haphazard piles of unwrapped gifts, you silently congratulated yourself. This, you thought with a smile, must be how lottery winners felt, the flipside of life's bad breaks and unanswered prayers. The outgoing invoice numbers were never questioned, and as winter wore on, you'd chat with Gill at Wednesday night's dart league. Gill had gotten into coke, his scraggly mustache often powdered white, his stutter chemically agitated into a spit-producing, percolating labor. Some nights you'd snort a line or two with him off the condom machine in the bar's mildewed bathroom, but when he got around to asking about the latest shipments at the docks, you quickly changed the subject back to hunting and darts.

...you light another cigarette, four drags before your cough returns, and when you finally stop and wipe the tears from your eyes, you spot a dead dog on the shoulder, a big dog, a retriever or a setter, its matted fur bristling in the breeze, a sunshine glint on the collar's metal tag, and perhaps the man and boy will claim the dog later, another parcel of rotting meat for their truck bed, and before the next odometer tick, you pass a belly-up squirrel, a mangled possum—has the deep snow forced these animals to forage along the road or have they always been there, your eyes oblivious to the carnage...

The Wednesday night bartender was the one who let slip that Gill had given you the shaft, an offhand joke as he worked the taps how Gill should be the one paying for the night's rounds after the eight large he'd made on some construction site deal. You'd been blindsided before, gotten beaned by a fastball in your high school baseball days, had three ribs cracked by a dropped two-by-four, but you'd never had the wind knocked out of you like you did that night, your white knuckles gripping the bar railing, your bones as brittle as November corn stalks. You said nothing, declined Gill's offer to check out the wristwatches and Cabbage Patch dolls waiting in his trunk, but over the next few days, the knowledge of his betrayal festered beneath your winter-pale skin. You'd been the one who'd told him about the spools, the one who'd risked his job, who'd balanced his family's wellbeing atop Gill's tee-tee-teetering schemes. That Saturday, you confronted Gill in the windowless garage he rented outside town, the unheated space crammed with car stereos and new, rubber-fragrant tires. The galvanized pipe lay on a workbench littered with pot seeds and coke-smudged cassette cases, and you were only aware of the first blow, the pipe striking Gill's temple before he could raise his fluttering hands in defense. After that, the metal-on-flesh thuds reached you in fading echoes, the sound of a bass-thumping radio being played in a distant room (did you hit him three times? a dozen?). When you were done, the pipe slipped from your fingers, struck the concrete with an earsplitting ping, and rolled lazily—the garage filled with its hollow, metallic song—until it came to rest against Gill's motionless body.

Remembering a scene from a movie (but had the character gotten away with his crime?), you mopped bleach over the far-flung bloodstains. You wrapped the pipe and body in the white shower curtain Gill had rigged up to hide his metal shelves stocked with triple-beam scales and the bottles of baby laxative he used to stretch a quarter ounce of coke into a half. Then you slumped against a cold wall, gagging on the bleach's chlorine stink, your jackrabbity heart bounding in your chest.

You turned off the lights to deter the coke-seekers and bargain hunters, but the knocks still came, and each jiggle of the locked handle squeezed the breath from your lungs. In gray degrees, the shrouded form lying beside your bloodstained boots separated itself from its murky surroundings until it seemed the white vinyl had grown iridescent, an accusing light generated from within.

The shovel rattled in the backseat and your headlights jittered ahead over the logging road's rutted grooves. The trunk's weight shifted with every wheel-bucking bump. The pines and firs stretched over you, the moon and stars choked from the sky, the air thick and cool and utterly still. You parked and killed the lights. The body balanced over your right shoulder, the shovel clutched in your left hand, you set off into the woods.

Your father had shown you the trappers' footpath that followed a seasonal creek down to the river. You walked the trail for fifty yards and turned abruptly into the brush. Your father had died the year before, and you wondered, despite your lack of beliefs, if he was somehow near you now.

Gill had always seemed so insubstantial, bird-like with his slight build and nervous tics, a guy you outweighed by a good fifty pounds, but now your shoulders burned as you weaved your way through the thick growth. Saplings clawed at your legs, and the pine branches swatted your face. You waved the shovel before you and cursed the darkness. You thought of the trail and panicked, fearing your staggering path might prevent you from finding your way back to the car. The body fell with a muffled thud, and you stood over the faintly radiating cocoon, the panting bellows of your lungs the only sound to reach your ears. The digging proved harder than you'd expected, the earth bothered by roots and stones, and you had to fold the stiffening body, knees to chest, to fit the tiny hole.

… mountains of dirty, plowed snow hem the vast hospital parking lot, and after two laps you find a space, your ill-timed engine shuddering into silence, and you unscrew the lid of the pint bottle stashed beneath your seat and throw back a shot, then another, and outside, quick steps propel you across the macadam, and you spit a dark, red glob on a cinder-crusted snow bank and the biting wind snakes up your pant legs, the cold tingling on the dewy alcohol residue around your lips, and the sun disappears behind the hospital, your body shivering in the shadow's temperature drop, and you shovel gum into your mouth, hoping the minty flavor will mask the taste of whiskey and blood, and as you near the entrance, navigate your way between the wheelchair-bound, the crutch-users, the bandaged and bruised, and the entrance's double-set of automatic doors whisper hello, the lobby's warmth tickling your stuffed nose, and you ask for directions at the main desk, make a stop in the perfume-scented gift shop for an overpriced teddy bear and a balloon that proclaims IT's A BOY! in blue, curlicue letters, and in the main corridor your ridiculous balloon bobs above your head, your steps slowed by a pair of bed-pushing orderlies, their oblivious, IV-tethered cargo as white as the bed's sheets, and you study the other passing eyes, the dazed and mournful and relieved, the workaday weariness of doctors and nurses and maintenance workers, and how unreal the place seems, this man-made cusp between life and death, and the elevator lights flash, a climbing of floors and a tally of heavenly pings, and the nurse standing beside you brushes your arm as she exits, the cinnamon smell of her coffee lingering after the chrome doors shut, and finally, it's your turn, and you step off and all you have to do is follow the muffled cries, and you count seven behind the nursery's thick window glass, all swaddled tight, their scrunched heads topped with knitted caps the color of ice cream, and some cry, some sleep, while the one nearest you blinks his clouded eyes against the assault of harsh light...

The next day you burned your clothes in a rusted drum behind the loading dock. The wind whipped the flames, and the swirling smoke stung your eyes, the thinning, gray ribbon climbing into a slate sky. Weeks passed, months, and the knock on the door that had kept you up at night never materialized. At the bar, you overheard rumors about Gill's disappearance, the most prevalent speculation that he'd run off to Florida after burning a couple of Jamaicans in a coke deal. With each passing year, you think of him less ... and more.

The fear that once consumed you has distilled into something more subtle, something finer and grittier, an ashy scrim through which your days are filtered. Food doesn't taste as good as it once did, and the bar's jukebox has lost its power to make you sing along.

Unwelcome images of Gill's decomposing body sometimes drift into your thoughts. Alone in your bed, you have pictured the rotting flesh and the feasting of worms, the slightly richer shade of green for the grave's grass. And some nights, you pull back further, rising over his grave, above the fragrant pines and firs, and you imagine the mice that ate the worms and the coyotes that snapped up the mice, and you feel as if Gill's carbon-laced residue has been spread as far as you can see.

Would you have forgiven him by now? On some level at least? Perhaps you'd still play darts with him. Perhaps you'd still be married. Perhaps you wouldn't need booze to fall asleep each night. Perhaps your daughter would call you more than once a month. Perhaps nothing. Perhaps everything.

... your daughter, propped in her hospital bed, smiles at you, sweat-teased curls springing from her hair, the tips brushing her flushed cheeks, and there's a nurse there, the room so small you have to wedge yourself into a corner so she can finish changing the boy's diaper and all you can really see at first is a pair of improbably tiny, needle-pricked heels cradled in the nurse's tender grip, and when she's done swaddling the boy in a sky-blue blanket, she steps aside and there's your grandson in a glass crib hardly bigger than a shoebox and he isn't crying, not a peep, and you study the peaceful face, the puffy, slitted eyes and cone-shaped head, a single finger reaching out of the swaddling blanket, and your daughter says, "Hold him, Dad," as she reaches onto the nightstand for an instamatic camera, and you slide your hands under the barely stirring bundle, your callused palm cradling the boy's neck and head, and as you lean over, you listen to the glass-trapped echo of his breathing—a sound high-pitched, congested, shallow, and persistent, his tiny lungs fighting to adjust to a strange world, and carefully, carefully, you bring the bundle closer to your chest, and when your bodies meet, you think about the purity of a soul without secrets or sin, and you think about the new generation of dart-throwers at the bar who've never heard Gill's stutter, never sifted through his trunk's improbable treasures, and a teary welling mingles with the blood in your throat, and your hands tremble when you bring the boy closer and kiss his smooth, round cheek, and as the camera flashes, you cry softly for him and for yourself, cry for the living and the dead and the fateful roads a man travels between the two…

my totally
awesome funeral

No viewing parlors with their embedded stink of old women's perfume and phony propriety. Throw a bash at my crib instead—ain't nothing like a house party—the price of admission a single wood scrap salvaged from the cobwebbed corners of basements and garages. Arrange a heap by the door and let the handiest and most ambitious guests hammer these misfits into my farewell vessel. Buy me a suit coat at the flea market, a sherbet-colored eyesore at least three sizes too big, and fill my pockets with verses of poetry and the old photographs that never made it into the family album, the shut-eyed portraits, the embarrassing shots of pale skin and tummy rolls taken from our beach vacations. Tell the undertaker to work a smartass grin onto my face. Paint *Hello!* on one closed eyelid, *Goodbye!* on the other. Entertain my son with a magic trick, and if he laughs, do it again. Ask my wife if she's lost weight. Buy the expensive beer and wine I never thought I deserved in life and make sure no glass goes empty. Play music all night long—Jelly Roll, Louis and the Hot Fives, and once the vibe grows ragged and sloppy, crank out "Iron Man" until the speakers crackle and the stomp of beat-keeping shoes sends every shelved knickknack tumbling to the floor. Carry me to the backyard and lay me on a picnic table beneath the stars—I've always preferred the company of outcasts and smokers. Drink to absent friends. Drink another just because you can. After my wife and son have gone to bed, let the hardcore partiers highjack me for one last ride—shotgun!—and no matter the season, roll down the window and let the wind lash my hair. Drive to the old quarry and drag me to the north face's steep cliff, the one I was always afraid to jump from into the cold, deep water below, and prop me against the cliff's crowning forty-foot hemlock while my friends yell and sing off-key into the darkness, a serenade echoed back from the circling vista of stone.

Hold the service at sundown the next day at the old drive-in, the one with the waist-high weeds straining between the macadam cracks, where the rusting speaker poles cast stretching, sundial shadows over a moonscape of broken glass and wind-swept trash. Monkeys, there must be monkeys, monkeys in red fezzes and roller skates, burning sparklers grasped in their paws. And while you're at the zoo, procure a giraffe or two to lope around the perimeter, their curious heads poking through the screen's tattered panels. Give the children noisemakers and encourage them to blow and toot until they're forced to lay their swooning heads in their mothers' laps. Hire a marginally talented mime to wander among the mourners—his glass wall routine both symbolic that we spend our lives trapped in little boxes and also a reminder that we should be eternally thankful that most of our boxes don't have mimes. Let my son wear his Superman cape if he wants. Break into the projection booth, switch on the static-spitting speakers, and broadcast a tape of a newborn's first cry. The recording can be of any baby, it doesn't matter. Tell my wife she looks great in black. Construct my eulogy with dialogue snippets culled from old Brat Pack movies and deliver them with a straight face. Relay this single message from me: "I had fun. Really." Adorn my old girlfriends in pink widow's veils and Victoria's Secret smuttery, and have them sing an A Cappella version of "Just a Gigolo."

As the light fades from the sky, stuff my casket with the drafts of my stories that went nowhere, the novels that sagged beneath the weight of their own pretensions. Let the giraffes wander the lot's edges, their shambling grace on display as they nibble the offerings of the surrounding trees. Allow my wife and me a private moment, a final goodbye before nailing the coffin shut with one last ill-fitting piece and dousing the wood with lighter fluid. Commission a dozen archers to shoot flaming arrows—high, arcing trajectories that trace the bruised sky like so many shooting stars. Hug the person next to you as the arrows thud into the wood. Stay for a bit to study the knotted smoke plumes, the orange sparks that leap higher than the rest, but leave, with monkeys and giraffes in tow, before the flames die.

After I'm gone, visit the monkeys and giraffes at the zoo. Part of me, I believe, will be waiting in their dark eyes. Unspeaking, unjudging, I will gaze upon you with all the wonder and amazement you deserve.

vacation
in ten parts

I. Hear the palms rustle. Hear the murmuring waves, the ocean's fury muted by the inlet's rocky cliffs. Wiggle your toes in the sun-baked sand, and with squinting eyes, commit the postcard scenery to memory—the white crescent beach, the teardrop bay, the steep, overgrown hills that press upon the shore. Struggle with the fact that in five days' time you'll return to a city of icy sidewalks and wind-swept trash. Have you really landed in paradise?

II. Spear fishing, the Philadelphia lawyer devolved, your Princeton degree abandoned for a hunter-gatherer's killing stick. "Throw it with authority," urges Bill, the resort owner. You raise your weapon, but don't throw, a captive of the moment. Knee-deep in unreal blue, the water shimmering with your prey, you study your wife's reflection in Bill's wide, mirrored sunglasses. The truth? the paralyzing truth? truth is you arranged this vacation to discover something beyond adventure and relaxation. Truth is you hoped the trappings of island beauty would shed their magic into your heart. But in this spear-wielding instant, with your wife's warped image painted across another man's eyes, you realize a thousand miles' distance can't alter how she appears to you now, in reflections, in glimpses and accidental fragments, and on the increasingly rare occasions you turn her way, she's barely there, a two-dimensional presence in a three-dimensional world. No more substantial than a waft of smoke. A rustle of leaves.

III. Your supporting cast:
   A. Stella, the widow of Nashville's largest car dealer. The rim of her straw hat wavering in the breeze, sketchpad balanced across her lap, she filters the pristine scenery into charcoal gray. For hours she sits by herself beneath a giant beach umbrella. The sandpipers barely notice her.
   B. Rolph and Bernice, the young Germans whose lean gym-bodies ripple like contour maps of good health. Out in the bay, their twin-mast schooner rocks gently from its moorings, their itinerary an echo of the sunny posters lining your travel agent's office—Martinique, St. Lucia, Cyprus, Bali. First impressions had them pegged for drug runners or scam artists, but at Sunday night's pig roast, you learned Rolph was the baron of a fifteenth century Black Forest castle. "It's all rather clichéd," Rolph explained in polite, unemotional English. "Suits of armor in the hallways, stone walls, tapestries sewn by a local order of monks." Bernice fished a pineapple slice from her drink and added with a smile, "Such a drafty, old place."

C. Manuel, the dark-skinned houseboy, perpetual motion on wiry legs. Count the sand-flinging back flips he performs for Stella—five, six, seven in a row. He pulls you aside, thumb and forefinger pressed into a dainty oval and brought to his puckered lips, a motion followed by a finger laid on the side of his nose. "You ask," he says, "and Manuel get, OK?" Why isn't he in school? but it only takes a few hours until you, too, succumb to the island's vague regime, its sense of time swelled and distorted by the afternoon's heat, the evening's lingering twilight.

D. Bill, the resort owner. You envy his island, his paradise niche, envy his meticulously groomed boyishness, the short pants and untucked shirttails, the calves muscled from years of beachcombing. He is the modern Robinson Crusoe, his message in a bottle replaced by his web page, his sextant forsaken for a satellite dish aimed at the bay's expanse of sea and sky.

E. Claire, Bill's live-in, statuesque and blond. A Scandinavian refugee who hasn't yet mastered the nuances of English pronouns, the words beyond her halting vocabulary acted out in pouting, exasperated charades. She sunbathes topless, rising every half-hour or so to take a languid dip. Try not to stare as she strolls past and collapses once again upon her towel, the ocean drops freckling prisms upon her tanned skin.

F. And your wife. Don't forget her.

IV. *"Tiburón! Tiburón!"* yells Manuel, a chirping, alarmed soprano that rouses you from a stuporous nap. *"Tiburón!"*

and while the word is a mystery, no interpreter is needed to translate the urgency in his voice. Sit up on your towel and watch the boy's frantic approach. His thin arms wave, the pose of a gangly bird attempting flight among the scattered sandpipers. *"Tiburón!"* he cries between heaving breaths that highlight his stack of bony ribs. The boy reaches Bill, who pauses in his host's duty of baiting Stella's long fishing pole. Manuel points up the shore. Bill and the boy run off, and still susceptible to the logic of dreams, you join the others who follow in their wake, your wife hanging back to assist Stella in her struggles with her pole and line. Rolph and Bernice jog ahead, their platinum watches glistening in the sun. Claire strides beside you, and you run a little stronger, a little straighter when you see the bouncing rhythm of her grapefruit breasts. Follow the curving beach to the bay's far end and stop when you reach the stranded shark. The beast has rolled onto its side, its smooth, off-white belly exposed. A useless fin points to a single, lonely cloud. Manuel pokes an investigating stick at the jagged teeth, the barely functioning bellows of its vertical gills. An onyx eye reflects the hot sun. A wave larger than the rest rolls in, and the monster twitches in response. Its massive tail kicks up the surf, and you flinch as the drops rain over you.

V.   Study your wife through the fine scrim of mosquito netting. Peaceful, her slumber, her legs tangled in crisp, white sheets, the cotton ripe with the ocean's briny scent. Moonlight touches the netting, a luminous curtain surrounding her motionless body. Lean closer until you detect the rhythm of her breathing, a sound that runs like a slender thread beneath the crumbling surf, the ceiling fan purr. Eyes closed, you focus on the sound, the exhaled parcels of life snared in the delicate netting.

VI. Stella corners you after your morning jog, an unadvised route that took you off the resort's trails and into the nearest town, a locale distressingly third world, tin roof shacks, dirt roads crammed with rusting cars and donkey carts and shoeless children. Concern wrinkles Stella's already wrinkled face, and she asks if you believe Bill's assertion that he's never seen a shark before in the bay. Sweat stings your eyes, and your parched throat begs for water. "I'm sure he's telling the truth," you say, and relieved, Stella's small talk barrage turns to your wife, your practice, and finally, your exercise habits. Yes, you tell her, you've run a marathon, a blatant lie to hasten your exit. Back home you'd never say such a thing, but in this setting of strange fruits and sunning lizards, your lie doesn't trouble you because here you are only an imitation of yourself, a facsimile, the you of deep histories and mortgage payments left back home in your closet among your tailored suits and silk ties.

VII. The nightstand clock's red digits hover in the darkness. Each successive number marks another minute of sleeplessness, the alarm set for an ungodly hour because your wife wants to watch one more sunrise before your flight. Step outside and softly shut the door behind you. The bungalow's white stucco glimmers in the moonlight like a bleached bone. On the sand behind the main house,

Manuel tends to a fire burning within a large ring of stones. Familiar forms pass between the fire and the open-air, thatched roof bar. Tinny notes from a steel drum trio mingle with the rising sparks, a dance of music and fire swirling up to a star-choked sky.

VIII. Watch your step along the winding path leading down to the beach. Tread carefully over the rocky terrain, your way marked by shadows and moonlight and the infrequent porch lanterns of the other bungalows. At the edge of the firelight, the gutted shark hangs from a tackle line. Its enormous jaw sags, teeth rows exposed, a laughing giant overseeing the night's festivities. Friendly faces smile in recognition as you perch atop a rickety wooden stool. Nod a hello to:

A. Stella, who places a salmon-pink shell atop her pile of bills and accepts Manuel's offer to dance to a steel drum rendition of "That'll Be The Day." The ocean breeze musses her snowy hair, the red chiffon scarf knotted around her throat. She executes an arthritic hula, and her forced enthusiasm underpins a confession about a widow's loneliness she divulged before your afternoon snorkeling expedition.

B. Claire, in a half-buttoned white Oxford shirt and candy cane bikini, huddled at the far end of the bar with Rolph. She laughs a bit too loudly, her hand resting on the knee of Rolph's carefully ripped jeans, her hair a blond cascade as she leans closer to his whispering lips. Bernice, a white lily tucked behind her ear, joins them. Firelight glimmers in the black spheres of her pupils, a condition you recognize in all three of them. Bernice lifts her waiting beer from the bar, and the napkin beneath the bottle flutters off on the breeze, a cartwheeling suicide-rush into the crackling fire. The steel drum beat infects her, drawing her onto the beach near the band where she performs a possessed, twirling dance, her long necklace of beads and shells swirling in an elliptical orbit around her neck.

C.   Bill returns carrying stacked cases of beer. Sweat glistens on his brow. Veins branch across his beefy forearms. Claire pulls herself away from Rolph and aims her slurping straw toward the last pulpy swallows in her glass. The cash register opens with a ring, the drawer a kaleidoscope of foreign currency, the fine papers and irregular shapes, the vibrant inks that give life to mysterious monarchs. Bill asks Claire why she didn't take your order while he was gone, and Claire gathers her tiny black purse in a huff, snapping, "Don't care if him wants a drink or not!" before storming off to join Bernice's shaman's dance.

D.   Manuel heaves a log onto the fire, another plume of sparks released. His teeth flashing white, the boy cries, "*Bien! Bien!* " encouraging the dancing of the three women. A shift in the breeze ushers in the shark's fishy stink, and when only you are looking, the boy creeps toward the bar and deftly sweeps Stella's loose change into his hand.

IX.   Bill makes you a Hurricane, this one on the house, an apology for the poor service. A shudder drops down your spine because the taste is stronger than you remember. Rise

from your seat, and drink in hand, wander to the fire. Politely
refuse Manuel's call to join the dance, but then Claire grabs
your wrist, a pull that topples your glass and its pastel-
hued contents. "I'll take care," Manuel says, and he picks
up the glass, the sandy fruit slices and paper umbrella,
waiting silently and patiently until you place a dollar in his
palm. Turn from the fire and walk to the sea. Your shadow
grows, a dark patch over the rippling sand. Take off your
sandals at the surf's edge and let the water rinse your feet.
The wind sneaks beneath your shirt, the rippling material
caressing your stomach. Stroll along the bay's curving arc
until the waves overtake the steel drums' song. Water foams
on the sloped beach, and each new swell erases your last
footprint. Hearing voices, you pause. Three silhouettes
weave in and out of the firelight. They walk with arms
draped over each other's shoulders and waists, a stumbling,
tittering procession, the firelight captured in their half-
empty beer bottles. The tallest one suddenly breaks from
the group and runs to your side. She is even more beautiful
in the ghostly light. The surf entombs your toes in wet sand.
Without a word, Claire presses herself close and kisses you,
her breath fiery with alcohol, her tongue as wet and washing
and rhythmic as the breaking waves. She steps back, leaving
you momentarily dizzy, the swift undertow toying with your
sense of balance. She runs ahead, splashing through the
surf on her way to join Rolph and Bernice as they push
their dinghy into the water.

X.   A smooth, sandy trail runs from the spot where Bill and
      Manuel and the one-eyed cook dragged the shark from the

sea. The sputter-hum engine of Rolph's dinghy rips into the quiet. Alarmed monkeys howl from the trees. Claire stands in the bow, arms outstretched, a modern, shameless Venus. The white lily from Bernice's hair bobs on the tide. The dinghy cuts its engine and pulls alongside the schooner, and the three revelers climb aboard, their laughter a faint ripple in the air. Step into the surf and retrieve Bernice's limp-petaled flower. The moon hangs over the opposite shore, a halo above your hillside bungalow, and its celestial glow paints a shimmering path that stretches across the bay to the very spot where you stand. The schooner's tall mast ticks a weak metronome beat, its narrow deck a dance floor for the tiny, grinding forms of Bernice and Claire. Take off your shirt and shorts and fling them onto the sand and then wade deeper into the bathish water.

You think of your wife's image in Bill's sunglasses, the her of glimpses and reflections, and you realize this poverty of vision runs deep inside you, a dark current that is gradually eroding the sense of who you are (look no further than your recent, pre-vacation behaviors—your shoving match with the driver of a gun rack-sporting pickup truck over a mall parking space, the curses you flung at your partner outside Judge Adlee's chambers). A wave pushes against your thighs, and the light spray strikes your exposed sex. When you and your wife first started dating, you went swimming on Saturday mornings at the campus natatorium. In your shared lane, your bodies cleaved the overly chlorinated water, while above you, the misty air glowed beneath the skylights. She was the real swimmer, a state medalist, a fact she never boasted about, and when you entered the pool, she always allowed you to set the pace. You know she did this to make you comfortable, and in turn, you struggled to be strong for her when your fatigued body cried out for rest.

A half mile, maybe less. Draw a deep breath and glide into the luminous path. Hear the tiny splashes you create. Hear the deceptive emptiness of the water. A cloud passes over the moon. Soon you are alone and questioning your strength, enveloped by both darkness and beauty, your life reduced to the simple knowledge that only a combination of heart and muscle can deposit you on the other shore.

three teeth

three teeth. You can pick them out if you hit PAUSE just right. Probably not a person in the entire valley who hasn't seen that video from the Eastern Cheerleading Finals. They even showed the tape on the eleven o'clock news in Scranton, my face circled and highlighted, the scene slowed into a dreamy rhythm, Tina North's elbow clipping my jaw and three white specks flying like summer moths from my mouth. My head turned for a second, but my clapping hands didn't miss a beat, and when the count came to hoist Tina into Valley High's trademark Flying Angel, I was right there, sucking in the blood already puddling on my lips. They showed the clip at the end of the broadcast, one of those light pieces meant to make people think the world isn't just killing and robbing and whatnot, the slot usually saved for shuffleboard-playing monkeys and toddlers smacking whiffle balls into their fathers' groins. "Ouch!" cringed Allison Davies, the perky eleven o'clock anchor. "That must have really *stung*!" There was this gleeful revulsion in Allison's voice that pissed me off, a 'Thank goodness it wasn't me, but isn't it funny?' tone, and as I watched, my bruised jaw just beginning to shade thundercloud-blue and my mouth stuffed with sopping cotton wads, I took solace in knowing that, if there was a God, Allison's Mouseketeer inflections and hushed-up DUIs would keep her from climbing too far up the network's ladder.

Valley High brought home best overall honors from Easterns, our first title ever. On the long bus ride home, I put one of my teeth in the big silver cup, and when the other girls passed the trophy around, my bicuspid made the thing rattle like a shook-up spray paint can. The ice bag over my jaw turned the left side of my mouth into a distant place, my eye too numb to blink, the dull, heartthrob pain just beginning to find me, while in the bus's rear, a collective "Oh no!" rose from the Barbie clique as Tina pulled back the gauze on her elbow and showed off her wounds. The Barbies are the squad's stars, the fliers and tumblers, the girls with springy legs and expensive haircuts and light switch smiles, the ones who break out new panties before each competition so the ass they show is store-bought white. I don't begrudge the Barbies one smidge of their spotlit glory—I could never twist my frame into their basket tucks or gyroscoping cartwheels. They are the spires of this world, the eye-catching peaks, the ever-bubbly news anchors, while people like me, the spotters and the throwers, are the foundation, the ones hunkered down at the base of the human pyramids and smiling through the pain of knees gouging the nubs of our spines.

A week after the competition, Coach Habbershaw took a breather from his phlegm-clearing, collar-tugging lecture on human reproduction and showed the Easterns video. I slid down in my seat, blushing, and cupped a hand over my fat lip. Coach Habbershaw said he'd never seen one of his athletes take such a shot and keep on going, which I guess was as much a compliment as he ever gave anyone. After that, some of his players, the beefy lineman mostly, kind of adopted me as one of their own. "Hey Jonesy," they'd call when they passed in the hallway, nodding their big shaved heads and delivering fake jabs to my arm.

"Looks like you're one of the guys now!" Tina piped one day in the caf line. She was parading by, latched onto the golden arm of Brad Diller, our State-bound quarterback. On the Mondays after Brad had turned in some fourth quarter heroics, Tina made a point of wearing his jersey to practice, the oversized material draping her hundred-pound frame like a little nightie, the shirt's mesh and her blond curls locked in perfect, billowing harmony as she soared above us.

Our advisor, Miss Stallings, organized fundraisers to help pay for my dental bills. We had a bake sale, a silent auction, and when a reporter from the *Weekly Courier* came to cover our pre-prom car wash, Tina made a point of draping her arm over my shoulder and flashing her best Barbie pose just as the shutter clicked. The reporter was some kid fresh out of college, and Tina flirted shamelessly with him, bending his ear with stories of how she was *so* interested in journalism, having edited the school paper *and* yearbook *two years running*, her rubber gloves peeled off and her sponge drying while the rest of us sloshed suds on the lengthening line of cars. By the time the reporter left he must have forgotten about me because Tina was the only one he quoted: "Today we're here to celebrate our championship Cougar pride and to pull together as the team we are!"

I guess I could have been angry that Tina didn't mention me or the pile of dentist's bills Miss Stallings's fundraisers didn't cover. I could have been steamed because Tina never truly apologized for not tucking right, and goodness knows what catty

Barbie retribution would have awaited me if I had missed my assignment and dropped *her*. But I had more immediate things on my mind than holding a grudge, and after graduation, while Tina and the Barbie bikini squad splashed in the Senior Week surf, I was sitting white-knuckled in the dentist's chair, my opened mouth cramping through impressions and root canals, a gurgling suction tube hooked over my lip and the enamel-gritty smoke of shaved teeth stinging my eyes.

I've had my new teeth for a year and a half now. I'm almost done paying off the dentist, forty dollars every month, which is a good chunk of my part-time take home from working the register at Dekalb's Grocery. When I'm not ringing up produce and Pampers, I'm trying to keep up with my classes at community college. Sometimes, when I get nervous about a test or paper, I take a moment and trace my tongue over those false teeth, a gentle, wishful rubbing like the genie's bottle from that kid's story, and I tell myself that I've survived harder things. Next year I might enroll at State, but I won't run into Tina there because she's transferred to a New England school famous for its pottery studios and ultimate Frisbee team. I don't believe the rumors about her getting drunk at some frat party and pulling a train—which, if you're unfamiliar with the term, is too disgusting for me to explain. Still, I know things like that happen; sometimes the weaker ones crack under pressure, the pretty ones like Tina and Allison who tumble hard from their belief that what's important in life is a mirror's reflection and pixie-flying above an adoring crowd. Me, I know differently. And I've got the scars to prove it.

the real, true-life story of godzilla!

billy Glenn grew up in a dusty, map speck of a southern Iowa town. He hated the town for its smallness and isolation, hated its provincial ways, the communal thrill that accompanied the changing of the feature at the Bijou or the purchase of a new fire company engine. He hated himself for hating a town that loved him in return, the high school gym where his retired basketball jersey hung from the rafters, the Main Street diner where his favorite order, a cheeseburger with green peppers and onions, had been renamed the Billy Glenn Special. Most of all he'd grown to hate the town's water tower, a red and white colossus that stood guard over the endless corn fields. The roads leading to town ran arrow straight, heat-glimmering stretches where tar sucked at his wheels and only gospel stations broke the radio static, and when Billy drove home from college for summer break, he'd catch sight of the water tower from as far away as Grantville, a rusting star on the distant horizon. Miles passed, and as the tower lifted ever so slightly into the blue sky, Billy's muscles tightened involuntarily, spasms so intense he sometimes had to pull onto the shoulder and catch his breath. Lying across the car's sticky-

warm seat, hand clenched over his heaving chest, he imagined
the news bulletin interrupting the stories of salvation—Billy
Glenn, starting forward at State, second all-time on the Iowa high
school scoring list, found dead on a lonely farmland roadside,
the circumstances mysterious, his body robbed of oxygen, an
apparent drowning miles from the nearest body of water.

He left college after his junior year in 1959, military service
avoided due to the knee operation he underwent near season's
end. He tore the ligaments on an awkward landing after a practice
lay-up, a motion he'd performed in drills since elementary school,
only this time there was a different ending, a buckling in his joint,
a pain that radiated down to his foot, and his first thoughts weren't
of his team or his scholarship, not what his injury might mean to
his chances to go pro. He thought of the water tower. The trainer's
voice, the pull of athletic tape around a makeshift splint—it all
seemed miles away to Billy. Behind his shut eyes, he saw the
tower's fat belly and long, skinny legs. And he saw himself
gimping through town, the tower looming over him, its fading,
painted letters forever reminding him of where he was and where
he'd always be.

Wearing a skin-pinching brace, Billy Glenn hustled through
countless tryouts, and in the course of three and a half years, he
signed with four different semi-pro teams in the Midwest. Most
of the teams were owned by local businessmen, carpet wholesalers
or car lot owners, and the backs of their players' jerseys were
festooned with advertising. *Buy your next car at Hartman's!* or
Big Al's, the Savings King! They played in small, smoky gyms,
and the spirit cheers Billy had grown accustomed to in high school
and college were replaced by drunken curses, the angry plink of
pennies hurled onto the court. Sometimes an owner visited the

locker room, not to give a pep talk but to remind them of the bookies' latest line and of the stake he'd placed in the proper outcome. Deliberately missing a wide open jumper made Billy sick to his stomach, and after such games, he'd return to the cockroach flats his income allowed and guzzle cheap whiskey until he passed out.

Their circuit cut through the heart of the country. There were stops in Flint, Des Moines, Louisville, cities more or less the same in their size and gray drudgery. Inevitably they rolled through the college towns where Billy had once played, and framed in the bus's frosted windows were the great arenas, the bundled students hurrying to ivy-cloaked buildings. Billy saw these things and wondered where his life had gone so wrong. With a grimace, he gulped back more aspirin and closed his eyes until the cold, rattling bus ambled back onto the highway. Into the ashy winter twilight they drove, passing farmhouses and cut fields, and eventually they'd near a town and Billy would spot another water tower, its ugly alien form rising above the snowy flatlands. He'd smile then and rub his aching knee, momentarily assured he'd made the best with the cards he'd been dealt.

Evansville was the last team to cut him. He still had his shot. He set his picks with rehearsed, mechanical skill, found his teammates with crisp passes, but his quickness, that initial, reactionary burst, was gone, and he knew it would never return. For two weeks he holed up in his apartment, hobbling up the fire escape to avoid the landlord. The metal steps rattled in time with the whiskey bottles he hid beneath his coat, and the slush that fell from his boots struck the trash cans below with loud, incriminating plops. He couldn't last like this much longer, the drinking and the debts, the bologna and peanut butter diet, but he vowed he'd scrape by hungry and broke before returning to the one place where everyone knew him. He feared a town populated by the ghosts of his past, the boy who shoveled snow from the schoolyard basketball court and practiced foul shots long into the dark, the type of early, unwavering focus that caused his teachers and most everyone else to say, "Keep an eye on that boy. He'll go far." Most people's dreams were carefully hidden, and the disappointment of not attaining them was limited to private regrets, but the entire town had cheered Billy's pursuit, and by returning home, his failure would no longer be his alone. He'd be watched by the women of the United Methodists' sewing circle and by the men who pitched horseshoes behind the dry goods store, and in thoughts both expressed and not, they'd interpret his actions and moods, reading into them some sort of mythic, plain-hardened drama, the story of a young man whose desires had outstripped his talents. The strange truth was Billy Glenn had never given his town or its water tower a second thought until he'd gone to college and come up against players better than himself, and he'd gladly go back home tomorrow if only he could return as someone else, someone with a history as blank as a cloudless summer sky.

The call from Jim McSwain came on a snowy morning. The ringing startled Billy because he thought the phone company had already shut off his service.

"Billy, Jesus Christ, you're a son of a bitch to track down!" Wincing with a hangover's pain, Billy held the receiver away from his ear. Profane Jim McSwain, as his players called him, was the owner of the Gary Smokestacks, the second-to-last team to cut Billy. McSwain was a celebrity of sorts in Gary, the owner of a successful sporting goods chain, the star of his own TV commercials, hubris-filled outbursts in which his burly arms whipped baseball bats and hockey sticks like assaulting weapons, the rhinestone crown proclaiming him KING OF SPORTS teetering atop his square head.

"You need me for the Smokestacks?" Billy asked hopefully.

"Smokestacks are fine, Billy. What I got to offer you is something much fucking bigger."

McSwain went on, but a hinge-rattling knock at the door distracted Billy. "Phone company!" called a grumbling voice.

"I'm listening, Jim," Billy said, "but make it quick."

"We're going to play fucking ball again, Billy." Over the staticy line, Billy heard the click and puff of McSwain lighting one of his trademark cigars. "In fucking Japan."

As the phone man disconnected his line, Billy packed his duffel bag and lit down the fire escape. His size-fourteen footprints crossed the snowy yard, and he turned once at the sound of his landlord's threat to call the cops before he broke into a run. He didn't stop until he reached the Western Union office a half mile away where the wire Jim McSwain had promised him soon arrived. The telegram accompanying the money outlined his itinerary—take a bus to Chicago, then hop the first train to San Francisco where he'd meet McSwain and the rest of the team in three days' time at an airport bar called The Flight Deck Lounge.

During the cross-country trek, Jim McSwain's words twisted in Billy's head, how the Japanese loved all things American and why not basketball, too? Hadn't McSwain gotten to know the Japanese mindset during his service stint with the occupation force? McSwain boasted they'd be the ambassadors of the game, celebrities, that it was only a matter of time before the whole damn country was at their feet. With the snow capped mountains gliding past his window, Billy realized he didn't care a lick about an entire country falling in love with him. In fact, love was the farthest thing from his mind.

Duffel bag slung over his shoulder, Billy stepped into the dimly lit Flight Deck Lounge. The stink of his own clothes repulsed him. Less than fifty cents jangled in his pocket, and the rough stubble of his chin itched like mad. He recognized a number of the faces huddled near the bar fish tank. Stan Shapiro and Big Dale Brown were ex-teammates from the Smokestacks. The redhead who tapped the aquarium glass and made puckered faces at the fish was Derek Reeves, a shameless gunner from Ohio State Billy had played against in college. Casey Poe, a worn-covered Bible in his massive hands, had been released from the Globetrotters for "undisclosed reasons," which everyone knew meant too much booze. Speedy Luther Berry dealt a hand of black jack to Swoop Nixon, the one time Celtic who'd silenced the Garden two years before with an Achilles rupture so loud the folks sitting courtside ducked for cover, thinking they'd heard a gunshot.

"Stop right there, you mother fucker!" Pushing his way through the gin-sipping businessmen, a smoldering cigar between his ringed fingers, McSwain approached his player with opened arms. McSwain had lost a little more hair since Billy had seen him last, the wrinkles around his quicksilver eyes etched a bit deeper. "The last piece of the puzzle!" McSwain bellowed. He embraced Billy in a bruising hug and shoved a ticket into his shirt pocket. "Jesus, kid, you look like shit." McSwain yelled back to the bar. "OK, ladies, let's get this goddamn circus on the road!"

Far above the dark Pacific, Jim McSwain outlined the mission of the Tokyo Gladiators. The game had been introduced by GIs like himself during the occupation, and when he'd visited Japan last year, McSwain had discovered that amateur leagues had sprung up in a number of the major cities. The first part of McSwain's scheme had already been set in motion, and each of these leagues had agreed to select its best players into a type of local all-star team. For the first year, the Tokyo Gladiators would criss-cross the mainland playing exhibitions, and the following season, they'd ride the crest of their own buzz all across Asia, playing before standing-room-only crowds in Taipei and Saigon, Seoul and Singapore. McSwain poured champagne into plastic airline cups. "When they write the history of this league," McSwain said, "yours will be the fucking picture on the first page." He raised his plastic cup over his head, but a sudden burp of turbulence sloshed the champagne from his glass, a fizzing cascade that wet the hair and cheeks of a suddenly anxious looking Casey Poe.

McSwain went on, lecturing them on the peculiarities of Japanese customs and giving quick, Midwestern-accented lessons in basic phrases. Next to Billy, Luther Berry shuffled and cut his deck of cards, grinning each time he upturned an ace or face. Billy gulped down his champagne and rested his head against the tiny window. What a desperate crew they were, all of them either egotistical or fragile, out of luck or, like him, running from their pasts. His eyes closed, he allowed himself to drift into sleep. The rise and fall of McSwain's voice reminded him of the tent revival preacher who passed through their town every summer, and Billy grinned at the idea of Profane Jim McSwain as a man of the cloth. Perhaps McSwain couldn't offer him salvation, only a reprieve, but for Billy, a reprieve was salvation enough.

👑

Red eyed from champagne and jet lag, the Gladiators played their first game less than sixteen hours after landing in Tokyo. Already Japan was proving itself a vexing place, its eerily clean streets and suffocating subway cars, the bedless shoebox apartments McSwain had arranged for them. Whispers and giggles rippled behind their backs, and their approach to the gym doors was met with open stares, an occasional bow. Inside, the thunder of beating drums echoed beneath the ceiling's exposed girders. Screaming fans waved fluttering banners written in indecipherable Japanese.

"Un-fucking-believable," McSwain said. With an expert flexing of jaw muscles, he transferred his cigar to the opposite corner of his mouth. "This, gentlemen, is ground zero for something big."

The locker room was being sprayed for silverfish, and they were forced to change in a dank hallway. The gym ruckus intensified. "Sounds like a goddamn war in there," Stan Shapiro said. The new uniforms scratched Billy's chest. He looked down at the tank top's design, a snarling samurai warrior, one hand brandishing a sword, the other dribbling a basketball. Samurai … Gladiator, Billy guessed they were close enough as he and his teammates started their shoot around. Their skills were rusty at first, but soon they rediscovered their touch and the net shivered with repeated cottony whispers. For a moment, the display seemed to quiet the crowd. Then the home team jogged onto the court, and Billy flinched under the renewed avalanche of drums and whistles, foot-stomping chants.

"You've got to be shitting me," Big Dale Brown said.

The rest of the Gladiators stopped their shooting and gathered at midcourt to witness the disheartening spectacle. Clad in old Gary Smokestacks uniforms, the Japanese performed a two-line lay-up drill. Half shrimps, half stork-legged glandular cases, they dribbled with slapping ferocity, their downward focus broken only when they stepped into the paint and flung up shots that more often than not clanked wildly off the rim. Their infrequent goals were met with standing ovations, furious drum beats. As each player joined the end of the line, they paused to bow to the drop-jawed Americans.

"This ain't going to be pretty," Speedy Luther Berry muttered. "For either of us."

Jim McSwain huddled with his players at the foul line. "This whole thing is new to these backwards fucks, remember that. Now I want you to put on a good show, but don't fucking embarrass them. No bullshit, no cheap shit, no yucking it up, got it? The Japanese ain't keen on humiliation."

Big Dale Brown won the opening tip and Stan Shapiro flew down the court for an uncontested two. Derek Reeves stole the ensuing inbound and snapped a behind-the-back pass to Billy, who sank it from the top of the key.

"Take it fucking easy!" yelled McSwain.

Billy and the others backpedaled, glancing toward the refs who seemed oblivious to travels and double dribbles. The twig-limbed Japanese center heaved a shot that barely nicked the backboard. A collective "ahhhh!" rose from the bleachers.

The Gladiators did their best to keep the Japanese team in the game. Big Dale Brown, wanting to see if he might be ambidextrous, launched only left-handed hook shots. Billy stuck to jumpers that tested the absolute limit of his range. Shapiro made dramatic defensive swipes only to pull his hand back at the last moment, a gesture that reminded Billy of the stage slaps his theater major roommate had practiced in college.

Despite their lack of effort, the score started to pile up, and as Billy deliberately short-armed his first shot, what little joy that lingered within him died. At the other end of the court he simply stepped back, hands raised in a defensive charade that left lanes wide enough to drive a Buick to the hoop. Derek Reeves threw an errant, lazy pass, and not one of them gave chase to the Japanese fast break that required three successive beneath-the-rim put-backs to score. That's when Billy noticed the change in the crowd, the ebbing silence that seeped into the din, the cheers softer, shorter, lifeless.

"Try harder!" McSwain snapped during a time out.

"Try harder to lose?" Swoop Nixon asked.

"Yes, goddamn it!"

But it was too late. They'd crossed some cultural boundary of shame or honor or simple bad manners, and no amount of playacting could bring them back. By the second half the fans started filing out, lugging their silent drums and ripped banners, some even crossing the floor as the game limped on.

The following weeks proved no better. In long, sweaty practices before each game, McSwain and his players tried to coach their opponents. McSwain ground his chalk into white nubs as he set up plays that should have guaranteed a modicum of success, but the Japanese, while keen on drill, lacked the skills to execute. The crowds dwindled. Soon the Gladiators found themselves participating in bizarre promotional gimmicks orchestrated by the increasingly agitated McSwain. Big Dale Brown wrenched his back wrestling a sumo-in-training in Yokohama. In Kobe, they ran half-time suicide sprints against bike riding monkeys. When the handful of spectators cheered for the monkeys, Casey Poe broke down and cried like a child. McSwain lugged his gloomy troupe across the mainland, their lanky American frames no match for the dollhouse proportions of Japanese trains, and one by one, his recruits bailed. They lost Shapiro in Kyoto, Reeves and Swoop Nixon in Osaka. Before an exhibition held in the parking lot of a Matsumoto dog show, McSwain himself disappeared, taking with him the last shreds of his players' faith and the promise of overdue paychecks.

The rush hour bedlam of the Matsumoto train station had separated Billy from the others, and he arrived alone in Tokyo to discover he and his teammates weren't the only ones McSwain had stiffed. The doors to their apartments had been padlocked, and amidst the alley's fly-buzzing stink, Billy picked through cans of foul garbage for his few remaining possessions. He unearthed a pair of jeans, a single sneaker and his aspirin bottle, the alarm clock that had seen him through college, all of it coated with a slimy residue and speckled with fishbone shards. In a disgusted rage, he smashed the alarm clock against a cinder block wall. The glass face shattered. The casing broke open, and the springs and cogs and knobs scattered over the macadam. He overturned the trash cans and then kicked his way through his teammates' shoes and empty liquor bottles, their razors and jockstraps and letters from home. Overlapping dog barks echoed up the narrow alley. Angry faces leaned from opened windows, cursing him in an unknown language.

Billy cursed them back, but when a voice answered with what

he thought might be a threat to call the police, he fled the scene. The alley dogs hurled themselves against their fences, the chain link shaking, their jaws snapping at his scent. He was running again, just as he'd done from his Evansville landlord, as he'd done for the past four years. He ran for the sake of running, ran only not to be still, for it was then that he sensed the hopelessness of his situation. His knee clicking, he sprinted down one block, then another, jostling startled pedestrians, hurdling the broom of a shopkeeper sweeping his sidewalk. Cars honked as he zigzagged across a busy street. He glanced over his shoulder, scared he was being chased by cops or the people he'd bumped into, by the alley's howling dogs, by the whole basketball-hating nation.

Looking back, he didn't see the frantically waving boy on the bicycle pedaling toward him. When the bike struck Billy's side, he tumbled headfirst, his world in a strangely peaceful free-fall until he landed with a thud on the sidewalk. His pants ripped, exposing the long, white scar on his knee. The bike skidded until it collided with a newspaper box. The bike's rider, a small boy in gray shorts and a baseball cap, struggled to his feet.

"Mr. Glenn," the boy said breathlessly. "I sorry. I saw you. I came riding to catch you."

Billy recognized the boy as Hiro, the Gladiator's towel boy, one of a half dozen locals he knew in a city of millions. By now, a curious knot of strangers had gathered around them. "Jesus, kid, are you OK?" He picked up Hiro's bike.

"I came to see if any player was left, but no one was at apartment." The boy studied his scraped elbow. "Then I saw you running. I took short cut to catch. Team is gone?"

"Gone." Billy straightened Hiro's jacket and dusted it off. "You sure you're OK, kid?"

"You need job, huh? You need money. I get you job." Hiro clamped onto Billy's wrist. "Four blocks. Good job. You see."

Billy insisted on pushing Hiro's bike. This arrangement seemed to please the boy, and he grew more animated, and in fractured, percolating English, he explained that his uncle worked in a place called Toho Studios. A tall concrete wall hid the grounds from the street. He led Billy past the guard at the studio gate and into a macadam plain of warehouses, barracks and weaving trams. A man in army fatigues passed, another in a tux and long tails, a cave woman with a bleached bone twisted in her black hair. Running the other way was a circus lion tamer followed by a trio of clown-faced midgets. "Here, here," Hiro chirped.

They entered a cavernous warehouse. Billy blinked until his eyes adjusted to the shadows. "You fit, Mr. Glenn," Hiro said proudly. "You fit good."

He ushered Billy into a circle of white-shirted men. Hiro addressed the men in rapid Japanese, gesturing proudly toward Billy. The men looked Billy over from his freshly ripped pants to his unwashed hair, and then blossomed into a single smile. One sprinted off and breathlessly returned with what appeared to be a giant, green animal hide.

"See? See?" Hiro said. "You fit good. You big like Godzilla." At first Billy balked, hands waving in what he hoped was a gesture of polite refusal. The white-shirted men nodded and grinned through Billy's objections, and then offered him the suit again.

"Too big," Hiro explained. Kneeling on the concrete floor, he unlaced Billy's sneaker. "No one fit. Big trouble around here. But with you it good. Everything good now."

Under their urgings, Billy stripped down to his underwear and socks. The white-shirted men smiled. Two of them held the costume, and with the hesitancy of a wedding-day bride, Billy shyly guided himself into the rubbery suit. His hands and feet disappeared into the dark holes. The zipper hissed behind him, and for a moment, his world went dark. He hadn't anticipated the weight of the suit, the smothering effect of isolation and the moist, curling warmth of his trapped breath. He was cocooned, adrift in a black world, even his sense of touch robbed. Standing perfectly still, he listened to the rhythm of his nervous heart and wondered what pathetic turn his life had just taken.

With a twist from behind, a pair of tiny slits appeared before his eyes. A narrowed perspective opened where his new, nameless friends bowed toward him like happy pistons. One of them guided Billy's lumbering steps toward a full-length mirror where he beheld himself reborn as a buffoonish walking lizard.

"Godzilla very good!" one of the white-shirted men said.

The fact that Billy had never heard of Godzilla disheartened the producers who'd hurried down to see their new star. They spent the afternoon in an executive's five-row theater watching reels from the first two Godzilla movies. Every so often one of the producers would rise onto the little stage, sputtering mostly nonsensical English phrases while helpfully acting out the flailings of the angry lizard. Their compact shadows fell hard and crisp over the screen, and the projector light glistened on their glasses. Sitting in the dark, absently nodding to the producers' gibberish, Billy began to empathize with the monster, the two of them foreigners washed up on this crazy island, oversized castaways who seemed destined to suffer one beating after another.

He slept that night on a backbreaking cot in the director's office.

The director rousted him at six, imploring Billy to join him in his grunting morning calisthenics before feeding him a breakfast of orange slices, a hard-boiled egg and tepid tea. On the set, the tech crew watched unemotionally as Billy struggled into his costume. The eyeholes had been cut into the neck, and the monster's head sat atop his like an awkward, weighty hat. The director communicated with charades, wild arm swings punctuated with guttural impersonations of explosions and destruction.

The first shots called for Billy's clawed feet to stamp across a desert island set. Off camera, the director and his assistants gestured for Billy to react like the primordial beast he was. The tech crew yanked his tail with a system of fishing wire and pulleys, and their arrhythmic jerks caused Billy to stagger like a drunken frat boy. His neck muscles ached, but the one time he tried to remove the costume's head, he was roundly scolded. Between the baking studio lights and the suit's thick rubber, Billy began to feel woozy. Sweat rolled down his back, soaking his underwear and socks. His head spun from breathing stale air, and as he raised a balloon boulder over his head for the thirteenth take, he lost consciousness. The crew revived him with cheek slaps and smelling salts. When Billy's blurred vision came back into focus, they gave him a healthy thumbs up and promptly plunged the monster's head back over his own.

Before lunch the next day, Billy had gagged on the smoke of a spewing volcano, turned his ankle stomping a miniature village. A spark from a crushed power line defied all laws of probability and flew into his eyehole. Twice he failed to sidestep the swooping

Mothra, his chest absorbing the brunt of the creature's blow, unscripted topplings that thrilled the director but infuriated the set manager, who was forced to rebuild half a fishing village and a canvas mountainside.

Near day's end, Billy peeled himself out of his costume. Headachy, exhausted, he collapsed on a bench outside the set. He'd raced bike-pedaling monkeys and now he'd become a mutated lizard, and he wondered how much farther down the evolutionary chain he'd sink before accepting defeat and heading home. Little birds hopped around his sneakers, and their pointed beaks chirped a trilling tune he'd never heard before. At that moment, with the sun beating down upon his neck and his slumped shadow stretching before him, he understood how a man could miss something as inconsequential as the sounds of familiar birdcalls and recognizable voices. He kicked at the birds, but civilized creatures that they were, they only scattered a few feet before returning to peck for crumbs in his shadow. Their twittering warbles grew, high-pitched scales that jabbed at Billy's skull. He covered his ears, and when he heard muffled words of English entwining their incessant songs, he thought he'd finally cracked, the border crossed between simple foolishness and full blown, Dr. Dolittle insanity.

"Excuse me," repeated the gentle bird voice. "Mr. Glenn?"

Billy brushed the stinging salt from his eyes. Before him stood a young woman, noticeably tall by Japanese standards even though she wore flat-soled shoes. Black, bluntly cut hair framed her delicate face.

"Mr. Glenn, I am Masago Hideyoshi." She bowed. "I am here to assist you."

In precise yet slightly hesitant English, she informed Billy she'd been sent from the studio's central office to help establish communication with their American monster. She'd perfected her English during her two years at Penn before returning home to work in Toho's overseas distribution office.

"They realize I'm not an actor, don't they?" Billy asked.

Masago covered her smiling mouth. "An actor is not needed to play a monster. You have heard there was some confusion with the costume design. They were going to go back to the old one before they met you. Now they like the taller Godzilla. He is more … imposing. And they like you."

"Please, don't snow me."

"Snow?" she asked seriously.

"I've done nothing but mess up since I got here."

"Oh no, Mr. Glenn." Billy noticed her habit of leaning forward slightly when she spoke, and he wondered if this was tied to the custom of bowing or if it was some self-conscious reaction to her height. "The studio is very enthusiastic about yesterday's rushes, Mr. Glenn. They believe you bring a certain …" her downcast eyes seemed to study the crumb-searching birds, "… a certain athleticism to the role."

"Obviously they haven't seen me play ball recently."

Masago smiled, bowed. "Very good, Mr. Glenn."

The following morning Masago was waiting when Billy arrived on the set. She wore the same outfit she did the day before, a white blouse and a black skirt that fell below her knees. No rings adorned her slender fingers, no necklace for her throat. A clipboard clasped over her small chest, she listened to the director's instructions, then hurried to Billy with clipped, expedient strides.

"He says to tell you Godzilla is angry. Very angry." She glanced back toward the director. "Yet I believe in this scene Godzilla must be played with a touch of sympathy. He is a monster, yes, but that is not of his own doing. He is ... he is like a storm, harmless over the ocean, yet deadly upon landfall. He would rather abandon this world of men and be left alone, but peace is not his to have."

"Sounds like you have this guy figured out," Billy said, his voice muffled by the suit's covering.

"Monsters and men, sometimes there's little difference between the two, Mr. Glenn."

With Masago's help, Billy's work on the set came easier. She intervened on his behalf, persuading the director to grant Billy hourly breaks where she'd sit by his side, ready with salt tablets, water and tiny cucumber sandwiches from the studio commissary. With her help, he found an apartment in her downtown high-rise, and together, they braved the rush hours, Billy staying close to her side as Masago fearlessly led the charge through the city's subway stampede, a swirling odyssey of shoving and transfers that magically deposited them at the studio gates. Back in costume, his perspective narrowed to the width of rubbery slits, Billy sought her out among the off-camera crowd. With an arch of an eyebrow or an encouraging nod or a sour-faced wince, she gave him subtle clues whether to play violent or hurt, bewildered or contemplative. The director shouted his approval.

After particularly difficult days, they treated themselves to a cab. Caught in downtown traffic, they talked of the States and basketball, Godzilla and the tribulations of living a foreigner's life. One night they decided to stop at a restaurant, and over sake and rice, she peeled back the petals of her life, the father she knew only from a stern military photo, the young mother who'd died in a bombing raid less than a month before the war's end. Her face in the flickering candlelight reminded him of moon glow on a still lake, and he leaned closer to hear her soft words amid the boisterous, singing din of drunken businessmen. They were the same age, yet he wondered if two lives could be more different. An orphan, she'd scoured for her existence in the rubble and humiliation of post-war Japan, while he had grown up in the geographic insulation of Middle America, a stranger to typhoons and earthquakes, incendiary bombs and the high altitude whine of B-29s. She told him she did not believe in fate or God, only in the dignity of each moment, and as they crowded beneath her umbrella on the rainy walk home, stepping over puddles electric with neon and oil, he couldn't help but feel ashamed when he compared this quiet strength to his own cowardly habits.

Less than two weeks into shooting, an electrical fire gutted a portion of the set. Miniature Tokyo lay destroyed, the forest-green uniforms of the Japanese military gone, Mothra's wings burnt to their skeletal wiring. Masago and Billy stood in the smoky aftermath. Water dripped from broken pipes, the rhythmic plops joined by the harsh scraping of shovels scooping up charred debris. Thin, gurgling rivers snaked their way toward the floor drains. Above them, the sun burrowed a brilliant shaft through a section of destroyed ceiling.

"What now?" Billy asked.

"I go back to work." Masago stooped, picked a tiny railroad

car from a puddle. "And you can have a vacation if that is agreeable to you. Come to my apartment tonight. I'll tell you what I can about the shooting schedule."

At seven that evening, Billy rode the elevator to Masago's apartment. Near midnight, she cracked her door and discretely removed his shoes from the hallway. Women were still very much a mystery to Billy. There was the girl from his hometown, the one who cried softly after they had sex in the back seat of her father's Ford. In college there were the basketball girls, the cheerleaders or statisticians or regular hangers-on who circulated among the team, girls either too possessive or too clinging or too anxious to break his heart. In his semi-pro days the older players had introduced him to prostitutes, the sad and hard women who counted his money twice and then stared into the room's dark corners as he fumbled away on top of them.

Sitting close on the couch of her sparse, modern apartment, they kissed, their movements daring them closer, a meeting as inevitable as the joining of two streams. Before the moment their lips met, Billy hadn't thought of her sexually. She wasn't particularly beautiful, a bit flat-chested and pigeon-toed. More importantly, she was his guidebook, his compass, his sole link to this peculiar land. Yet in a heartbeat, they were naked, their clothes in soft piles by their feet. Her dark-eyed focus unnerved him for she'd rarely looked him in the eye before. The other women he'd known in this way would look him in the eye during every moment but this one. They stumbled kissing and groping into her bedroom. She whispered words he'd never heard, and he wondered if she'd forgotten his lack of comprehension or if she felt free because of it. Shade-slitted bands of blue neon stretched across the ceiling, and everywhere else there lingered a watery mix of darkness and smog-filtered moonlight, an illumination in which his hands appeared even darker and rougher against her milky skin.

♛

Red pen in hand, Masago settled herself on the couch and looked over the script. Billy watched her, amused by the way her lips moved, as if she were digesting the pages word by word.

"What are the odds?" Billy said. He'd been turning through the channels when he came upon a Godzilla movie. "Be honest. Which do you like more, old Godzilla or new?"

"New, definitely." She touched her pen to her flat nose. "Although I am not Godzilla's biggest fan."

"I'm crushed."

"Look at it," she said. On the tiny black and white screen, a hysterical mob stampeded between the cavernous walls of Tokyo's high-rises. Behind them, a fire breathing Godzilla blocked out the sun. Busses were crushed, buildings destroyed. Destruction rained down upon the unfortunate. "The world must laugh at how empty our country is, how we have this need to fill ourselves up with such fanatical nonsense. Our fathers filled themselves with thoughts of empire. Now we fill ourselves with fads and dreams of better dish detergent. The wonders of a new car. And monsters."

Billy rubbed her neck. "You think that's unique to your country? You should have seen the crew I came here with. Talk about meaningless dreams." He watched as Godzilla swatted back attacking jets. "Maybe filling empty spaces is the one, true international language."

Masago nestled against his side, her eyes fixed on the set. "I don't know if that makes me happy or sad."

♔

Some days Billy accompanied Masago to the studio. He pitched in where he could on the set, running errands, nailing backdrops. Most days, however, he remained behind. Half asleep as Masago kissed him good-bye, he woke only when the sunlight claimed its midmorning spot over the bed. He enjoyed his time there alone. Draped in one of her bright, silky robes, he sipped his morning tea and snooped in a polite, respectful way. The mismatched scraps in his apartment could have belonged to anyone, but her things, while few, seemed essential, important, each a tiny mirror that reflected another facet of who she was. He ran his fingers over her sugar bowl and candleholders, smelled the collars of her shirts. At night, she taught him Japanese, and soon, he'd mastered enough to venture out on his own. He visited the hushed Shinto shrines, strolled around the Tokyo University campus. Before Masago returned, he'd go to the grocery where more often than not, he left with what he thought he'd ordered. They'd eat to the tinny strains of her kitchen radio, and after, she smoked his cigarettes, her long body relaxing in poses worlds removed from the stiff-spined postures she assumed at work. Then they'd retreat to her room of watery light where the hard mat of her bed became a raft just large enough for their two clinging shapes.

One night, as they lay sweaty and naked, she softly kissed each of his fingertips. "Billy—isn't that considered a boy's name? Do they call grown men 'Billy'?"

"If you wanted to be formal, I guess you could go with William."

"How about Bill? Do you like Bill?"

"Everyone's always called me Billy, but I could live with Bill, sure." He listened to the sound of it, short and to the point. "Bill," he repeated, trying to align images of himself with the truncated word.

"They're almost finished rebuilding the set," Masago said.

"You don't sound too excited about it."

"I like coming home and finding you here," she paused, then added, "Bill."

"Not much we can do about it, is there?"

She lay with her head on his chest, and he felt the muscles of her face gather into a smile. "I could start another fire."

He grinned. "When we flew here, the guy who ran the team gave us this long talk on Japanese women. Obviously he never met you."

For a minute or more, she said nothing. Billy assumed she'd gone to sleep, and when she did speak, her words jerked him from his own blissful drifting. "After my mother died, I imagined myself as a dot. A tiny dot. Meaningless. When I saw girls my age on the street, a parent holding each hand, I saw them as sentences without beginnings or ends, each with a history infinitely deeper than mine. And I was just a dot. A period. A speck on the breeze." She kissed his chest. "All those things your friend told you about Japanese women stem from the notion of tradition, and tradition means much less when there's no eye for you to see your reflection in."

"Does that upset you?"

"If I hadn't been a speck on the breeze, I wouldn't have met you, would I? In that way we are much the same."

"Maybe so," Billy said.

♛

When filming resumed, Billy happily stepped back into his monster's skin. His smile masked by painted rubber, he stomped modern skyscrapers, withstood the piddling attacks of missiles and tanks. No longer did he recoil at the flash powder stink of volcanoes and bombs for he knew that once the smoke cleared, he would see Masago standing dutifully in the director's shadow.

The pace of their work quickened, fourteen-hour days, pre-dawn shoots. The fire had sent them over budget, and tensions on the set ran high. A sound engineer punched an extra who'd stumbled over his cords. The assistant director suffered a mild heart attack while arguing with the producer over the price of catered lunches. Some days were pure chaos, sets erected minutes before the cameras rolled, yet Billy remained calm amid the storm. No tragedies real or cinematic mattered because behind Masago's locked bedroom door, he'd discovered a place he didn't want to escape from. There, they'd sit half-naked on her floor, eating peanut cookies and unagi, feeding each other cut pear sections, barely noticing the building summer heat, the constant street serenade of honking cars, passing fire engines. As she slept in his arms, he whispered *I love you* just to hear how it sounded.

"I'm pregnant," she said softly. Her head was bowed, and it was impossible to see her face. They sat on her couch, and the kitchen light shimmered on her dark hair. "I didn't mean—"

"Shh," Billy said.

"I'm sorry for—"

He scooped her into his arms. His scarred knee momentarily buckled as he rose to his feet. Her tears wet his neck. Without a word, he carried her into her bedroom and shut the door behind them.

♛

The final days of filming were saved for water shots. Billy spent hours in the frigid tank, Godzilla emerging from the deep, stirred by atomic radiation, wounded Godzilla retreating to the safety of the sea. As he waited for the cameramen to load new film, he stood shivering, his eyes just above the water's surface. He moved his hand, watching the ripples he made. From beneath the camouflage of his costume, he studied the faces of the crew and imagined the hidden layers of life, the secrets people kept, the unguessed at worlds concealed behind locked doors. Masago stood by the director's side. She raised her eyebrows, silently asking if everything was all right. With the cameras reloaded, the director motioned for Billy to submerge. Billy held his breath and the water seeped into the eyeholes, an icy trickling that collected in puddles around his feet. He thought of the succinct sound of 'Bill.' He thought of the child growing in the watery world of Masago's womb, the mass of cells probably no bigger than his thumb. He'd seen the pictures in a college text, the fetus's alien appearance, the sea horse body and the miniature, vein-throbbing head. Muffled by the water, the director's megaphone order for action sounded like a monster's call, but Billy didn't respond. His heart drummed, and for a moment, he feared he was drowning in a five-foot pool, paralyzed by his own thoughts and dragged down by a waterlogged suit. The director called again, and one of the tech crew knocked on the tank's side. With an air-sucking gasp, Billy reared out of the pool, hands clawing the air. The sprays of water that flew from his scales wet the director's glasses and shorted out a row of lights.

Billy told Masago he'd pay for the procedure. He had the money, having signed a contract for two more films during the wrap party. He'd call McSwain for the number of the doctor who'd helped Swoop Nixon out of a similar jam. They were young, Billy told her. There'd be time for children later. For now they should just relax and not cancel the post-shooting vacation she'd planned for them at the Shuzenji hot springs.

Masago said little that night as she lay next to him. The next morning she called from the office. The ringing woke Billy from a dream of singing carp. She said she'd been asked to help proof a script for an English dubbing project and that she'd take the next train to Shuzenji. She wanted him to go ahead and secure their room, and she'd meet him that evening. The carps' song echoing in his ears, Billy agreed and promptly went back to sleep.

The train was hot and crowded. The engine lurched from the station and slowly settled into a peaceful, clicking rhythm. The city's glass towers gave way to lower buildings, tiny houses that blurred with the train's increasing speed. An elderly woman in a traditional robe glanced at him once and then stared down at her sandaled feet. Billy wondered what she thought of him. Did she see him as a monster, no different than the other monsters who'd left a trail of corpses and smoldering stones across her country? Was he just another man? Could he be both in the same breath?

A young family crammed into the seat opposite him, and their black-haired daughter gawked openly at the towering American. Billy waved, and the girl buried her face in her mother's lap. By the time the tiny houses faded into farmland green, the girl was asleep, her mouth opened wide, her head pitching thoughtlessly with the hurtling motion of the car.

He'd been an only child, and rare, the times he'd actually seen a child sleep like this, oblivious, peaceful, secure in the protective love of her mother. Ever since he'd left Iowa, he'd been on the run, either chasing a dream that wasn't meant to be or running from the knowledge that without that dream he couldn't really say who he was. Basketball player or monster. Billy or Bill. Years of running. And now, lulled by the the train's rock-a-bye motion and the image of a sleeping child, he became inexplicably tired. If he could only sleep like that child, lay his head on Masago's cool shoulder and sleep.

He called her from the train station the moment he arrived, and when there was no answer, he became excited. She was already on her way, perhaps boarding the train, and when she stepped onto this platform, he'd be waiting. He'd hold her, kiss her, Japanese customs be damned. He'd tell her he wanted this child, tell her he wanted his eyes to hold their reflection until the day he died.

In town he paid for their room, then hurried back to the station, but she wasn't on the next train. Or the one after that. He waited on a hard wooden bench, and after a policeman's stick nudged him awake the next morning, he walked stiffly to the phone and called the studio. Harsh morning sun streamed through the windows. On the other end of the line, the phone was passed among the secretaries until one was found who could relay the information that Masago had cleaned out her office yesterday.

Billy bought a ticket for the next Tokyo train. He seethed the entire way, kicking himself for mistaking the local line for the express. He hailed a cab at the station and smacked the seat like horseflesh in his urgings for the driver to go faster. Three blocks from their apartment, traffic snarled. Billy threw fluttering yen notes into the front seat and took off on foot. His knee throbbing, he ran the shadowed sidewalks. The elevator was out again in their building, so he charged the steps, taking two and three at a time until he reached the seventh floor. Doubled over, gasping, he hobbled to her door only to find it locked, a box of his belongings and his old basketball sneakers set neatly in the hallway. He pounded the door until it shook on its hinges, his assault answered by the perplexed, mop-wielding landlord who was busy cleaning the space for the next tenant.

In the years that followed Billy and Godzilla battled the likes of Baragon and Ghidorah, Rodan and Oodako and Ebirah. A new interpreter was sent, a jittery man half Billy's size, but by his third feature, Billy's grasp of the language had improved to the point where he no longer needed his help.

Billy tried to find Masago those first few months after her disappearance. He haunted the stores where she'd shopped, questioned the studio secretaries. He even got hold of a Tokyo phonebook printed in English and made halting, bumbling calls to every *M. Hideyoshi* listed. A year passed, two, and in time, he abandoned his hopes of reuniting with her.

It was 1969. Billy was in costume, a department store opening, a chain partly owned by the studio. Vibrant blossoms hung from the cherry trees, and a cool spring breeze kept Billy from getting too hot in his suit during the ceremonies. There were speeches, raffles. A band played covers of the latest radio hits. Children fidgeted in nervous anticipation as they waited for their parents to take a snapshot of them with Godzilla.

When the time came for the ribbon cutting, Billy lumbered over to the throng of identically dressed businessmen. A row of photographers lined up before them, and beyond them, a small crowd. Daydreaming, Billy scanned the on-lookers. At the crowd's edge stood a tall, thin woman with a little girl by her side.

"Masago?" Billy said, a muffled exclamation from beneath his disguise.

His heart racing, he stepped toward her, breaking flanks with the businessmen. It was her. It had to be her. She had been looking at him, and he was sure she knew it was him. The studio head cut the breeze-fluttering yellow ribbon. In the same instant, the reporters snapped their pictures, so many flashbulbs exploding that their starshine blinded Billy. The businessmen applauded enthusiastically. The band struck up a feedback-laden tune. Hands raised, Billy tried to shield his eyes. He waved away the photographers who only laughed and snapped more pictures at his antics. Popping afterimages dancing before him, Billy waded into the crowd, where all he found were laughing children who tugged at his lizard's tail.

the cuckold

e ven in my dreams, you are unfaithful, and in the land of sleep, I am denied the luxury of closing my eyes. Rarely do I see your face, but I long to, and you counter my advances with slithering escapes, a footwork display that would make Ali proud, the distance between us forever preserved. What am I allowed of you? Little more than haphazard glimpses, the tumble-touch of coal-black hair against a crisp blouse collar, a dismissive wave of your drink-cradling hand. The natural world—with its laws of diffusion and osmosis, displacement and renewal—yearns for equilibrium, and I now understand this balancing desire spills into dreams, for my stunted vision is offset by the painfully honed clarity of your voice, a tone so shimmering and true it travels not in waves but in molecule-cleaving particles. How fitting, your words' barbed sting, for the cuckold's deepest pain lies not in his ignorant past but in the all-too-aware present, in the unprotesting acceptance of his beloved's lies. In my dreams, you throw yourself at men with callused hands and horseshoe jaws, bullish shoulders and neon smiles. You kiss them with such passion, such need, that I can't help but stare, paralyzed once again by your beauty, by the selfish fire I once mistook for ambition, by your nearly flawless knack for betrayal.

I wake with a gasp. The crumbling darkness brings your unmade face into focus. Your mouth hangs slack, the corner of your lips glimmering with drool. You mutter something I don't catch and roll over. Even in sleep, you keep your secrets, and who, my darling, is holding you now?

killer

No one could talk about anything else. Twelve disemboweled bodies tangled in the riverside grass since the last snow melted— hookers, convenience store clerks, a schoolteacher, a pair of freckled twin boys. Impossible to turn on the news without confronting a blissfully unknowing snapshot of the killer's latest victim, without hearing the graveside wail of another anguished mother. Rumor said the governor had already called out the National Guard. Rumor said there might be more than one killer. How else to explain the police sketches' shifting details – with mustache or without, almond eyes or round—the slashed torsos the calling card of a cult's bloody rituals. The weeklong heat wave had turned our bedrooms into plaster ovens, so we lounged on our front stoops and exchanged our fears. Grasped in her thick fingers, Mrs. Addison's Jesus fan fluttered like a tropical butterfly, a jungle dance set to the salsa songs trilling from a distant radio. The Rodriguez twins squatted on the stoop and took turns braiding each other's long black hair. Joey Cintron lit his after-work joint, sucked five deep, cherry-burning hits and exhaled five, sweet clouds before passing the bad boy on, the resiny tip flavored with the oil and grease from his garage workbench. Shirtless boys played stickball on a field skewed by manhole covers and streetlights, graffiti-splashed mailboxes and abandoned cars. Mr. Gray's pain-in-the-ass terrier snapped at the mosquitoes hovering above the last dusty puddles surrounding the corner fire hydrant, a near riot just hours before, the children splashing in the hydrant's geyser spray, a police cruiser pulling up, threats of arrest as the cops wielded their tightening wrenches. "Why you arresting the kids for doing nothing when there's a psychopath running wild?" Mrs. Spadafora yelled from her stoop. Others picked up her cry— the Sum Parks and the Farley boys, the old men who played chess outside the bodega, Mrs. Addison, who waved her Jesus fan like an assaulting weapon as she struggled out of the comfort of her stoop chair. The taunting grew, a torrent of accented threats that chased the cruiser's hasty retreat.

"Wonder what he's thinking," Tiny Driscoll said. He pushed back his porch awning's frayed, limp tassels and stared up at the starless sky. The streetlight shimmered on the tanned dome of his shaved head.

"What who's thinking?" Mrs. Addison asked.

"The killer," Tiny said. "Wonder what's going through his mind."

The damp tips of Mrs. Addison's hair fluttered in her fanning breeze. "Hopefully a bullet, sweetie."

At first we gave little notice to the solitary runner, the shadowed form who flickered across our street before disappearing back into the alley. Probably a kid running from the cops, we told ourselves. Or maybe a backdoor man caught with his pants down or maybe a deal gone bad or perhaps just another soul driven crazy by the heat. Then came the first pack of pursuers, the lanky greyhound boys, thin arms and stork legs, and the ripples stirred by their swift, focused passing piqued our sweaty curiosity. The Farley boys set down their beer bottles. The stickball outfielders abandoned their groping under Joey Cintron's tow truck for their lost ball. "Here come more," Mrs. Spadafora said when the next small group darted across our street, young men less graceful than the lead pack but still swift. Tiny Driscoll hooked his dangling suspenders over his wide shoulders and ambled down from his stoop. There was a breath of heavy silence before we heard the ensuing sneaker stampede and the muted, echoing cries that blossomed when the mob poured onto our street. "It's the killer!" they yelled, pointing wildly. "The killer's up there!" For a moment we remained still, glued to our spots by heat wave lethargy and disbelief. The Farley boys, no strangers to street fights and general lawlessness, where the first to light out, and in a heartbeat we were all moving, a tributary drawn to a raging river. Beer bottles crashed, the stickball bat clattering onto the sidewalk but then picked up by little Willie Reese who waved the sawed-off broom handle like a sword as he admonished the rest of the fielders to follow him. Our own greyhounds led the way—Derrick Hill, the all-city forward, Dominique Brown, state runner-up in the 400—their paths picked through the jostling mob until they broke free to join the lead packs. The rest of us threw ourselves into the melee, some rushing forward, some falling back, our strides settling into the niches carved by aerobic levels and fast-twitch muscle responses. Mr. Gray's terrier scampered alongside and nipped at our dangling shoelaces. Fire escapes rattled as new arrivals clambered down to join the chase. A swipe of heavenly radiance cut over us, the searchlight from a police helicopter, moments of blinding illumination and long, dizzying shadows.

"Disperse now!" commanded the God-like voice, but the flawless mechanical rhythm of the helicopter blades only served to spur us on, the beating *whoosh-whoosh* amplified by the alley's cavernous walls, the din knitting the disparate rhythms of our hearts into a single, rushing pulse. Old newspapers and fast food wrappers fluttered above us like angry birds, the whipped-up gales putrid with the stink of sweat and rotting food and uncollected trash. Columns of soot and grime rose in gray tornadoes from the alley nooks, violent funnels that churned skyward only to settle back over us like a dirty snow. Joey Cintron wrapped his T-shirt over his gagging mouth, a bandit's style we quickly adopted. At each cross street our numbers grew, the Korean grocers in their flapping white aprons from Sun Street, the playground basketballers from the park, the frat boys stumbling out of the college bars, the high-heeled whores and the dazed crackheads, and with each step forward, we armed ourselves with makeshift weapons, car antennas and trash can lids, broken bottles and stray lengths of pipe, wooden stakes and baseball bats and torn-off sections of spouting.

On we ran, pushing, tripping and picking ourselves up again, our pursuit ending abruptly when the alley dead-ended onto River Street. "Where is he?" we asked, bumping into one another as we spilled onto the road. "Where did he go?" Mr. Gray's panting terrier sniffed our ankles as we stood atop the steep banks gnarled with spindly sumacs and tall grasses. Before us flowed the wide river, its watery scent rising over us like a wet veil, its black, glassy sheen distinguished from the night only by the faint headlight reflections of the cars crossing the cantilever bridge. We milled about on rubbery legs, hands grasping our heaving sides, the car-honking of blocked traffic ringing in our ears. The helicopter's searchlight crisscrossed over us, and in the beam's unflinching glow, we pulled our T-shirt masks from our faces and stared at one another through sweat-stung eyes, each of us silently wondering if the killer walked among us.

the baby cries

I. ● The baby cries. The baby cries. The baby cries. The physiology of his colicky sobs would stymie a busload of Einsteins; such a tiny body, such a staggering noise. You roll down the car window, hoping to vent his bawling, but you wonder—can sound be vented? where is that genius bus when you need to flag it down? Even on winter's iciest days, your father used to crack the window and hold up his cigarette, the pose of a blasé, motorcade-riding monarch waving to his adoring subjects, the smoke a fleeing white ribbon. But Einstein's dead, and as of last Wednesday, so is your father, and now neither of them are up for answering your questions.

II. Signal your last turn well in advance of your block. You are the lead ship in this sorrowful armada, the guide from the funeral parlor to the post-service gathering at your house (your mother is in no condition … and again, the heaviest responsibility falls upon you, the eldest child). The chilly current from the window nips at your cheek and dries the dampness from your eye. A rearview glimpse, your husband in the charcoal suit that doesn't quite fit the way it did when he wore it to his first post-college interview, and beside him, your son, hidden in the protective shell of his rear-facing car seat. "Hey, little man. Hey there," says your husband, but his tantalizing offers of a nook are drowned beneath the boy's tearful gale. Your husband slumps back into his seat and sighs dejectedly. "We've got to find that damn blanket."

A.   And the baby cries. And cries. And cries. Einstein scratches his tangled garden of snowy hair and accepts your father's offer of a cigarette.

B.   Adjust your rearview to witness the orange echoing of your turn signal. Guide the car down your development's winding streets. The procession twists behind you, and here and there, like speckled dapples on sunlit waves, you pinpoint the cars of the relatives you haven't seen all in one place since your sister's wedding.

III.   Last night you held the baby, drying his wet cheeks and whispering that everything was going to be fine, and could he please, please let you sleep—just for an hour—tonight of all nights? You rocked him until you both drifted off, your prayers answered by God or exhaustion, but with his first renewed squawk, you woke startled, momentarily confused by your surroundings, by the swaddled bundle in your arms, your son's slumbering expression replaced by grimaced strawberry cheeks, slit-squeezed eyes, a quivering, dimpled chin and a gaping, toothless mouth, a face so distorted that it came to you as a dreamy image, your baby's sweet features kidnapped by a stretched-to-bursting balloon filled with the breath of all that was pained and inconsolable in the world.

IV. Park well beyond your house and bail out with a parachutist's hell-bent determination, the door quickly closed to seal yourself from the incessant cries. While your husband struggles with the car seat, clutch your coat closer to your throat and witness the armada's docking maneuvers. The front wheel of your great uncle's Cadillac bucks onto the curb, and even the cocoon of metal and tinted glass can't mute his wife's scolding exasperation. An unintended choreography settles over the scene, the spirit of Busby Berkley resurrected in the one-by-one extinguishing of headlights and engines, in the opening and closing of car doors, in the last gray puffs of exhaust plumes rising into an equally gray sky. Your husband hands you the baby and jogs ahead to open the house. Navigate the gentle slope of your lawn, your heels unsteady over the dead grass and the last of the brittle leaves, and the baby, perhaps fatigued, perhaps shocked by an inhaled lungful of December cold, stops its sobbing. "That's a good boy," you whisper into the pink, seashell curve of his ear. Stand in the opened doorway, the baby's cheek nuzzled next to yours, the house's warmth touching your neck, and await the invasion of the sober figures who descend your lawn's slope. How will all these people fit inside?

A. Your alarmingly thin sister, already separated after less than a year of marriage, her dreams of a family vanished along with the husband who wiped out her bank account. Her speech at the funeral home service crumbled into a rambling account of family vacations and long-deceased pets, her voice cracking as she read the lyrics to some Dylan song she'd penned on a rumpled piece of hotel stationary. Her mascaraed tears ran in dirty streams until you stepped forward in an act equal parts compassion and embarrassment and helped her back to her seat. Despite the afternoon's deep blanket of clouds, she wears sunglasses, and the dark, oversized lenses twinkle with the cherry-burning reflection of the cigarette perched at her plum lips. You pray she'll survive the afternoon without popping too many pills or making a scene behind the barricade of a locked powder room door.

B.   Your mother in widow's black, her face obscured by the sheer veil hanging from her pillbox hat. How collected she is, her grief distilled into a series of graceful interactions. As a rebellious teen, you thought her rigid social codes archaic, even soulless, but now you've grown to appreciate her as the embodiment of suburban decorum, a woman who can pick up the phone and, sight-unseen, select the perfect corsage for any gown, who pens next-day thank-you notes with a calligrapher's precision. How perfectly she understands her role today, the linchpin between seldom-gathering clans, the afternoon's emotional barometer, the one others will look to for strength or comfort, and you have no doubt she will conduct herself accordingly, her behaviors setting a precedent she hopes her children will follow. Only later, alone in a bed suddenly too large, will she allow herself the luxury of tears.

C. Your father's parents, their wrinkled, Florida-brown hands linked, your grandmother leaning heavily on her silver cane, your grandfather's pained, arthritic stride further hampered by his oxygen tank tethering of clear plastic tubes. They haven't said a word all morning, a silence that only adds to their fragile veneer, and there's a poignancy in their labored procession that makes you clutch your baby closer.

D. And the rest—your father's half-deaf business partner; a young cousin on chrome crutches, his scholarship hopes mummified beneath an ankle-to-thigh cast, the white plaster graffitied by his football teammates; your brother, whose four-year-old son, once released from his car seat restraints, sprints ahead in a wobbly legged, momentum-building rush that ends with a headfirst tumble into flowerbed mulch.

V. The afternoon's overriding emotion? Relief first springs to mind, your father's suffering finally over, thank God and Amen, a period put to the cruel wasting of his dignity and awareness. Of course there is still sorrow, and throughout the morning tears have flared like wildfire sparks, some catching and spreading, most tempered with soft condolences and back-patting embraces. But mainly there is relief, for now you are free to forget his gray and sour-smelling skin, his hollowed cheeks and drug-slurred speech; now you and everyone else are finally free to remember him as you wish—as a child, a college roommate, a brother, a Christmas visitor, a bridge partner, a lover, a father. Stand aside and welcome each of these memories into your home. But other, more private emotions simmer beneath your hostess's smile. Nuzzle your baby's sweet-scented head, the downy hair smelling of your breast milk, and coo the same powerless assurances you've been whispering these past few sleepless nights. The unsettling tension accumulates in his bones, his momentary peace replaced in troubling degrees by the faint, seismic twitching of tics and scowls. "There, there, honey," you say. "Be a good boy for mommy." And herein lies the conflict: today your maternal duties do not mesh with memories of your father, memories in which you are the child being held, the one hearing whispers that all is well with the world.

VI. "Let me," your sister says, taking the baby before you can warn her of his impending eruption. Your still-outstretched arms are swiftly filled with the arrivals' shed coats, a bulky mass of wool and leather and unwound scarves, and from the staticy mound rises a garden of distinctive scents, your sister's Winston Lights, the spicy patchouli oil you can't smell without thinking of Aunt Mary's Christmas cards. When you place the coats on your upstairs bed, you pause, your palm smoothing the rippled landscape of your grandmother's patchwork quilt, the familiar scraps of old dresses and faded jeans you helped her sew as a young girl on a summer visit. True, you've never shared your family's addictions, their smoking and drinking and pills, their need to stand in the spotlight or upon a moral high ground, but at this instant, you understand the nature of selfish temptation for it takes all your strength not to stretch your weary frame across the quilt and tumble into its deep sea of hibernation dreams.

VII. Downstairs, you discover your mother arranging the serving trays and dishes across the dining room table, the plastic wrap skins pulled from refrigerator-cooled spinach dip and cheese cubes, vegetable trays and cold pastas. A quick glance into the living room finds your husband groping under the Christmas tree's lowest branches to plug in the string of white lights. Your sister bounces your fitfully whimpering son on her hip, her pursed lips leaving faint, plum impressions on his forehead. Her dark glasses have been pushed atop her head, her mascara-circled eyes exposed. How different is she than your baby? The two of them so fragile, both clinging to their teetering emotional perches, hers complex and intricately haunted, his unable to stray beyond the black-and-white of brainstem and reflex. You worry about her pain and disappointment, fear her history of impulsive love affairs and dramatic sabotage. Would she still let you hug her the way you did when you were kids? Your mother brushes by, jostling you from your drifting. "Silverware and napkins first, dear," she says, a correcting tone that resurrects the dormant pulse of the rebellious teen who thought her so foolish. *Calm down*, you tell yourself. Her penchant for orchestrating life's most inconsequential and maddening details is just her way of coping, of exercising a bit of control over the world's engulfing chaos, and in recent years, you've become a bit more sympathetic for you've discovered these habits creeping into your own actions, a genetic hardwiring that provides a mild, cringing shock each time you find yourself obsessing over color schemes or anniversary gifts. Relatives crowd around the table, plates are filled. Someone turns on the kitchen radio, the tuner twirled in a garbled march that ultimately settles on a station playing Christmas carols. Your son's gurgling spurts accumulate into a sobbing torrent, and you turn instinctively, nearly tripping over an eight-year-old second cousin who's lowered herself onto all fours in an attempt to coax your spooked tabby from beneath the table. Your grip tightens on the extra forks you've retrieved from the kitchen ("*Dessert* forks, honey," your mother said, handing you back the dinner forks you'd laid out), your knuckles bony white, the tines gripped in your trembling hand like a bouquet of silver thorns. And the baby cries. And cries. And cries. The distressed wails rise into a tidal wave that washes over the voices around you. You feel choked by the table's shuffling press of bodies, by your mother's Miss Manners scrutiny and your sister's tinderbox instability. "Stop your crying!" you want to scream. "Stop your goddamn crying!"—a public crumbling that would expose your most shameful, nagging apprehension, your fear that if you can't handle a crying infant, how can you possibly manage the years to come, the emergency room visits, the slammed-door arguments, the calls from disappointed teachers, the broken-curfew nights…

VIII. Your husband appears in the dining room entrance. "The blanket, honey?" Snapshot bursts tumble through your thoughts, and you see the blanket, a hand towel-sized swatch of nubby, colorful yarn with the inexplicable ability to soothe the boy, in a dozen different locations. Stuffed between the couch cushions. Speckled with clinging dust beneath the crib. Balled up and forgotten in the depths of your diaper bag. Concentrate, you tell yourself, and you close your eyes in an attempt to shut out the voices, to stifle the shrill sobbing that twists through your mind like a rusty corkscrew. As a child, your mother claimed a prayer to Saint Anthony would lead you to what you'd lost, but this afternoon, your heavenly connection has been interrupted, the frequency pirated by images of your father doing the hokey-pokey's two-step with Busby Berkley while Einstein furiously diagrams chalkboard equations relating the inverse relationship between the duration of your son's tears and your sanity. Set out on your blanket-seeking journey, and as you travel from room to room, meticulously scanning the knee-high niches of a child's world, you notice the distinct strata that have settled over your house:

A. The TV room, where the men have unbuttoned their collars and suit coats of black and gray, their ties loosened, their hands filled with beer bottles and snack plates. The paneled walls vibrate with the collective groans and cheers triggered by the football game playing on TV.

B. Despite its chill, the sunroom has been claimed by the teens, girls with braces and blossoming curves, boys who rub their peach-fuzz chins and grumble in alarmingly deep baritones about the inanity of their parents.

C.   The kitchen, the wives' domain, with their talk of carpools and household finances, the young ones in mid-thigh black dresses and high heels, the mothers in more sensible shoes whose rubber soles squeak each time they peer into other rooms to see what mischief might need their attention. (Yet these distinct divisions are unified by the conversational snippets you overhear about your father, his business partner who imitates the improbable, choppy swing that netted your father, a golfer who rarely broke a hundred, a hole-in-one; your uncle recounting the weekend they hitchhiked to Atlantic City and danced the Mashed Potato with Miss Alabama and Miss Tennessee, two pageant losers whose lacquer-sprayed hair stayed unruffled while their debutante-ish demeanors melted away on a sloppy river of sloe-gin fizzes.)

D.   The children are the afternoon's nomads, their routes repeatedly crossing yours as they chase each other in a giggling, duckling parade. Untucked shirts and rumpled blouses bear the spills as yet unnoticed by their mothers. Clip-on ties dangle from suit pockets, and a few unwittingly carry static-attached tinsel strands, thin ribbons that flutter like starshine banners in their hurried wake.

E.   You discover the blanket in the laundry room off the garage, the prize nestled like an oyster's pearl in the dryer's metal drum. The garage's scents of oil and gasoline stir faint recollections of the sleepwalker's steps that led you here last night after your son had rechristened the blanket with spit-up. Set the dryer for a quick, warming spin and thank Saint Anthony for coming through.

IX. "Snow!" shout the children. The smokers have gathered by the garage's opened doors, their inky silhouettes stark and flat against the hushed curtain of white. *I'm coming, honey*, you think when you hear the baby's distant cry, the wail that reaches you with the prickly distinction of the princess's mattress-buried pea. *Hold on, little one, hold on.* Detours hamper your progress—your eight-year-old second cousin, having lost interest in your cat, now darts in front of you on her mad dash to smudge her nose and fingers against the kitchen window and watch the snow; your little nephew, who tugs on your skirt with one hand and grabs his crotch with the other as he breathlessly asks for bathroom directions; your aunt, who reminds you for the fifth time that she wants to exchange e-mail addresses before she leaves. You enter the dining room, and as your cousin Beth's fiancé steps back to let you through, his shoulder strikes the ornate mirror you bought on your Bermuda honeymoon. The glass shatters when the mirror hits the floor, the frame's perimeter of seashells and ocean-worn stones spit out like teeth knocked from a boxer's mouth. Others join you as you squat and carefully pick up the shards, Beth and her profusely apologizing fiancé, your broken-legged cousin who uses the rubbery tip of his crutch to push the far-flung shells and stones your way. "Don't worry, please," you say, trying to calm both yourself and Beth's mortified fiancé. Partial reflections swim across the mirrored fragments, eyebrows and ears, groping fingers,

the fleshy bits of the room's improbable nexus forged by
blood and marriage and shared rituals. The still-warm
blanket draped over your shoulder, you sweep the broken
bits into a dustpan, but as you carry the debris to the kitchen
trash can, you become concerned. The baby isn't crying …
isn't crying. Even Einstein halts his chalk-grinding
calculations and directs a worried glance your way.

X.   In the living room, the Christmas tree lights soften the
crow's-feet wrinkles around Aunt Mary's eyes. She sits in
a straight-backed chair, a pie plate balanced on her touching
knees. She grabs your hand as you pass, anchoring you in
her patchouli oil current. "He's so beautiful, honey," she
says. The baby lies on a quilt stretched over the living room
rug. He gurgles and spits, his dark, wet eyes glinting with
sparks of Christmas tree lights. His pudgy legs kick with a
spastic, happy force that rocks him like an overturned turtle.
Your sister sits on one side of the blanket and plays peek-
a-boo with an unfolded napkin, the game paused every so
often to wipe the drool from his laughing chin. Your mother
sits on the other side of the quilt, her widow's black gloves
placed neatly atop the coffee table, her fingers tenderly
brushing the baby's mat of fine hair. Others gather nearby,
their chairs drawn closer, their trance-like attention fixed
on your son. Your grandfather grins behind the clear plastic
of his oxygen mask, while beside him, your broken-legged
cousin perches awkwardly at the sofa's edge, his crutches
propped beside him, and in his oversized hands, he holds a
child's stuffed football, which he waves in a bell-jingling
attempt to snare the baby's attention.

XI.   Kneel beside your mother, and when you rub her back, she
      leans into you, her head resting against your shoulder. Hand
      the tiny blanket to your sister, your meeting fingers
      exchanging a quick, comforting squeeze. Using the blanket,
      the game of peek-a-boo continues, the baby responding with
      a finger-flexing, wide-eyed excitement that triggers a mask-
      muffled laugh from your grandfather. A friendly debate
      ensues, your mother insisting the child has her eyes, your
      grandfather pulling aside his mask to contend that the boy's
      square chin is a carbon copy of his own, your sister's
      ringless finger tracing the curl of his ear and asking if
      anyone else has noticed that she and him are among the
      family minority with unattached lobes. It goes on like this,
      the associations growing more detailed, more ridiculous
      and amusing, the way his upper lip curls when he smiles,
      the musical toots of his burps and farts. Einstein sighs
      defeatedly, tosses aside his chalk and plunks down at the
      foot of the blanket. Busby jumps atop the coffee table, and
      with his hands held in a director's crop, yells, "Yes! Yes!"
      as he pictures the scene shot from his swooping crane. Your
      father settles down next to you and holds his ghostly fingers
      above the baby's mouth. He only wants what all of you
      want, to claim an exhaled bit of the child for himself, to be
      reminded once more of those brief, irretrievable moments
      that can only be appreciated by those who have lost them.

beneath the net

Your first dream ended on a Reno undercard. A left hook hollowed you to the core, your insides a column of dead air, the punch a whistling, thousand-pound bomb whose impact turned your thoughts to dust. How expertly you'd been played—five rounds of jabs and straight, quick rights, just enough leathery *rat-a-tat* to keep you on your heels, and then... The canvas scratched your back, and your moth-fluttering eyes beheld the other-worldly vision of a half dozen suns burrowing through cigar-smoke clouds. Impossible to tell where your dislodged mouthpiece stopped and your tongue began. Somehow you made it to your feet, oblivious to the world's new silence, to your cornerman who'd already thrown in the towel and was ducking between the ropes to rescue you, your boxer's instincts working you like a puppet on strings, the deeply engrained belief that you could no more quit than you could stop breathing.

Jean Harlow movies. Radio songs like "Moonglow" and "Cheek to Cheek." The whores who gathered in the alley behind the gym, sundown vampires whose bodies turned cold the moment their backs touched their stained sheets. The girl from your hometown, the preacher's daughter who, on the night she finally stopped saying no, whispered a prayer of forgiveness as your hand reached beneath her home-sewn dress.

This was all you knew about love.

You loaded freight cars and rousted hobos in the Santa Fe yards, sheared llamas in Utah, paved mountain roads in Colorado. On the radio, you listened to news reports from Europe and Africa and the Pacific. The world seemed intent on consuming itself, armies on the march and whole countries vanishing, and truth be told, you didn't much care one way or another. In each new town, you'd find your way to the gym, watch the fighters, sometimes wrap your hands and hit the bag … and around the corner from every gym was a bar … and just outside, the whores who looked right through you, knowing.

When the war finally came, you tried to enlist, faking your way through the physical until the bored doctor took a peek at your ruptured eardrum and told you to get lost. And there you were again, the fighter unable to fight. You hitched a series of rides to California, the desert crossed in a pickup bed shared with a mangy dog and caged, squawking chickens. The moon shone across the dead sea, and you pulled your tattered coat tight around your shivering body. Who were you, anyway?

Army engineers had rigged football fields of camouflage over the airplane factory's hastily erected holding areas and warehouses, the loading bays and slope-roofed hangars. The camouflage reminds you of seaweed tangled in a fisherman's net, and as you cross the vast parking lot, the frayed cloth strips flutter on the warm breeze, the net heaving with the rhythm of a restless ocean. You gaze up, the sky cut into the tight squares of a giant crossword puzzle, the clouds and blue, the faint morning moon and winter's evening stars.

You smoke your morning cigarette until the lit nub warms your fingers, nod a hello or two, but no one knows a thing about you, your boxer's past, the home you left long ago. A sleepwalkers' parade files past, faces obscured by the net's ever-shifting play of shadow and light, and you think of the deeper camouflage of a man's life, his heart wrapped in actions and stances meant to mask the sorrows that were his alone.

♔

You spot a woman at the plant. Tall and blond, pointed knees poking her overall's enveloping blue with every step. Her arrival as one of seven in a backfiring Ford reminds you of a midgets' circus trick. You set your alarm twenty minutes early just to plunk yourself in her path, smoking and kicking stones into the plant's backhoed trash pit. Below you, the maze of oily rags and paper scraps and broken wooden skids bristles with the traffic of scurrying rats. *Tat-tut-tat* scold the netting's strips of olive cloth.

Her story comes to you filtered through a dozen tongues. Her husband's body left on some jungle-island speck, and what more did you really need to know? On your way home, you stop at the gym and hit the heavy bag for the faraway glint of her green eyes, for the way the shadows fall across her face beneath the camouflage net, for the itching, melancholy lust that's taken root in your heart. Afterwards, you take a shower ... grab a beer ... and with your last three dollars, you find a street corner girl, and in the perfumed dark, you imagine her speaking in a voice you have yet to hear.

Her name, your foreman tells you, is Gail.

Hello, and can she hear the nervous sputtering in your gut, your throat's dry desert of apprehension? The Ford's six other women, in their work boots and babushkas and bobby-pinned hair, walk right past, but your blond lingers by the trash pit's edge and accepts your offer of a cigarette. *OK*, she says when you ask if you could meet her for lunch, but the cafeteria's din plays tricks with your bad ear, so you suggest a retreat to the wide, opened doors by the supply depot. *Want a chaperone?* the Ford's driver asks, and her squinting eyes fix you in a tail gunner's stare.

Outside, you sit on empty metal drums, your lunch pails balanced on your laps. The sparrows that nest high in the depot's exposed girders swoop around you. You tell her about the night in Reno, but then feel ashamed, your misfortune petty and selfish compared to hers. Flustered, you play the clown, walking on your hands as pennies and match packs rain from your pockets, tossing up crust strips for the darting birds to pick out of midair. Her laughter eases the embarrassment of your buffoonery.

Look, she says. Near the depot doors, the netting slants down, its stretched edges anchored on metal poles, and it's here that the net jerks with the wing-flapping struggle of an entangled sparrow. You and Gail stand side by side, half-blinded by the sun as you study the bird. Gail drags over one of the drums and climbs on top, momentarily posing like the surfing girls you've seen at the beach. She motions you over and, without revealing the vaguest hint of her plans, hoists herself onto your shoulders. Her boot heels dig into your ribs. Impossible to see what she's doing, her actions relayed by the faint tug-of-war she wages to release the bird, a curse she immediately apologizes for, the moment's awkward sexuality rapidly fading beneath the strain of holding her for so long. A feather drifts before your eyes, then another, and finally, the struggle ceases. She slides down, holding you, one of her overall bib straps coming undone on the way. Blushing slightly, she refastens the strap's hook. Bloody pecks dot her hands.

♛

Here's what you've come to know—

She prefers Basie over Sinatra, Cagney over Gable. She has hidden talents for pitch-perfect whistling and blowing concentric, slowly dissolving smoke rings. Her head swirls with facts and lists she can recite at a moment's notice—the Seven Wonders of the Ancient World, the roll call of Snow White's dwarves, the batting averages of the entire Gashouse Gang. But the deeper parts of her, the parts you alone want to know and possess, are only hinted at in the way she hums along with radio tunes you've never heard, in her unnerving habit of abandoning a conversation in mid-sentence to stare out the nearest window, her forgotten cigarette wasting away to a gray, ashy column.

♛

On a rainy November evening, you take her to the movies, and as the newsreel plays, many in the crowd sit forward at the sight of your factory's bombers trundling down a palm-lined runway. How unlikely, the planes' rumbling flight, their tons of hastily-welded metal flung into the sky and arranged in winter geese formations. The bomb bay doors open, revealing a seaside town's tight grid of houses, and then the bombs' flight, moments of silent anticipation, a breathless waiting that reminds you of a swimmer's rise from a lake's silty bottom. The bombs' strangely graceful cascade dwindles to invisibility before being reborn in dusty, rapidly multiplying blooms. *Give 'em hell!* one man yells, his cry cheered and applauded through the darkened theater.

I want to go, Gail says, already gathering her coat and purse.

Ten minutes later, you're climbing her apartment's rattling fire escape, four flights of narrow steps slick with rain. Her window is open, and the curtains drape around you as you straddle the sill. She waits for you in the middle of a dark, sparsely furnished room. Her palm gently pushes you back, and one by one, she undoes the buttons of her dress.

I loved my husband, she says.

I want to be a good man, you answer. *I want to be good to you.*

She stares at you, unblinking, intent, and you think if the entire building fell down around you, she wouldn't notice, a singularly focused state of mind you can only compare to that night in Reno when you willed your uncomprehending body off the mat. Her dress billows to the floor, a soft moat which grows with the addition of her slip, her bra and panties. The streetlamp below shines onto the ceiling, a spotlight shaft that divides the room into night and day. She steps toward you, hiding nothing, and it's not until you hold her that you realize you're both trembling, your naked, pressed-together hearts beating like the wings of the sparrow she once saved, a creature desperate to leave the false trappings of this earth and return to the sky.

professor asher's magnificent party hat

S now fell outside Professor Jim Asher's office window. The lights lining the campus sidewalks captured the trailing flecks of white and the bundled students hurrying to the semester's last night class. Jim Asher picked out the familiar ones headed to his fiction workshop—Crystal Martz with her trailing red scarf, the hulking figure of Sal Nardone in his football jacket and paddle-wide hiking boots. They walked side by side, and in the shadows between them, their fingers laced. Jim Asher smiled, his suspicions confirmed. Behind them, the snowflakes dotted the black shoulders of David Hess's long overcoat. Steam rose from the coffee cup gripped in his fingerless gloves, and the tip of his cigarette glowed orange as he inhaled one last puff. With a casual flick he launched the butt into a snow bank.

From the clutter of his desk, Jim Asher gathered his students' stories. A cross-section of his red pen comments caught his eye, bits of applause and appreciation, the gentle hints that seldom found their way into rewrites. Jim was halfway out the door before he turned back to survey the bookshelves above his desk. He liked to start each class by reading a passage from a story or novel he thought beautiful. He traced the nudges of the books' spines—Vonnegut, Fitzgerald, Chekhov. Without a hint of premeditation, his finger settled on the hideous purple cover of his first novel.

Crazy Water had been published when he was twenty-seven, and for a brief, illustrious moment, Jim Asher had been the newest star on the literary horizon. Fawning write-ups splashed across the newsweeklies' glossy pages, his sickeningly sober jacket-flap photo on the cover of *Poets and Writers*. The auctioning of the movie rights was quickly followed by a Book-of-the-Month Club selection. His publisher rushed out his story collection before *Crazy Water* made it into paperback. While his literary journal credits had been admirable, Jim feared his collection was inconsistent, ripe with the stink of his feckless MFA sensibilities, and the collection's lukewarm reviews hurt his feelings more than he let anyone know. The same publisher took *Among the Living*, his second novel, but his editor pushed back the book's release date and, instead, pestered him with rewrite requests for "accessibility" and "broader female audience appeal." When she suggested Jim change his main character into "someone you wouldn't mind being stuck in an elevator with," Jim tore up the contract in an uncharacteristic fit of anger. A mid-sized publisher with a solid reputation picked it up, but within a year after *Among the Living*'s release, the press folded. Now both *Among the Living* and his story collection were out of print, and with it, Jim Asher felt as if two giant chunks of his life had been lost forever.

He flipped through the pages of *Crazy Water*. How odd his own words seemed sometimes, a sensation like looking back at old photographs, the dated haircuts and ridiculous clothes, yet beneath it all lay the person he once was. He stopped at the night swimming scene, two naked lovers in a stranger's backyard pool, and with each sentence, the notion of his younger self became clearer, a mirror's reflection given the depth of time. In his thoughts, his submerged characters slowly rearranged themselves into an image of the kitchen of his old apartment, the table cluttered with his ink-smeared notebooks and manuscript pages, a tiny space he happily shared with his newlywed wife, Steph, who taught English at the local high school and often brought home paper piles to rival his.

Flipping the light switch, Jim exited his office. Hints of tinsel and holly sprigs adorned the doors of the other faculty offices, and as Jim strode past, the festive covers of their taped Christmas cards fluttered like a host of single-winged birds. The only things hanging on his door were his nametag, class schedule, and office hours. Christmas had snuck up on him this year, the season's usual announcements gone, his bachelor's apartment barely furnished, let alone decorated.

A few students greeted Jim's classroom entrance with hellos or comments about the weather. Sal Nardone peeled off his jacket, and with a limbo dancer's finesse, slid his bulk into the desk beside Crystal Martz. The ashy stink of cigarettes wafted from David Hess's coat as he arranged the last of a dozen desks into a circle.

"My last workshop," he said to Jim. "Doesn't seem possible."

"I know," Crystal said. Her scarf, now unwound, lay in her lap like a coiled snake. "Where did the time go?"

Jim squeezed into the circle and handed back their stories. For the next hour, he asked each of them to read a favorite passage from their work and then give a self-critique of both their story and their semester's progress. Crystal Martz blushed slightly as she read her dorm room love scene. Sal admitted he was uncomfortable at first writing from a woman's point of view but now he didn't mind it at all. Tina Bates, an exchange student from Dublin, said she still couldn't balance dialogue with exposition. "Guess it stems from me habit of runnin' off at the mouth. Me bleedin' characters do the same damn thing."

"What about you, David?" Jim asked.

The young man stroked his carefully trimmed goatee. "I have too many ideas. My head's swimming with them."

"Christ!" blurted Tina, adjusting her cateye glasses. "We should all be so bleedin' unfortunate!"

"Professor Asher?" David asked. "I've heard whispers that there's some long-standing tradition for the last meeting of this class. Is my information correct?"

The others smiled. Sal Nardone sat up expectantly, wriggling behind the confines of his desk.

"The word's gotten out, has it?" Jim said. "You know what they say about loose lips."

"They make for bleedin' sloppy kissers!" Tina said. "Now enough of the bullocks, professor."

"OK, it is tradition that the last night of a senior fiction workshop goes down to the bar for the final hour of class."

"Only an hour?" asked Sal.

"It has been known to stretch out a little longer, Mr. Nardone."

David Hess stood, sweeping his black coat over his shoulders. "What are we waiting for?"

The conspicuous squeak of their wet shoes in the hushed, cavernous hallways triggered giggles among the bundled escapees. Jim Asher glanced into the passing classrooms, the eyebrow-arching professors and the envious students. Their giggles crumbled into laughter as they hustled down the echoing stairwell, and with a door push and a bracing gust, they stepped from the bone-dry heat and radiating fluorescent buzz into a night painted by falling snow. A one-inch coating layered the parking lot cars. Two cars were quickly brushed off and filled, and with fishtailing, honking exits, they headed to the bar, shouting promises to claim their tables. David, Tina, Crystal, and Sal joined Jim for the half-mile walk to the bar.

They trekked across campus, abandoning the regular geometry of the unshoveled sidewalks for shortcut trails, their footprints skirting the iced-over fountain, the founder's white-shouldered statue. Sal plunked the statue with a snowball to the chin. Tina tried to do the same, her arm reared back in a ridiculous windup, the throw of an unathletic woman raised in a soccer-loving nation, but her unpacked snowball disintegrated long before it reached its target. "Bullocks!" she snapped. "Is there some secret Yank ingenuity I'm missin' out on?"

The snow muffled the sounds of Main Street's few passing cars, and the flakes swirled in an endless dance beneath the streetlights. Sal took Tina aside until she understood how to pack a decent snowball, and with her first stop-sign plunk, Tina raised her fists and danced a triumphant jig in the empty street. Crystal's red scarf lifted like a battle flag as she ran toward Jim only to pounce into a boot-skiing, surfer's pose that propelled her halfway down the block. Jim smiled at the scene. The dichotomy of the adult-child always fascinated him, the mixing of mature bodies and limited experiences, their flirtations with imported cigarettes and existentialism, their clinging belief to the notion of romantic love. They still had hopes and dreams they believed stronger than the weight of the world.

"'What silly games we make of our lives,'" Crystal said, struggling to balance herself as she slid between David and Jim. She was quoting from *Crazy Water*, the scene where the protagonist has just watched his best friend faint at the altar. "'The goals we set and the lies we use to comfort our egos.'"

Sal hurled a snowball in a high arc, a pearly dot consumed by the darkness above the glowing streetlamps. "'And in time, our lies become our truths, our lives erected on a foundation of excuses and regrets, the roads not taken expanding into a roaring superhighway journeying deep into our shadowed souls.'"

Tina climbed onto a church's brownstone steps and solemnly held a gloved hand over her heart. "'And so I drove, the pedal down, the desert wind whippin' my hair, speedin' faster into my soul of lies, faster toward the black horizon where I prayed I would find salvation or death or even a good night's sleep.'"

"You kids need to start expanding your reading lists," Jim said.

"*Crazy Water* was an important book to a lot of people our age. The ones who read, at least." David paused, cigarette clenched between his teeth, the warm shine of a lit match captured in his cupped hands. "It spoke to modern fears without whining, and it let us laugh at ourselves at the same time. That alone is an accomplishment."

Sal and Crystal and Tina scampered ahead, slipping, weaving paths as they dodged each other's hurled handfuls of snow. "Their rendition just now sounded like it had a bit of whining," Jim said.

"There's a fine line between whining and honest introspection." David exhaled a smoky cloud and ducked a snowball thrown by Tina. "Personally, I liked *Among the Living* better. I mean *Crazy Water* was a blast, but *Among the Living* had this kind of appealing desperateness. Now your story collection was OK, but the pieces you've been writing recently, like that one in the last issue of *Bay Street Review* or the really long story in the *Penn Quarterly*, I think they're really some of your strongest efforts."

In workshop critiques, David's icy wit and deft turn of phrase had set him apart, his contributions brutal but honest, and his elaborately defended opinions had swayed the group on more than a few occasions. Sometimes Jim felt David chose his stances for the sake of being argumentative, the intellectual bully flexing his muscles. Now, as David brought his cigarette to his lips, he appeared less sure of himself, the student tentatively placing himself on the same plane as his teacher.

A rush of warmth and rock star covers of Christmas songs greeted them inside the bar door. The early arrivals had staked out a large corner booth in the rear. Jim separated himself, waving off David and Sal's offers of money and insisting the first round was his. Wedging himself between occupied stools, he tried to catch the bartender's eye.

A good crowd tonight, lots of laughter, enough empty seats to avoid the claustrophobic feeling the place had on a weekend night. Orderly constellations of Christmas lights circled the booths and bar, and their shine delivered a delicate, flattering illumination on the front door arrivals, the red-cheeked youngsters who brushed snow from their sleeves.

Jim ordered three pitchers and carried them, one in each hand, the third cradled precariously between the other two, until Sal hustled over to help. Puddles of melted snow had turned the hardwood slippery, and Jim walked his path with hesitant, deliberate steps. He was accidentally bumped once by the dartboard, another time by the pinball machine. The spilled beer wet the cuffs of his jacket. Mistletoe hung from the exposed, wooden ceiling beams, and the dangling clumps of green snagged at his hair as he passed beneath.

Jim set the pitchers on the table. He'd expected a rousing welcome, but was greeted with only distracted thank-yous, his students' attention fixed on the muted TV above the bar where a Christmas cartoon played. Santa steered his rickety, overloaded sleigh through a blinding snowstorm. A teddy bear and yarn-haired doll emerged from his bulging bag, a pair of pint-sized co-pilots who helped pull the reins. Jim had watched the show's first airing when he was a pre-teen too old to believe in Santa, and as he peeled off his damp-sleeved coat, he noticed how deeply entranced the others were in the cartoon's antics. They anticipated each line of dialogue, and shouted warnings before the evil, Christmas-foiling villains appeared.

"I love this bleedin' part," Tina said. The shifting TV light reflected in her glasses. "Hits me straight in the damn heart."

David, who'd just tilted his last pinball round, joined them, taking the seat directly opposite Jim. The spillover who couldn't squeeze into the booth pulled up chairs. Jim had deliberately planted himself in an end seat, an easy exit should the proceedings turn glum, but by the time the pitchers were refilled, his fears had been put to rest. Perhaps the snow contributed to their effervescent mood, or perhaps it was the mix of Christmas lights with the gaudy bar neon, or maybe it was the looming stress of finals week—whatever the cause, their corner of the bar had turned decidedly boisterous. Their loud voices competed with the jukebox tunes. Their communal eruptions of laughter rattled the aim of the Thursday night dart league. Empty pitchers were quickly filled. Rounds of schnapps were brought, and the ashtrays filled with crumpled butts. Their alcohol-lubed conversations veered recklessly between topics—the use and misuse of the second person in literary novels, childhood trips to the emergency room, first loves, and worst breakups. To emphasize her selection in the category of favorite dead rock star, Tina rose and belted out a possessed, hair-swaying accompaniment to the jukebox's playing of "Me and Bobby McGee." The dart league throwers acknowledged her performance with a round of whistling applause. Crystal laughed until she cried, and between hyperventilating gasps, she begged Sal to get her a drink of water. David stubbed out another cigarette. He was seemingly preoccupied, and Jim followed his gaze to the approaching black-haired young woman in paint-flecked bib overalls and a camouflage hunting cap. Jim recognized her as a student from his Advanced Comp class—Mary, Maggie, Meg—the names swirled in his thoughts, none of them quite right.

"Got room there, Professor Asher?" she asked.

Jim scooted over, the others following in a domino rhythm. The girl sat and the side of her leg pressed against Jim's. She leaned forward, a pose that communicated her true intent hadn't been to sit next to Jim but to place herself directly across from David.

"Hi, Mel," Crystal said brightly. *Mel*, thought Jim, and he silently repeated the name again, hoping it wouldn't slip from his short-term memory.

"Crystal, Tina, Sal, everybody." Mel accepted an offer of a beer, and Sal filled her mug. With a quaffing gulp, she downed half of it and turned to Jim. "You've got class tomorrow at nine sharp, Professor."

"That makes two of us."

"I'll be there with my proverbial bells on." She wiped foam

from her lip. "Maybe real bells if the spirit hits me."

David grinned. "You always knew how to make a grand entrance."

"And your forte, Mr. Hess, seems to be exits."

David's cigarette-holding fingers pointed to her head. "Isn't that my hat?"

She took off the hat and shook out her long, straight hair. Her elbows anchored on the table, she placed the hat upon her raised fist and held it away from her face as if admiring it for the first time. With a finger from her free hand, she bothered the dangling earflaps. "Used to be your hat, didn't it?"

"Finder's keepers," David said.

"So sayest the weepy loser." She put the hat back on her head. "I'm here on official business, gang. Mark's having a New Year's party and you," she then turned from David and nodded to the others, "and all of you are invited." She stood, finished the rest of her beer in a single swallow, and kicked the toe of David's boot. "And no excuses. Maybe if you're lucky you'll get back your lovely chapoe."

She made her way back to the bar, the camouflage hat magically floating above the crowd. Jim refilled his beer and David's. "I assume there's something between you two beside shared headgear."

"I've come to learn that a circle of friends can be more tangled and fanged than a nest of vipers," David said.

"They dated for over a year," Crystal explained, counting out a pile of wrinkled ones. She grabbed an empty pitcher, but paused before leaving. "Why did you guys break up anyway, David?"

David shrugged. "Just wasn't meant to be."

"Oh, they were hot and heavy, they were." Tina helped herself to one of David's cigarettes. "And he's got the pictures to prove it. Our little friend here's quite the amateur shutterbug."

David lit a match for her. "They were life studies. Very tasteful. Very artistic."

"You can talk an art chick into anything," Sal said. His broad shoulders sagged beneath the attention his remark garnered. "At least that's what I've heard."

Tina exhaled, her lipstick a bright, red ring on the cigarette's filter. "Life studies my ass. My theory is—"

"Here we go," David said.

Tina elbowed him in the ribs. "My theory is your so-called life studies attracted most of the world's perverts in the pre-pornography days. Start with Titan and Bottecelli and plow straight ahead to Balthus, Touelous-Latrec, Gauguin, and Klimt. Every last one of them a bleedin' perv."

David shook out his last cigarette and crumpled the empty pack. "So what you're saying is the new Van Gogh is probably wallowing beside some strip club brass pole right now?"

"That's exactly my point." Tina held up a soggy bar napkin. "And the next *Les Demoiselles d'Avignon* will be sketched on a bleedin' napkin with a dirty joke printed on the other side!"

Near midnight, Jim rose a bit unsteadily from the table. The dart league throwers were gone, replaced by a trio of tipsy sorority girls who hit the wall as often as they did the board. Jim laid down his remaining singles and patted his jacket pockets for his gloves. "Time for me to call it a night, folks."

"Me, too," David said. "Got a paper to finish tomorrow morning."

They bid their farewells, waved to Sal and Crystal who shuffled a clinging slow dance in the jukebox light. Jim buttoned his coat as he weaved through the bar, absently yet cheerfully acknowledging the calls of "Merry Christmas, Professor Asher!"

Outside, the snow still fell, lighter than before, the fattened flakes pushed along on a wind that had grown stiff and biting. A beeping municipal plow rumbled down the street.

"Got to tell you, Professor, I enjoyed your workshop," David said, his voice raised above the scrape of steel against macadam. The truck's orange strobe flashed across his face. The plow passed and he resumed his normal tone. "No bullshit or sucking up."

"Thank you. Without the bullshit as well."

"You have a way of making it come alive. You communicate that fire." David patted his chest, and the long, black material of his overcoat ruffled in reply. "You believe it. You've made it happen." They stopped at a corner. A blinking traffic light suspended above the intersection bobbed on the same icy breeze that tussled David's hair. "And that's why I want to ask if you'd be up for reading something I've been working on outside of class, the beginning of a novel."

They stepped from the curb and crossed the street. Usually Jim's response to such a request was a flat, reflexive *no*. He could barely read the first drafts of *Crazy Water* without being sickened by his obviousness and sentimentality, his reliance on clichéd images and stagy dialogue. Yet when he looked into David's waiting face, he saw the reflection of a desire he once knew well.

"Sure," Jim said. His right foot slipped on the powdery coating outside the dark-windowed coffee shop. He quickly righted himself and tried to offset his clumsiness with a joke. "Just put a few of your snapshots in as payment."

David's lips crinkled into a mischievous smile. "You feel like getting high?"

Jim stopped. "We're talking about pot here, right?"

"My old roommate's a botany major and a part-time farmer with a grade-A crop."

Jim's exhaled breath formed a curtain that momentarily veiled his world. "Grade-A, huh?"

They walked a block and a half. "He's on the third floor, the lit window." David squatted and packed a snowball. "Only problem is his buzzer doesn't work." With a grunt, he hurled his snowball, a toss that missed by inches, a white spattering marking the brick just above the window.

Jim joined him, and together, they took aim at the faintly shining glass. Jim's first throw hit the fire escape landing, and with his next errant toss, a twinge shot through his shoulder. David's aim proved better, and on his second glassy plunk, a vague form appeared in the window.

"Rocking," David said.

Jim rubbed his shoulder. "Rocking indeed."

Between coffee sips, Jim graded the last of his Advanced Composition class's papers. A dull ache filled his brain, a pain intensified by the early morning ruckus from the floor below, an apartment occupied by a brutish cell of the college lacrosse team, young men fond of bass-thundering rap and backyard wrestling matches. Jim squeezed his temples and tried to summon his reserves of patience already worn thin by his papers' misplaced commas, the sentence fragments, the promising notions that crumbled beneath ghostly support.

He swallowed two aspirin, then another for good measure. Kneeling, he groped beneath his bed for his missing shoe, but his search netted only a gagging swirl of dust. He'd lived here for nearly six months, the lease taken over from one of the department's graduate assistants, yet most of Jim's belongings remained stuffed in the milk crates and boxes he'd lugged in on moving day. He finally located his shoe, and as he sat to lace it, he noticed the answering machine's blinking red light. He pressed the button and began gathering his papers into a folder, but stopped at the sound of his wife's recorded voice.

"Hi, Jim, it's me. The lawyer says you haven't been by. Will you please do it soon? It'll only take a few moments. And call me so we can make some Christmas morning plans, OK?" He played the message again, this time listening to his daughter's playtime shouts in the background.

He opened his apartment door, and a large brown envelope fell onto the tip of his shoe. He recognized David's handwriting and hazily remembered his agreement to read his manuscript. Jim scolded himself for being drawn into the task, and he hastily placed the envelope in his already bulging folder. In a stairwell made loud by his footfalls and jangling keys, he devised a plan; he'd skim the pages after class, jot a few encouraging margin notes, give him the old 'stick-to-it' speech and hopefully be done with it.

He squinted in the morning's sunshine assault. A snowy sheet cascaded onto his pants when he opened his car door. He threw his folder onto the passenger seat, but the turn of his ignition key was met only with a single, metallic click. He tried again, his foot pumping the gas, and then understood he must have left his headlights on when he'd returned from the mall before last night's class.

He usually walked, campus was only five blocks away, but

today he was running late. With the folder tucked tightly against his side, Jim strode briskly up Main Street's salted sidewalks. The wind blew the snow piled atop the power lines, and the plummeting white slices struck the macadam with shattering grace. He passed the corner apartment he and David had pelted with snowballs the night before. In a stranger's slovenly, poster-covered living room, Jim had smoked himself stupid, lung-burning bong hits, coughing until his eyes teared. When the time came to leave, he could barely peel himself off the couch and shuffle the short distance home, and he wondered what David and his green-thumbed friend thought of him, a supposed man of words reduced to grunts and giggles.

The bells in Old Main's clock tower rang nine times as Jim approached his lecture hall. His hustling pace had triggered a damp sweat beneath his jacket. The cold numbed his face, and he worried that his room's dry heat would trigger a runny nose, his final lecture punctuated with tissue grabs and lip dabbings.

A two-lane road cut across the intramural fields that led to the faculty lots behind the lecture hall. A sleek yellow sports car skidded on the road's final turn, the low-slung rear bumper gouging a snow bank. The car belonged to Richard Karnow, a computer science professor and, Jim suspected, the man who'd recently started seeing Steph, Jim's signature-waiting, soon-to-be ex-wife. It was difficult enough for Jim to accept that Steph might be dating, but the fact that it was Richard Karnow made it doubly hard. Richard was the unofficial faculty squash champion, a noontime jogger clad in ridiculous short-shorts and bright headbands. What hurt most of all was Steph's decision to seek out his polar opposite, a choice Jim saw as a symbolic statement meant to distance herself not only from him but from the memory of the young woman she'd once been, the one he'd fallen in love with in their undergrad workshop, the two of them staying up half the night to make love and dream aloud of the novels they'd one day write.

A brittle voice called as Jim neared the lecture hall doors. "Hold the train, conductor!"

A hunched, silver-haired woman wobbled toward him. Dr. Sally Pruce was the English Department head, a woman who hadn't changed her eyeglass frames since she published her first poem in 1949, her stubborn sense of style now imitated by the hip, flea market-scouring undergrads. The clatter of her ankle braces accentuated her frailness, the legacy of a childhood from the days of polio, and the rattling sound had Jim shaking off the image of a skeleton beneath her enveloping overcoat. Jim opened the heavy door, a task made difficult by the entrance alcove's wind tunnel effect.

"And who said chivalry was dead?" she asked. She paused, a bright smile compounding her face's network of wrinkles. "And give a Merry Christmas to that pretty wife of yours and your daughter, will you? How old is she now?"

"Tricia's five—"

A burst of wind howled across the open field. The distant pines bowed and shook off their snowy caps, and when the gust struck the alcove, its current hit the bricks and crashed back upon itself. Coffee cup lids and flecks of snow bombarded them, Dr. Pruce's gray hair standing at a frightful attention. The cold, metal door handle tugged against Jim's grip, and his shoulder, already strained from last night's snowball-throwing escapade, ached as he tried to maintain his grasp and save the door from slamming against the dawdling old woman. A second, trailing gust blew open Jim's folder, and a half dozen of his papers flew out like so many white doves escaping a magician's hat.

"Dear!" Dr. Pruce exclaimed. With a brace-rattling step, she attempted to pick up one of the swirling papers.

"I've got it, Sally," Jim said, still holding the door while stomping on the paper. He dejectedly watched the tumbling, fluttering exodus. "You go in, please. I'll take care of this."

"Well, if you're sure, Jim—"

Jim smiled weakly. "I'll tell the girls you said Merry Christmas."

He scampered off after his papers. He found one snared and ripped in the bare branches of a brick-hugging shrub, another bogged down in a half-frozen puddle. His shoes crunching over the snow, his socks damp and icy cold, he drifted onto the field and rounded up the others. Two, three, four times, he bent to pick up a paper only to have the breeze whisk it from his fingers, his footsteps a crazy, twisting path leading away from the lecture hall.

He was out of breath by the time he reached his classroom. He smoothed back his disheveled hair, dabbed a tissue at his running nose. "Well, what a morning it's already been." He took off his coat and scarf, placed David's manuscript envelope on his desk. "I'm sorry for being late, so without further ado, let's get this party started." He held up the folder. "Here I have your final assignments, some of which are in a strange condition I can barely explain."

"We saw," said Tim Deibler, a lanky, bent-nosed wrestler who sat by the back window. He flashed a thumbs-up. "Very entertaining stuff."

"Glad you were amused, Tim." Navigating aisles cluttered with backpacks and purses and shed coats, Jim handed back the compositions. "My apologies," he said each time he delivered one of the damaged papers.

"Is this due to some after-effect of last night's activities?" Mel asked quietly when he gave her one of the more mangled papers. Last night's camouflage hat had given way to a French braid, her overalls replaced by a zipper fleece. She pressed the soggy-edged paper against her jeans' thigh, one side then the other.

Jim reached back to the young man behind her. "Next time we meet in a similar situation, do me a favor and tell me to go home."

"Hey, Professor Asher," called a student in the back, "I can't read your comments. They're all smeared."

"Mine, too."

Jim closed his empty folder and leaned against his desk. Most of them were sophomore English majors; a few, like Mel, just fulfilling core requirements. He sighed. "In the spirit of the season and to atone for my bumbling, I could be persuaded to bump everyone's score five points."

"How about ten?" Tim Diebler called.

Jim took his glasses from their case. "How about three, Mr. Diebler?"

"Five's fine, Professor. Perfect."

Jim launched into the day's lecture, the Zen of Continuity. Examples were slapped on the overhead projector, key phrases highlighted in pink, and Jim's projected shadow loomed large on the screen. The same grouping of hands shot up each time he asked a question, reflexes as sharp as trained animals, their mouths pecking out the answers. Jim turned off the overhead and wondered what, if anything, he'd accomplished these past four and a half months.

"Ms. Uhlig," he asked the most persistent of the hand raisers, "outside of another human being, what is the most beautiful thing in life?"

The young woman stared as if he'd asked the question in a foreign language. She flipped back through her notes.

"How about you, Tim?"

Tim diverted his daydreaming gaze from the back window. "What's that, Professor?"

"Go back to sleep, son." Jim turned to the rest of the class. "There is no right answer is there? The much clichéd eye of the beholder serves as beauty's final judge, and thank God for that. And for these two eyes, the written word is the world's most beautiful thing. There are twenty-six individually meaningless letters and a handful of punctuation marks, but string them together right and you can create a universe. And I'm not talking exclusively about fiction and poetry. Writing can have a functional beauty that breathes life into your e-mails, the notes you slip under your girlfriend's door, even a dry-as-sand corporate newsletter."

He paused. Tim Diebler was reabsorbed in the snowy world outside the back window. Ms. Amy Uhilg halted her copious note taking, her multi-colored pen bobbing with a gunslinger's twitch. Mel looked up from the intricate doodles that had blossomed in her notebook margin.

"Take Warhol. I don't think his soup cans and Brillo boxes were solely concerned with the banality of a consumer culture. Quite the contrary, I think they addressed the beauty of such a culture. That Brillo box you pass in the supermarket was put together by some artist, the colors added just to catch your eye, to please your senses. A person can do the same with language. If you're going to write, why not make it something worthwhile, something wonderful, something with a little life and spirit? Why not create a sentence or paragraph that adds a little something to this world instead of feeding upon it? Maybe Warhol was truly and simply saying, 'Here is this box. Isn't it beautiful?' I…" Jim sighed, "I think I've lost my train of thought again."

He took off his glasses and folded them back into their case. Mel sat back and grinned, but the blank stares of the others made Jim feel foolish. He clapped his hands and checked the clock. "Well, that's it. There are ten minutes left in the semester, and I'm afraid I've said all I have to say. So I now give you each a gift by giving you back ten minutes of your life. Put it to good use. See you at the final."

"You almost had it there," Mel said as she walked past. "Just couldn't reel it in."

"And Hemmingway thought he had it rough with that oversized tuna."

After a visit to the lobby vending machines, Jim Asher settled down in his office chair. He had an hour until his next class. He took a sip of his soda and peeled back the crinkling wrapper of the cream-filled cupcakes that were about to pass as breakfast. He undid the clasp of David's envelope, and when he slid out the pages, a pair of photographs of a naked young woman fluttered onto this desk.

The lacrosse players had been at it again. Crushed beer cans littered the apartment stairwell, and wadded sadly by the foyer door lay a giant pair of graying underwear, the name *OX* magic-markered on the spent elastic. Outside, Jim noticed a young couple loading a car with laundry bags, computer components, armfuls of hanging clothes. Halfway through finals week and the trickling exodus had begun. In three days these streets would seem like something out of a ghost town.

Frigid gusts buffeted him at each intersection. Sparkling pinwheels blew off the sloped roofs. He gripped his jacket against his throat and questioned his decision to walk to the student union to meet David for lunch. With his other hand he carried David's manuscript envelope, photos included. In his office, after his first, recognizing glance, he'd quickly shoved the pictures back into the envelope, but later that evening he couldn't resist another look. The flash had bleached portions of her skin, the Polaroid's lack of depth diminishing her curves. In one pose she stood in a doorway, her hands raised high against the frame, her legs crossed at the ankle; in the other she lay on her side across a quilted blanket, her head propped on a fist and a book opened beside her. In the days since, Jim had returned to the pictures often, his attraction due less to her nakedness than to her apparent comfort, the shameless ease with which she held herself.

He paused on a sidewalk and allowed a pair of sofa-lugging students to pass. "Thanks, Professor Asher," the trailing one huffed when Jim stepped forward to hold the door. He walked on, and as Old Main's tower rose like an ominous moon over the houses and bare trees, he thought about how *Crazy Water* had changed his life. The book's notoriety had assured him a teaching position, if not here then in some other parallel universe college town. Twice a year the royalty checks came, figures not enough to live on yet still surprising to Jim. In the decade since its release, his words had brought him cushy speaking gigs and financial semi-security, offers of easy sex (which he'd always declined) and free drugs (which, outside the occasional joint, he hadn't accepted since Tricia was born). And now, they'd brought him naked photos of an unsuspecting student he'd have to face later that afternoon at her final.

A stuffed, upright bear guarded the student union lobby. A scarf sporting university maroon and gold ringed the beast's neck, a matching wool cap atop its matted head. Skylights dotted the high ceiling, and today, they cast a brilliant, crystalline glow. An ocean of voices echoed and overlapped. Jim blew his nose and scanned the room's nexus of institutional quality sofas and chairs. A nasty flu bug was making its way through campus, and Jim thought of winter's hungry look, the pale skin and chapped lips, the watery, bloodshot eyes.

He spotted David sitting alone in a booth beside a large window, and he wondered what the next hour would bring. The story pages were fine, the writing sharp and, at times, sublime, but what could he say about the pictures? Just holding them made Jim uncomfortable, the envelope practically radiating its own accusing heat. He ducked into the snack line before David noticed him.

Steam billowed each time a hair-netted counter worker lifted a soup vat lid. The welcoming aroma of brewing coffee penetrated Jim's stuffy nose. The line inched ahead. Jim gazed out the frost-bordered windows. A groundskeeper scattered salt on the sidewalk. A decapitated snowman guarded a patch of lawn, his charcoal-eyed head lying nearby on the trampled snow. Coffee and danish in hand, Jim walked through the room's gentle bustle, his path often altered by the activity of peeled off gloves and unwound scarves, handshakes and farewell hugs, the bickering study groups. He settled in across the booth from David.

"So you're not a health nut," David said.

"Could qualify for the nut part if the other night's actions are any indication."

"You were the life of the party."

"Please." Jim squinted in the avalanche of snow-reflecting light. "Pretty bright spot you picked here."

"I thought it was Hopperesque."

"So this is your last hurrah? Your victory lap of the student union."

"I'll hang around until the lease runs out in mid-January. Give myself a month of victory laps."

"Don't underestimate a victory lap's power. It's a phenomenon that occurs less often than you think."

"Advice taken."

"So what's next after you stop running?"

"Then I work. And write. Get this novel together in a year, year and a half, something I can take in-hand to grad school." He held his fingers over his steaming cup. "Pretty nebulous isn't it? Most pressing thing on my schedule is deciding what to do for New Year's. It's a dilemma because the only thing more depressing than a New Year's Eve party is sitting at home and not going to one."

Jim tested his coffee with a hesitant sip and considered his own New Year's plans, the invitation to the Rosenblatt's party. The past six years, he and Steph had gone, but Paul Rosenblatt was also one of Richard Karnow's squash partners, and Jim couldn't bear the possibility of running into Steph on the arm of another man.

Jim slid the envelope across the table. "Listen David, the other night outside the bar, I didn't mean to give the impression—"

Jim choked on his words when Mel abruptly appeared and

threw herself and her oversized canvas purse into the booth next to David. "Hey Professor. David." She was bundled in a blue down coat whose zipper sported a collection of frayed ski tags. "What's that?" she asked, nodding toward the envelope. "Some clandestine, literary shenanigans? Our Advanced Comp final?"

David smiled. "Top secret shit."

"Very," Jim said unsteadily. He withdrew the envelope and placed it on the seat beside him. He studied the loose sleeves of her sweater, her red nose, her breathing, actual presence no match for the memories of David's pictures.

"My ass." Mel sneezed, and Jim handed her a napkin from the tabletop dispenser. "Thanks," she said. "Half the fucking world is sick this week."

"I feel fine," David offered.

"You're a special one, aren't you?" She blew her nose, and Jim slid the napkin holder toward her. "So you know why I'm here, don't you?"

Jim placed an anchoring hand over the envelope that now felt as if it were on fire. Mel wiped her nose and turned to David. "Mark's New Year's Eve party?"

"I'm considering an appearance," David said.

"Did I miss something somewhere on how being a self-serving hermit is the in-thing now?"

"All the cool kids are doing it," David said, ducking her playful swat.

"Mark's graduating, too. And so are Alice and Sal. Chances are this will be the last time we'll all be together."

David sipped his coffee. "Professor Asher and I were just talking about New Year's. Maybe it's exactly what I need to cap my college career—a couple hours of drunken slobbering, some amusing sideshows of the inevitable emotional meltdown, maybe a post-midnight fistfight. Yes, sir, sounds like a blast."

Mel blew her nose. "And your favorite holiday is?"

"Christmas," David said.

"That has nothing to do with the baby Jesus and everything to do with the fact that you're a greedy SOB." She waved her crumpled napkin at Jim. "How about you?"

Jim jerked to attention. "Thanksgiving," he said after a moment's thought.

"Good choice. That's my number two after Halloween."

"Hey, what about my hat?" David asked.

"Maybe it'll be at the party." She gathered her napkins and shoved them in her coat pocket. "See you at the final, Professor."

Jim watched her struggle through the incoming lunch crowd. "She seems rather insistent that you attend."

"I think she's becoming swept up by nostalgia."

Jim handed over the envelope. "I made a number of comments. It has potential. No bullshit, as you so aptly put it the other night. There are some structural concerns that I think you should look into, but that's a judgment call. I'll be willing to check out a rewrite but don't tell anyone else in workshop or the offer's off. And please, no more pictures."

David took the envelope. "So what are your New Year's plans?"

12/25

I keep thinking back, a driver obsessed with the rearview mirror, imagining the ghostly image of myself, a man untouched by bitter knowledge. A year ago I woke beside

Steph, Trish crawling over us, begging to go downstairs and open her presents. Today, I'm envious of that man … and also ashamed of how oblivious he was, blind to what was happening all around him.

My life was once a house. Now its foundation has crumbled, leaving me with a collection of unconnected rooms, tiny stages where I'm left to play out my days, an actor unsure of his lines or motivation.

On the drive to see Steph and Trish this morning, I passed our old apartment. Blinking blue lights ringed the windows, garlands on the rickety fire escape. I thought of the three cramped rooms, a stove with a stubborn pilot light, rattling pipes. There were times I'd so hated the place's dollhouse proportions that I'd kick my way from one end to the other, books and clothes and shoes flung against the plaster walls … but this morning, as the car behind me beeped that the light had changed, those blinking blue lights shone like a borderline, a boundary I could dream about but never cross.

Strange, the garage entry into the house where I'd once lived, another disjointed stage, the scene of Steph's tearful confession last spring—that she no longer wanted to be married, that she'd felt this way for some time—her voice still echoes there, captured in the unchanged setting, the dented trash cans and half-filled fertilizer bags, the mildewed magazine piles waiting to be hauled to recycling, the oil stains beneath my shoes. Trish appeared in the doorway that connects the garage to the laundry room, no cries of 'Daddy!'— just an initial, silent stare, a hesitant greeting for the ghost returned to flesh, the haunting presence who took his deep voice and muddy boots and sink-ringing whiskers and then vanished from her day-to-day life.

And this marking of time occurs in the present as well. Too quickly the morning passes, the happiness of moments marred by their ephemeral nature, Trish running, her bathrobe flapping open, butterfly wings for her warm, little body; her sleep-matted, downy hair; the crinkling static of her flannel pajamas.

Later, alone in the kitchen (another side stage, hushed voices not meant to carry beyond the immediate walls), Steph and I argued—my reluctance to sign the divorce papers, my thinly veiled Hail Mary attempt at reconciliation. Hurt, I brought up Richard, something I'd promised myself I wouldn't do, his name bubbling in my gut like bad gas, the uttered release bringing no relief, only an intensified discomfort.

As Steph made breakfast, Trish and I retreated to the garage to play with my present to her, a new soccer ball and miniature net. Some of her kicks sent the ball rippling into the net; some missed, wild bounces and ricochets, the windows narrowly avoided. A kitchen scent reached me, Steph's traditional Christmas morning feast of chocolate chip pancakes ...and here I was once again, locked away in a side room, just another setting of an increasingly fragmented life, the leading man haunted by the past and mesmerized by the fleeting, melancholy beauty of the present.

👑

A red bulb lit the second floor landing. Jim pulled a cold-skinned champagne bottle from beneath his coat. Cutout snowflakes bordered the door of 2B, and behind the door drummed a party's muffled chaos, music and raucous voices, the piercing screech of noisemakers. Jim checked the watch Steph had given him last Christmas. Only an hour remained in this year of crumbling foundations.

A young blond woman burst through the door before he could knock. The stampeding rhythm of her platform clogs halted when she paused beneath the red light and brushed the confetti flecks from her jacket's fur collar. "Hey, Jen," asked a young man hidden amid the doorway-bordered throng, "how about buying a bag of ice, too!"

"And two—no, three—packs of Marlboros!" begged a female voice.

Plastic cup in hand, David appeared in the doorway. "Professor Asher, I assume." He placed his cigarette in his grinning mouth, and with his free hand, executed a grand, inviting sweep of welcome. "Welcome to the jungle."

Bloody veins colored the young man's eyes, and when he spoke, he leaned slightly forward, a pose of confidentiality far removed from his usual reserve. He draped Jim's coat over his arm and presented Jim's champagne bottle to Mark, the lanky, redheaded host. The freckled young man immediately opened the bottle and sloshed the fizzing liquid into the plastic cups thrust his way.

A brunette with elbow-high, black satin gloves and mismatched contacts of blue and gray fitted Jim with a cone party hat and secured its band with a chin-stinging snap. Noisemakers trumpeted, a cry that reminded Jim of horribly wounded geese. The kitchen's sticky linoleum pulled at Jim's shoes as he jockeyed for position in the keg line. Sal and Crystal sat side by side on the stove.

"It's awesome you came," Crystal said.

Sal offered up his meaty hand. Jim completed the ritual with a fainthearted high-five. "Right on, Professor."

The foam overflowing from his cup, Jim ventured into the living room. The press of bodies had ratcheted up the room's heat, and the fogged windows held their faint reflections. Hints of marijuana smoke flavored the air. Mark handed out paper bang-snaps, and their exploding bursts lent the party a nervous, hiccupping rhythm. Techno music pulsed from the stereo speakers. A melee of possessed dancers shook the living room, and one by one, the cheap ornaments dropped from the corner Christmas tree, a hundred broken shards to reflect the party lights.

"Top of the evenin', Professor!" Tina Bates called. In her chunk-heeled boots and bunching, black leather skirt, she climbed atop a kitchen chair. She dipped a wand into a plastic bottle, and with a pursing of her lips, exhaled a bubble storm. "Happy bloody New Year, you Yankee wankers!"

A bubble burst on Jim's cheek, a soapy film on his skin. Tina blew more, a cascade of transparent orbs, some popped by burning cigarettes, some cradled momentarily in loving palms.

On his way back to the keg, Jim stumbled between David and his debating friends. Their conversation twisted in odd, looping shapes, and Jim sensed a hint of other drugs, a chemical sugarcoating he saw reflected in Mark's saucer-wide eyes.

"Lust," Mark stated, the neck of Jim's champagne bottle still clutched in one hand, a pitcher of beer in the other. "Without a doubt, lust is the most delicious emotion."

"Got to be love," Crystal said. "It's the basis for anything worthwhile man has ever done."

"Save love for the dwindling ranks of the romantics, and lust, my dear Mark," David spoke out of the corner of his mouth as he lit a cigarette, "is the soul's Chinese food. Its satisfaction is, regrettably, temporary."

"I think Chinese food is the shit." Mark filled Jim's cup from the pitcher. "How about you weighing in here, Professor."

A bang-snap exploded on the nearby wall, a powdery gray residue marking the spot. Jim's attention had wandered to the narrow hallway behind Mark where Mel, in a hooded sweatshirt and baggy jeans, and two other brush-wielding girls were busy painting some sort of mural.

"Chinese is OK with me." Jim sipped his beer. "As far the most delicious emotion goes, I'll let you know when I find it."

Countdown updates were shouted above the din—*Thirty minutes! Twenty minutes! Fifteen!* On his way to the dance floor, Sal delivered a tattooing high-five that had Jim flexing his aching hand to make sure his fingers still worked. Jim claimed a chair and spied on Mel over the rim of his raised cup. She and the other girls painted with aerobic class movements, continually shifting places, rising and kneeling, stretching onto their tiptoes, brushes raised high then lowered in sweeping arcs. The second time she caught him staring, she left her friends, and Jim's heart sputtered at her approach.

"Look who's made the scene."

Smears of pink and indigo marked her jeans. She dabbed her tapering brush on a makeshift, cereal box pallet. "Mind if I brighten up your party hat?"

"Is it that dreadful?"

"Dreadful but not irredeemable." She brought herself closer, and her soft, gray sweatshirt brushed Jim's shoulder. The cardboard circumference of his hat scraped across his scalp as she began to apply the paint.

"How's your hallway project coming?"

"It's a wonderful mess. The whole too many cooks thing. Place gets repainted after Mark moves out, so no damage done." She circled him like a barber, her brush strokes nudging the hat this way and that. "This, though, will be my masterpiece."

"I'm honored." Her thigh touched the outside of his leg. "I hope you enjoyed class."

"I did. I mean it was comp after all, but still, it was OK."

He took a sip of rapidly warming beer. "It can be pretty dry material, I'm afraid."

"Once you got away from the commas and semicolons and that sort of shit, it picked up. Made me think about writing a little differently. That part of it was pretty cool."

She stood directly in front of him, and when she leaned closer, her breasts pushed against her sweatshirt. Jim cleared his throat. "Maybe you'd like to take a workshop."

"Can't." She abandoned her long strokes for a series of dotting points of color. "My semester's full of studios. And gym, which I've been putting off. Anyway, I'm not a multi-talented kind of person. Don't even know if I'm uni-talented."

"So my hat's not a masterpiece?"

"Your hat," she said, finishing her work with a bold, emphatic stroke, "is simply your hat. Only now it's uniquely and totally yours."

"Five fuckin' minutes!" Tina cried.

Champagne bottles appeared, bargain brands in dark green bottles. The countdown continued, and Sal opened a window, snow blown in from the ledge, an icy wind knifing through the smoke and stale air as he lit bottle rockets and sent them whizzing into the night. The champagne bottles' plastic corks ricocheted wildly, the partygoers ducking for cover as if under attack by angry bees.

Streamers and confetti and Tina's bubble storm marked midnight's arrival. The gunpowder stink of Sal's bottle rockets lingered long after he'd shut the window. Jim had a sip of champagne, then quickly returned to his beer in an effort to wash the putrid taste from his mouth. The party reeled in exchanges of kisses and hugs and handshakes, and Jim felt himself adrift in the swirl of bodies, temporarily grounded only when he came upon a familiar face. "Happy New Year," Mel said, giving his cheek a kiss before melting back into the crowd.

A waifish girl toured the living room with a bottle of tequila, pouring shots directly into open mouths. Voices grew louder, the comings and goings more frantic, the whole party seemingly under the influence of a vibrant power surge. A clogged toilet produced a temporary hallway river, and the drunken guests continued to slip and slide even after David and Sal had mopped up the mess. Jim sat on the end of a tattered couch that had been pushed into a far corner. He politely declined the offers of passing joints, his beer exchanged for water. Mark plunked himself down next to him with a cushion-springing twang and thrust a pen and a worn-covered edition of *Crazy Water* into Jim's hands.

Mel and David shimmied at the fringe of living room dancers. She'd lost her sweatshirt, and was now pared down to a tight pink T-shirt, *GIRL* written in glittery letters across its front. She and David moved with a grinding, teasing intimacy that betrayed their ex-lover status. How beautiful they were, their souls unfettered by worries of health or lost promise, their smiling faces as bright as winter stars.

David abandoned her at the next song's start. She stood alone, her feet planted but her hips refusing to abandon their swaying rhythm, her eyes leisurely taking in the party's panoramic scope until she noticed Jim. When her beckoning finger couldn't lure him from his seat, she came to him, clamped her warm hands around his wrists and pulled him to his feet.

Jim struggled to find the kinetic beat that seemed hardwired into the bodies of the other dancers. He debated how to hold his hands, his body a network of kinks and complaints, his feet seemingly distant objects. An image surfaced in his head, the shameless, garter-exposing twist his Aunt Edna had performed at his and Steph's wedding, and Jim's performance grew even stiffer.

"Let loose, baby!" Mel said. She reached out with both hands and tussled his hair. "Shake it!"

By two a.m. the party had turned the corner toward sloppy, the waifish tequila girl vomiting off the fire escape, Tina embroiled in a profanity-laced, barely coherent argument with Sal. Jim wandered to the bedroom and unearthed his coat from the pile atop Mark's unmade bed, trying not to wake the passed out form of the blond who'd run out for cigarettes and ice just as he was arriving. Jim found David's heavy overcoat and draped it over her motionless body.

Sliding his arms into the coat's sleeves, he met up with David by the front door. A crumpled, unlit cigarette was clenched between his fingers. "Slipping out, eh?" David asked.

"Hours past my bedtime."

"Me, too, only who's counting?" He placed the mangled cigarette between his lips.

"So you'll be hitting the road soon?"

David lit a match but seemed unable to make the connection between cigarette and flame. "Yep."

"Where's the first stop?" Holding David's wrist, Jim guided the match to the cigarette's tip.

David puffed, waved out the match. "Tonight I'm thinking Montreal." He exhaled. "Kind of a Paris substitute until my finances get straight."

"Send me a copy when you get your first story published. I'll be able to say I knew you when."

"You keep writing, too, man." He clutched Jim's shoulder and squeezed tightly. "You're a real inspir—"

"Out of the way, boys." Mel, bundled in an army jacket and wool scarf, stepped between them.

"Where're you going?" David locked her in a hug, his goateed chin raking her neck. "You're the one who talked me into coming to this hellhole."

"Like you had anything better to do." She pushed him away. "I'll be back. Just running home to get something."

"My hat?"

"Number one on my list."

David followed them onto the landing, a stagger-step that just missed escalating into a stumble. "Happy trails!" he called down the stairwell. He waved, his hand striking the wall, a shower of orange sparks raining from the cigarette's tip.

Jim opened the door for Mel. Outside, flurries twisted out of the sky. "You really getting his hat?"

"He wouldn't remember if I came back or not. He's probably up there either getting ready to pass out or trying to put the moves on the first available piece of ass." Behind them came the shriek of breaking glass, and together, they looked up to see tumbling, light-reflecting glass shards and a single shoe plummeting from Mark's apartment window. "When does life stop being the search for the coolest clique?"

"What makes you think it stops?"

She brushed a fine, snowy film from a mailbox's rounded top. "I used to love going sledding when I was a kid. I tried it again last week. You know that little hill behind the art studio? We found some cardboard scraps by the dumpster and used them."

"How was it?"

"Soggy. Not nearly as good as I remember it." She stopped beneath an intersection streetlight and gazed up. "It's like a soft avalanche, isn't it?" Breathy steam rose from her mouth, and her long lashes batted at the falling flakes. "A soft, beautiful avalanche."

A yellow sports car slowed to a stop at the intersection's red light. Framed in the windshield's scraped portal were the intently staring faces of Steph and Richard. The light changed, and Richard's gear attack caused the car to lurch like a woken beast. The engine coughed, nearly stalled, and the yellow car bucked its way up the street, its rear end shimmying wildly.

No vehicle existed that could return Richard Karnow to his youth. Jim couldn't go back and enjoy bad champagne. He couldn't go back and write *Crazy Water II*. He couldn't return to waking beneath the same warm blanket beside the person he thought he knew better than anyone else in the world. All that he had for certain was this tiny stage, this New Year's morning of darkness and snowflakes.

He grasped Mel's hand, and together they walked silently toward her apartment. He remembered an afternoon at the art museum where he'd held Tricia's hand, a gentle leading through priceless wonders, and a similar emotion filled him now. His eyes strained to see this night through Mel's perspective, to understand what these hours meant to her.

"This is my stop." Mel climbed onto a stoop, her eyes level with Jim's.

"I'm two blocks down."

"Long walk on a cold night."

He leaned forward, kissed her slightly parted lips, then pulled back. The moist cloud of her breath broke over his dry skin. He held her tenderly, his cheek resting against hers, his heart brimming with a love he could never fully explain to her.

"I'd better go," he said.

"Don't you want to come up?"

"I do." He smiled. "But I can't."

He paused at the end of the block and watched the light flick on in her apartment. There was no point in trying to recapture a ghost. To have lived such a time and be reminded of it every now and again was enough of a gift, and all the way home, Jim concentrated on the memory until it glowed like a coal deep in his belly, a warmth that carved the tiniest niche against the blustery night.

amelia imagines
herself in terms
of a circle

A circle is a two-dimensional figure in which each point is equidistant from the center

a melia wonders if this is the shape of life, each of us standing at the center of an empty space entirely our own. When her boyfriend Daryl holds her, the two of them naked on his floor mattress, his room midnight dark and his apartment building throbbing with music and footsteps and a dozen muffled conversations, the radius of Amelia's circle dwindles until it is no wider than an eyelash. On the morning bus, surrounded by strangers and insulated by her headphones' serenade, the circle swells, an all-engulfing boundary that emanates from her beating heart and swallows the entire city. But be it near or far, there is always a line she draws around herself, a radius measured not in centimeters or inches but in a hundred finely shaded nuances, in laughter cut short and eye contact avoided, in her refusal to join Daryl in his nightly telescope peekings into the vista of lit windows surrounding his apartment. What fills Amelia's circle? The wispy notions of daydreams. The silent words of her books. But most often, the space is occupied by an acute awareness of herself, an atmosphere filled with a repelling charge that keeps the world at bay.

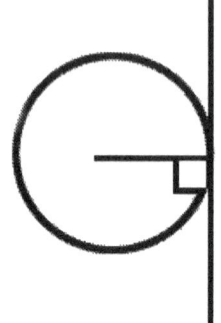

A tangent is a line which intersects a circle at a single point

A tangent shares a lone point with a circle, yet a circle possesses infinite tangents. Amelia thinks of just such a design when she studies the intricately woven willow branches that form the dream catcher above Daryl's rumpled mattress. Daryl claims his grandfather was a full-blooded Chippewa, an assertion Amelia finds either lovable or maddening, depending on her mood. Chippewa legend claims the willow hoop only allows the passage of pleasant dreams. Amelia told Daryl anything she could buy at Spencer's could hardly be classified as a tribal artifact, but the secret truth is she's never had a bad dream in Daryl's bed. Most likely this is due to a combination of their post-sex exhaustion and the mind-numbing weed Daryl stuffs into his bong, but some nights, as Daryl snores beside her, Amelia imagines the nightmares meant for her glancing off the willow's curved arc, the lines' barbed tips zooming back into the darkness like little malevolent arrows. Amelia wonders what happens to the dreams meant for her. Do they fade into infinity? Are they shunted off into the shadows where they wait to ambush her another night? Will their payload of distressing images plunge kamikaze-like into an innocent dreamer's sleep?

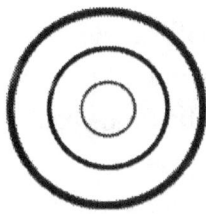

Concentric circles share the same center but possess unequal radi

You're pregnant, her doctor says, and with the words, Amelia is overcome by a new strain of vision, a heartbeat-gapping conversion that casts her surroundings in a suddenly queer light, not brighter so much as heavier … denser … as if the visible spectrum had bulged from its time-honored constraints and sprouted a new color beyond violet. Amelia detects this unnamable hue in dots and splashes that swiftly fade if she looks too long. Perhaps, she thinks, this shade serves a different function than its brothers, its role not to discriminate and categorize but to hint at the interconnectedness of all things.

Over the next ten days, she often lays a hand over her belly and thinks of the growing mass inside of her as both the seed of this novel color and also as her new center. And then Amelia thinks how she was once the center of her mother's life, and her mother of her grandmother's. And so on. And on. And on…

Daryl accompanies Amelia to the clinic, his temper ready to flare in case the pro-life crazies block the door or shove pictures of mangled fetuses in her face. But the morning brings an icy rain, and the three protesters huddled beneath umbrellas keep a respectful, almost disinterested distance from the clinic's entrance.

Inside, Amelia finds a waiting room of somber girls, a fidgeting boyfriend or two, the smell of wet coats. She pretends to read a magazine article about rising oil prices until her name is called.

Ninety minutes later, she limps back into the rain. Woozy, her knees as liquid as the sidewalk puddles, she leans against Daryl, his arm anchored around her shoulders. The same trio of gray-haired women stands on the sidewalk, and the plunk of raindrops on their umbrellas provides an oddly harmonic counterpoint to the hollow *click-click* of their rosary beads.

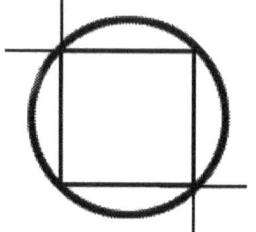

An inscribed angle equals half the measure of its intercepted arc. The opposite angles of an inscribed quadrilateral are supplementary for they intercept two non-overlapping arcs that comprise the entire circle

The half dozen candles surrounding the bed are part of Daryl's sex ritual, a series of maneuvers and props Amelia once thought cute. The blowing snow whistles between the slats of the fire escape's metal, and in Daryl's room, the candles' flames twitch, the space chilled despite Amelia's efforts to line the windows' gaps with scarves and singleton socks. Hugging herself, Amelia rises and hunts down her sweatshirt. A splash of come drips from between her legs, then another, and the pearly puddles mark a Hansel and Gretel trail to Daryl's telescope. Amelia stoops to look through the eyepiece. A black circle surrounds the indistinct shine of the not-so-distant windows, the scene blurred by the falling snow. Amelia adjusts the focus and brings the unappreciated middle into view, a vertical shaft of continually dancing flakes. Beautiful.

Settling back onto bed, she's momentarily blinded by the sudden, violent flash of Daryl's instant camera. Daryl smiles and claims he took her picture because he wants to remember how lovely she looked on the night a blizzard brought the city to a halt. Amelia holds the picture, watching her image arise from the field of black, and presto, there she is, captured in the Polaroid's murky, unflattering hues. *My turn*, she says, snagging the camera. Daryl mugs, posing with a smarmy leer and flexed muscles. Lining him up in the viewfinder, Amelia thinks of herself and Daryl facing each other from opposite sides of a circle. Yes, they see each other, see their allotted sections of arc, but their individual visions tell only half their story, each of them blind to what the other truly perceives.

The flash clicks, the room flooded in a pulse of harsh illumination.

Pi is the ratio of a circle's circumference to its diameter

When expressed as the fraction 22/7, pi appears rigid, immutable, yet its exact value can never be known. Pi is both irrational and constant, its digits refusing to terminate or surrender to pattern. Despite its mystery, pi's ratio holds just as true for a pinhead's micrometer radius as for the behemoth satellite dishes NASA aims into the heart of star-speckled desert skies. Computers have calculated pi to twenty-million-and-counting decimal places, but the inexhaustible digits are at this moment still outpacing Silicon Valley's most heralded microchips.

Amelia navigates a cart through the supermarket aisles. One of the cart's wheels emits such a piercing squawk that a few shoppers openly scowl. There's not much in her basket—two cans of tuna fish, a loaf of bread, noodles, cereal, half a chicken breast and quart of milk—the telling items of single life. She and Daryl have declared a hiatus, a cooling-off period she's hesitant to rekindle, especially now that he's taken to late night, drunken phone calls. As Daryl's ramblings veer erratically between anger and crippling self-pity, she wonders what she ever saw in him.

Another cart reaches the checkout at the same time, and Amelia defers to a mother whose toddler fidgets in the cart's backward-facing seat. The mother takes the cart's front, transferring her items to the cashier's shimmying conveyor belt.

Amelia diverts her attention to the checkout's racks—the tempting displays of chocolate goodies; the tabloids' lurid tales of Hollywood's latest infidelities and addictions, stories which, like their neighboring sweets, amount to little more than empty calories. Amelia tries to interest herself in the headlines, but she can't divert her attention from the suddenly calm toddler, a waif with fine, blond hair and wide, blue-gray eyes. The two of them exchange stares, a type of unashamed voyeurism that makes Amelia a bit more sympathetic to Daryl's telescope snoopings. There's something going on here, something as simple as one number posed beside another, something which radiates out from this point like a still-water ripple, linking them all in a way both concrete and maddeningly indefinable.

the species crown—
a novella in days

5/30

My therapist suggested keeping a journal. Her rationale—writing down the whos and whats of my days might help me sort things out. She said looking back over a crumb-trail of entries could make the present's forest seem a bit less overwhelming. A journal would allow me to become a witness to my own life. Whatever.

My previous impression of journals was limited to junior high girls and their admissions of secret crushes, and so let this be my first journal secret—that fifty-minute-hour on Dr. Owen's squeaking leather chair was fucking excruciating. The things I'd imagined myself telling her—the things I'd *hoped* I'd be able to tell her—welled in my throat, a logjam of good intentions and unrevealed confessions. How could I tell a stranger something I can't even bear to utter aloud? I've tried to, you know, alone, drunk or hazy with pills—or both!—just me naked before the mirror on the back of my bedroom door, but I can't, not without losing my cool in one form or another.

Shit.

6/2

I didn't go in to clean out my desk on the day designated by the transition team. There was bound to be a scene or two, the inevitable tears, perhaps an altercation which would be swiftly hushed by the rent-a-cops the corporate boys would bring in. Maybe I should have gone, started a bit of subtle instigating and then sat back and enjoyed the ensuing ruckus, but my mischievous inclinations were sunk by the near-coma I'd put myself into. I didn't come around until one-thirty, a resurrection on my apartment floor, the stacks of cardboard boxes surrounding me initially disorienting, my first cobwebbed thoughts wondering if I'd woken in the proverbial roadside ditch my father was always warning me about. I spent the remainder of "T-Day," as my ex-boss Everett had named it, lugging those boxes out to my car, settling with my landlord and nursing my splitting head (it wasn't a good day to be outdoors for a man in my condition—the harsh sunshine throwing everything into unforgiving relief, a perfect light for hopscotching children and Impressionist painters, but not for a man suffering from the temple-squish of tequila and unpurged pharmaceuticals). Everett left five messages on my machine. Ivy League Everett. Fuck him and his suspenders.

So, twenty-four hours late and still slightly woozy, I arrived for my last day of work. At least there was plentiful parking in the MELCO lot. The rest of the pink-slippers were gone, vanished, and the thought of soon joining them brought me a whiff of joy. Reflections of high, feathery clouds floated across the building's tinted windows, and I might have even thought the scene beautiful had I not known the brain-decaying shithole that lurked inside. MELCO—MAKING CONNECTIONS THAT LAST—and it's funny how I'd never noticed the sign before that moment, the placard held between two ass-crackers from maintenance as they ginger-stepped down a pair of rickety extension ladders. My last empty box slapping against my thigh, I studied the new sign waiting in the dewy grass. RODOSCOPE INT.—A WORLDWIDE NETWORK OF CARE.

Long live Rodoscope, comrades! I shouted. Long live their worldwide network of care!

Fuck off, the fatter one sneered, and I saluted them with a clenched fist and shuffled inside.

On the ground floor, I stopped by the empty employees' gym. A wall of mirrored panels doubled the glistening rows of chrome weight machines and computerized stair-steppers, stationary bikes that beeped out their riders' brisk heart rates. Setting down my box, I opted for one last go-round with the heavy bag. THWAP, THWAP, THWAP, until the jolts numbed my wrists and a sweaty, alcohol-scented glow beaded on my unshaven lip. The jarring violence awoke my senses. I punched and jabbed, left hooks high and low. The motions loosened my knotted back, and I vaguely hoped the shock waves would travel further inside, a seismic jolt straight to my soul, a dislodging of some undeniable emotion.

Stepping back, I studied the swaying bag and wondered if the emotion I was experiencing (and I say *wondered* because how can a person who no longer trusts something as elemental as his own instincts truly know an emotion from his ass?) was freedom. Ahead of me waited a summer of leisure, a situation made possible by a decent severance package and my upcoming house-sitting gig for my aunt and uncle. Mine was now the freedom of empty space, of blank calendars and uncluttered days stretching to the distant horizon. It was the freedom of the ocean seen from a cruise ship deck, the stars at play outside John Glenn's Mercury capsule ... a freedom I suddenly found consuming ... vast ... disorienting. I stepped to the bag. Double jab, right cross, and the crisp smack of leather-on-leather made me reconsider, and perhaps I was better off defining the day's experience as finality, the act of placing a period at the end of a life segment. Somewhere in the caring worldwide network of Rodoscope, my finality and freedom were being resurrected into some other drone's burden, more hours for the same paycheck, a looming cut in benefits. Long live Rodoscope! With my last breathless THWAP, THWAP, one of the maintenance ass-crackers paused in the door and called out, *Look, it's fucking Rocky!*

Ping, ping, ping sang the elevator's tally of ascended floors, a harmony for the treble-rich Musak I pray never to hear again. The car heaved a sigh and the doors slid open, but for a paralyzing moment, I didn't get off. Not ten feet in front of me, Everett and his suspenders balanced on a chair, his Gucci loafers tiptoeing as he tore down a hallway banner wishing *Good-bye and Good Luck!* If I were a real man, I would have kicked that chair from under his feet, but instead I opted for a cowardly scurrying behind the office's opaque windows.

After a week of apartment packing, my desk was a no-brainer. Toss memos and coffee cups and spent Walkman batteries, keep the hip-shaking hula doll, tear down my wall of post-it notes, empty my drawers. The trashcan filled with loser football pools and scratched lottery tickets and green Lifesavers, bar matchpacks, tokens, a pair of Everett's suspenders I'd swiped from the gym locker room on a dare, a wilted spider plant I'd watered with cold coffee, a button I thought in one of my more ambitious moments I might be able to sew back on my shirt. I saved the squeaking handgrips and nearly depleted aspirin bottle, the Visine and my tattered thesaurus (an invaluable tool for a word-impaired smartass like myself), and when I stepped back … my five-and-a-half year MELCO stint had been erased, and not a trace of Stanley H. Watson remained.

Perhaps I can't define freedom without my trusty thesaurus, but one thing I could enlighten Everett and the rest of the MELCO family about is absence. Experience has taught me that absence, by its very nature, implies a past presence, and thus forces one to consider ghosts, to weigh memories, to sift and judge. What more proof do I need than my odd, strained relationship with my mother that the absence of a desired thing is infinitely more powerful than its physical, tangible reality, that the present is an eyeblink, the future only a whispery promise, but the past possesses depth and texture, and nothing haunts a man like the history of the things he's lost or the wrongs he's inflicted. How else to explain the dark lure of obsession or remorse or the sentiments of middle-aged regret that find their voice in classic rock radio lyrics like *You don't know what you got till it's gone*? Standing before my bare cubicle, I wondered when this sense of absence, even for a place I despised so thoroughly, would strike me. When would I grow nostalgic for the lobotomized task of routing freight trains and truck lines, paths sometimes detoured through unlikely cities, places picked out of boredom, choices determined by the arc and zig the routes made across the map, switching yards selected not for maximum MELCO profits but for their poetic sounds— Ringaloo and Oshkosh, and my personal favorite, Fiddler's Elbow? When would I yearn for the halo shine of my computer screen, the grainy buzz of fluorescent lights? If that day ever comes, I vow to enact my second-amendment rights, drive to the nearest Wal-Mart and buy the first handgun I see. God bless America.

Before I could make my exit, Elaine spotted me, just like I knew she would (or, as I—at some level—probably wanted her to), and here is the second of my journal confessions, our not-so-discrete office affair, our shameful and intoxicating swap of bodily fluids. In the foyer, she slipped a beauty-shop nail through my belt loop and gave a tug that made my hula girl's wiggle seem downright lascivious. Here's the first wave of dirty details: her breasts flattened slightly against my wrinkled shirt, a hint of fluorescent glimmer on her plum lips, my eyes drawn to the simple cross that pulled all attention toward her cleavage's shadowed canyon. Her lavender perfume hit my cobwebbed brain like a shot of smelling salts. Wake up, Rocky! and yes, my little Rocky, the stupid trooper he is, stirred for one last round.

Let me show you out, Elaine said. I knew she'd gone to bat for me with the transition team, and for that, I was thankful. But of course "out" entailed a detour, a partial anagram, another belt loop tug and another fall from grace, a supply closet pit stop full of tugs and pinches and gropes and bites. Dark behind the closed door, and the stink of janitorial supplies contaminated the air. The walls and shelves amplified our exchange of naughty, breathless words. Metal shelves shook, an earthquake for two, our positions twisting into acrobatic tangles, balancing on boxes, a rolling chair, my pants swaddled around my ankles just to add a degree of difficulty. But the frenzied motions struck me as somehow desperate, undeserved, and this thought caused me to fall away from the physical moment and into the split screens that are forever playing deep in the recesses of my mind, the competing images that portray the two halves of my life … my drinking and sneak fucking, the self-imposed silences I subject my girlfriend Michele to, and the single, unutterable secret that's haunted me since childhood ... and playing beside that, the slapstick version of myself, the clown who scrambles to mop up the messes he's created, gestures essentially hollow for I often fear the vexing language of human decency lies beyond my comprehension. Guilt, I can no more escape it than I can explain it (yet I've looked up all the thesaurus's mysterious synonyms— *blame, error, fault, sin, transgression*). With my thoughts snared in my split-screen thicket, I feared I was going soft. In a panic, I called up the projection booth and ordered some appropriate stock footage to fill my split screens. Bridget Bardot tummy down in the Riviera surf! a partner-swapping threesome with Mary Richards and Rhoda! a funkytown orgy with the Soul Train dancers! Wake up, Rocky! Toot, toot! Beep, beep!

6/6

I've been having lunch these past few days down by the river. Puffy clouds dot the pastel sky. Bees pester the yellow lilies. Sunshine on the flowing water, a duck waddling parade on the sloping shore. Anchored boats rock gently beneath the bridge. The current laps against the bridge's massive brownstone stanchions. Young, hand-holding couples stroll past. The stock footage of an early summer afternoon. I've been trying to forget my awkward parking lot good-bye with Elaine, her twice-repeated request to call her sometime, my head swimming with notions of guilt and absence as I kissed her rouge-smudged cheek.

    Today, between bites of relish-smothered hot dog, I focused on the bridge, the dwindling span straining toward the far shore.

Near its middle, pigeons gathered, tiny specks on the stone railing, and the semis that rumbled past scattered the birds into the air. Through the miracle of the split screen, the birds' flight became my own. I pictured the scenario in terms of the unspoken but never absent equations of trajectory and velocity, potential and kinetic energy. I saw my leap and subsequent fall like the arcing map-paths of the expresses I'd once routed from Boston to Dallas … and when I adjusted the scene's framing and watched it Cinemascope-big on my reunited split screen, the balancing on the rail and the mesmerizing sheen of water, the deep knee bend and ensuing leap into a high school physics question (*A man jumps from an 80 foot bridge; considering the wind is calm* …), there was no corresponding pull in my belly, no cringing reflex, only the imagined, all-erasing rush of wind in my ears and the weight of absence in my belly and the cool acceptance of equations swirling in my head.

6/7

My aunt called earlier tonight. Straight off, I knew something wasn't right, her speech full of hesitant ticks foreign to her usual candor. We talked about her neighbor's yapping dog, the recent heat, and she thanked me again for agreeing to housesit for them and, more importantly, for looking after my cousin Bobby this summer. Then came a fretful pause before she blurted out her true reason for calling. Bobby has discovered masturbation. He's like clockwork she said, the bedsprings twanging, whimpering moans, and sometime during the summer, when the time is right, would I mind talking to him about it? Please?

Relieved, she digressed to happier subjects—the upcoming

retirement party for her and my uncle, the latest update from their trip's itinerary, but my thoughts wandered back to Bobby. I pictured him standing before me, the grease and faded ketchup stains marking a Phillies T-shirt that could have enveloped my frame like a tent. I saw the grime from his laborer's job at a tool factory that blackened his wide chin, saw the way the corners of his lips twitched with nervous anticipation. When his fingers weren't lacing and unlacing, they were forever tugging on various parts of his body—his nose and ear, his shirt and hair. And I imagined my aunt in her kitchen and the photo that hung on the wall behind her, Bobby and me in our little league uniforms, a sunshiny day before Bobby's accident, and in my head, another split screen (is it possible to split an already split screen? dividing and subdividing until my life ceases to be a whole thing and instead crumbles into a nonsensical mosaic?), and now playing were the reels of Bobby's life, before and after scenes and my role in the matter, and unfortunately, there was no guest star billing here.

Stanley, my aunt said, *are you there?*

6/9

Spent an hour today in traffic on the Schuylkill Expressway's snaking river turns. Too early for rush hour, and in the opposite lanes, the happy, Friday afternoon beach exodus, the sun-worshipers sneaking off to the Jersey shore. A soot-coated, graffitied truck idled in front of me, and with each lurch forward, oily clouds belched from its corroded tailpipe, my head dizzy from the fumes and my mood growing fouler with each crawling yard. Siren wailing, a police cruiser navigated the shoulder, an ambulance close behind. Horns blared, a harsh mid-tone amid the booming low-end thud of rap on a nearby jeep's stereo and the happy, high-pitched whistling of unencumbered beach cars in the east-bound lanes.

Finally, after three lanes funneled to one, maneuverings accompanied by a multitude of exchanged unpleasantries that only confirmed my worst notions of my fellow human beings, I became aware of the holdup's source. Two cars with crumpled doors posed like fang-baring animals, the sprung trunk of the first rising up to meet the hood of the second, the meshed tangle surrounded by a moat of diamond-sparkling glass. Paramedics attended to the bleeding forehead of a dazed, shoeless, business-suited woman. On the roadside, near the driver's door of the second car, a policewoman snapped photos of a white-sheeted form.

The horns and shouted threats fell silent, the booming stereos muted. A breeze fingered the edges of the sheet, and as I passed, I gave in to the baser instincts of rubbernecking curiosity, and wondered what lay beneath that rippling swatch of white, whether death brought peace or torture or the ultimate empty calendar. This was what my pill and booze escapades flirted with. Lights out, all split screens shut down, the show over, and I wondered what was the crime of leaving a theater before the last reel if you had no stomach for what you'd seen so far?

And here's another confession—the car crash I suffered at eighteen was no accident; it was a solo, backroads swan dive, a sloppy choice, the stuff of amateurs I realize now. Too imprecise, too haphazard, too many variables of hope and safety. Angels of mercy—or so they appeared through my blood-streaked eyes in the moments before I slipped into a three-day coma—cut me from my twisted chrysalis of metal, and out emerged this damaged butterfly, short two internal organs and one baseball scholarship. Surgeons have revisited my body for follow-ups on my hip, my elbow and knee, leaving a network of scars that makes it impossible to shower without rehearing the shriek of breaking glass.

6/10

I went with Michele today to clean out her classroom, and there I was, the guest star projected into another feature, this time as Gulliver in a first-grade Lilliput, an out of place giant in a landscape of knee-whacking tables and chairs, belly-button-high coat hooks. On the walls, scraps of writing on wide-lined, yellow paper, 'GOOD BUY MISS HAZEN' and 'HAF A NCE SUMMER,' quivering, unsure letters, the penmanship of children and stroke victims. Michele and I were the only ones there, still I detected an echo of bustle, a whiff of bristling activity—shoeboxes jammed with markers, an aquarium where goldfish swam behind finger-smudged glass, a pair of safety scissors underfoot, and above, papier-mâché planets held in their orbits by fishing wire. A tangle-woven bird's nest sat on Michele's chair. A dried beehive hung beside the flag. On the chalkboard, the outlines of eighteen tiny hands, their owners' names printed below—John and Kristine, Eric and Kathi and Gene.

Almost three years ago, Michele and I met on a blind date, and it's funny how the things hinted at that night are the traits I've grown to appreciate most about her—her unnerving, almost cutting honesty, the amusing contours of her thoughts, the claptrap memory that allows her to rattle off the vice-presidents of the twentieth century or the starting nine of the '80 Phillies in a single breath. Other facts I learned that night—she was the recent survivor of a messy divorce and had missed Sunday Mass only once in the past decade, that she mistrusted men who drove sports cars and swore she would never again kiss a mustached lip.

I watched her, blond ponytail swishing as she strode through her classroom, confidently navigating the children's maze. Before leaving, she insisted on making one last shot with the Nerf basketball. Her first two attempts rimmed off the hoop hung over the cloak closet door. *One more*, she said, clapping her hands until I threw her the ball. *Can't officially start summer on a note like that.*

As she aimed, her left eye squinted, giving her face a lopsided appearance and drawing into focus the general misshapen quality of her features, a playground-broken nose that bent to the right, the corner of the lower lip she sucked in when she balanced her checkbook or lied to a pestering telemarketer or lined up a tricky basketball shot. Even her breasts are a bit lopsided, one slightly larger, its nipple positioned like a wandering lazy eye. Her next shot went through—yeah!—the net shivering. She raised her hands in triumph and planted a wet, raspberry-sputtering kiss on my cheek.

She turned off the lights. Goodnight, kids! Goodbye to this year's memories, the tears dabbed and the band-aids applied to stinging paper cuts. Goodbye to chalk dust and high-pitched voices, the push-pulling brand of Munchkin chaos she was paid to corral and lead. On the playground, bloody yells and screams from a kickball game, a youthful celebration of freedom, and in my car, a variation on the same theme for Michele was already unwinding into her summer mode, the rigidity of schedules and clocks falling away, time turning liquid, flowing … and yet another variation noticed by me alone, her summer freedom genuine, her smile sincere, but like tails on heads, the underside of my empty calendar was tainted by my weaknesses and lies, my talent for self-sabotage.

Is she blind?

6/11

I stopped by my aunt and uncle's to drop off a few things, a slow shifting of belongings from my car and my temporary digs at Michele's apartment (her landlady nosy, nosy, always asking roundabout questions, the curtain pulled aside whenever I get out of my car … or am I being paranoid?). I spotted my uncle's colossus halfway down the block, their new RV painted in the soft hues of a summer twilight, the sun's last, long rays igniting its chrome and mirrors, its bulbous hubcaps, a glistening sheen just short of blinding. All hail the Roadmaster 3000 Luxury Land Cruiser! the name carried proudly on the spare tire covering, the kind of regal title that triggered a corresponding trumpet call in my brain. Ta-da! and yes, here was irrefutable evidence that truth in advertising was possible. Microwave, stacked washer and dryer, satellite dish and GPS—pricey, for sure, but this wasn't a hem-hawing purchase. No, the Luxury Land Cruiser (ta-da!) was for the consumer in touch with their desires, the official vehicle for apocalypse believers (which I don't believe my aunt and uncle are) and recent retirees (bingo! both newly presented with pewter plates acknowledging their decades of service to the Lower Merion School District). This LLC was born from my aunt and uncle's drifting, bedtime discussions of all the places they'd only seen in stock footage glimpses, Carlsbad Caverns for my uncle the science teacher, Hoover Dam for my aunt. My finger squeaked over the LLC's just-washed hull. This was their ocean liner, their spaceship—a capsule to propel them into their notions of freedom and all the other dream spaces they cared to claim. Ta-da!

Passing through the LLC's substantial shadow, I considered my aunt and uncle's house, my soon-to-be temporary home. Brick with white vinyl trim, a two-car garage, an immaculately landscaped garden, the plush-enough-to-sleep-on grass soft, soft beneath my sneakers. During the summer vacations of my childhood, my father would drop me off at his sister's, and here, I became the guest star of a summer replacement series, three months of wholesome poolside shenanigans and proper adult supervision, a contract that regretfully ran out each September.

I lifted the front door's elephant-trunk knocker, but the threshold step brought on a paralyzing memory flood, a tide that whisked this guest star back to the summers before Bobby's accident when this was the home, the family I wished was my own. Here was the setting on my first split screen, and on the other, my real home, a self-absorbed father and the mother who left us not in a satisfying theatrical blowup but in quiet shifts of expectations, in increments, by the molecule, the sub-atomic particle, a slow dissolve. A fade to black. Gone.

Bobby was with his group home buddies, my aunt at her pool aerobics class, and I think my uncle was glad to have some time alone with me. We talked a little about the RV (ta-da!), a lot about Bobby, a conversation that ended with an awkward pat on the back and a thankful, teary glint in his eye, a choked-up moment he then defused by leading me on the just-in-case tour through the house. In the basement, my uncle's silver hair glowed faintly beneath the naked bulbs. He pointed out the water main, the furnace shut-off, the finicky nuances of the hot water heater, the breaker box, the sump pump—all the appropriate switches and nozzles marked with dangling tags. In the kitchen, he demonstrated the proper way to disassemble the garbage disposal in case Bobby fed something inappropriate into its spinning blades. And upstairs, in a bedroom that would soon be mine, he pulled a locked army trunk from the rear of his closet and unearthed a chrome-glistening handgun. He placed the gun, sleek and clean, its weight perfectly balanced, into my hands. The reflection of my eyes played along the barrel. Absorbing, the gun's precise, beautiful lines, my thoughts drifting again onto a split screen where the gun was my costar in final, gut-wrenching scene, and I barely heard his warnings of recent neighborhood home invasions, his brief lesson on how to flip the safety and load the clip.

6/12

The LLC started with a surprising purr (ta-da!). A good omen, I thought, the rumble of power reassuring, the small mountain of metal providing a degree of insulation from the inhospitable world. The harsh *tsk-tsk* of lawn sprinklers hissed in the background, the just-cut fragrance of onion grass. Neighbors gathered, and there was Mr. Lehman, a smoky wisp of man who lived next door, his wriggling, yapping Chihuahua in his arms. How bent and frail Mr. L looked, a man I already thought ancient when Bobby and I were kids, and I felt a pang of remorse for the way we once tortured him with stealthy pranks. I studied my aunt and uncle, the gifts and hugs their neighbors bestowed upon them, and I wondered whether there was an unconscious movement to imitate stock footage in our own lives or was this spectacle a real, heartfelt bon voyage? The Chihuahua, an irritating dog with an equally irritating name—Chappie—jumped from Mr. L's arms and assumed a tail-quivering shit position among my aunt's begonias.

Posed before their RV in their sunglasses and sailor caps and matching Hawaiian shirts, my beaming aunt and uncle could have been poster children for prudent retirement planning. Perhaps *this*, I thought, was what freedom truly was, a happy escape made all the happier because this very spot was their final destination, because somewhere at the core of their leaving wishes lay the ultimate desire to return home.

And beside me stood Bobby, one weighty paw resting on my shoulder, the other hand distractedly bothering his nose, tugging his chin. *The pool, Stan*, he whispered in my ear, *Mom said not to bug you about the pool, OK?* Mr. L asked if anyone had seen Chappie, and Bobby leapt to the rescue. Ignoring his father's pleas to let the dog go, Bobby wormed his way between the begonias and emerged with a yellow flower in his hair and Chappie in his grasp, the leaf-shaking runt held at arm's length and offered back to Mr. L, Bobby's proud expression quickly dissolving as the beast let forth with an arcing urine stream. With a twist, Chappie sprang from Bobby's grip and scatted a *Born Free* sprint across the yard.

The final goodbyes were saved for mother and father and their man-child son, tearful declarations of love and reminders that I was boss in their absence. As his mother hugged him one last time, Bobby stared over her shoulder, his concentration held hostage by Chappie's sniffing return to the blooming begonias.

Dabbing her tears, my aunt gazed back as she climbed into the LLC's entry portal. Bobby waved only after I told him to. Toot-toot, went the LLC's horn, its backup warning alarm beeping until my uncle shifted into drive. Nails scraping over the sidewalk, Chappie scampered to the curb, his nub tail a nervous blur, barks as piercing as ice pick stabs. We stood waving until the behemoth was out of sight, and then Bobby turned to me. *The pool, Stan. What about the pool?*

Bobby led the way to the back of the house. Above, a wooden deck jutted out from my guest star's bedroom, and beneath the deck, a shaded patio bordered by ferns and hostas. A narrow strip of grass separated the patio from the pool, and beyond, a slope of yard, a cherry tree where there was once a tire swing (wasn't there? I wondered, or was it just a stock footage mirage?), a breeze-trembling weeping willow, a red and green birdhouse I'd helped my uncle build, my aunt's neat-rowed vegetable garden. His bare feet slapping across the pool's apron, Bobby retrieved the long-poled skimmer.

Hypnotizing, the swirl of pool leaves and the surprisingly deft turns that captured them. Hypnotizing, the swirl of years, and paralyzing, the weight of guilt, and mesmerizing, its undiluted power all these years later. Bobby and I, nighttime commandos raiding Mr. L's tomato plants, a mad dash over the rolling dewy lawn, a fall into the pool, but with a *thump*, not a splash, too close to the edge, Bobby's pudgy, half-naked body sprawled in stunned peace, his stolen tomatoes bobbing on the rippling waves, the curling reservoir of blood forming around his temple.

Sure, I said, entranced as my cousin snared leaves in the skimmer's delicate net, we can open the pool.

6/14

I took Michele to lunch today, Charlie B's, an homage to our past, the sight of our blind date. Outside, Michele picked up a severed doll's arm, dirty plastic punctured by dog's teeth, and smiling at me, she slid it into her purse.

Someday soon the doll's arm will make its way into one of her assemblies, a cigar box or wooden soda crate, one of the cupboard spice racks she's unearthed at the drive-in's Saturday afternoon flea market, and adorning each shallow space, her treasure finds, 3D collages of scraps and broken remnants, the chewed doll arms that made no impression on me. Science-minded folks like my uncle define species through hierarchical checklists, and in my thoughts, I jotted down this doll-arm vision right beneath our contrasting summer freedoms on my and Michele's scoresheet of differences. Her blue eyes spot the muddy thimbles, the metal scraps and fabric swatches, the incidentals my Gulliver stomps right over. And this special vision goes even deeper than gutter diamonds, for it also serves as a type of ironic radar, a contraption akin to Hemingway's fabled shit detector, but kinder, more self-effacing. With it, Michele divines humor in the distractions and easy entertainments of her fellow man. Parades and AM bubblegum pop and trained monkeys send her into chuckling tizzies, but the absurdity of these follies only depresses me, each one another tally on a scoresheet that sometimes seems to stretch for miles.

There was trouble at the next table. A sleeves-rolled-up salesman grilled his waitress, his order late and his lunch hour dwindling, short-tempered, rude words, a threat to call the manager if his food wasn't served soon. Michele swirled a straw through her icy daiquiri and glanced at me.

Asshole, I said, loud enough to cut the din. When the salesman glared at me, I didn't look away. *No drama today, OK?* Michele pleaded. But I couldn't stop my stare-down, a lowering of myself to the knucklehead's level, the two of us erasing the evolutionary marks from our checklists until we resembled a pair of hair-bristling beasts, the tension broken only when the oblivious waitress stepped between us and placed a club sandwich in front of the moron.

Michele squeezed my hand. She has her own sad stories, her parents dead, a divorce from a two-fisted alcoholic, and I knew she shared my conviction that just beneath every breath lay the hidden and delicate backbone of our days, the sorrows and disappointments, the tragedies we lock in our hearts and then spend half our energy trying to shield from a prying world—and still another mark for my checklist, for she accomplishes this with a compassionate grace while I am prone to lashing out, confronting the waitress bulliers of the world.

She brought my hand to her mouth, kissed my fingertips, but I reflexively pulled away, disgusted by the thought of her lips touching the same fingers that were inside another woman not so many days ago. I wiped my hand on my napkin. Perhaps I am sympathetic to strangers and waitresses because I understand hidden pains and deep histories, but in the schizophrenic logic of the split screen, I atone for this kindness by inventing a thousand indignities for myself and the ones I pretend to love.

And during our shared dessert came the day's big surprise—my Michele wants to get married—*to me.* It's time, she says, to move ahead or say thanks for the memories. She asked for no answer, but said we'll discuss it again at summer's end. Oh boy.

Back at her apartment we tumbled into bed. Michele playfully tongued the snaking, pale scar over the spot where my spleen once lay, the sensation both numb and prickly. Naughty, the stolen moments of being beer-buzzed while my RODOSCOPE nee MELCO comrades were slaving away. Delicious, the embrace of Michele's willowy legs around my waist ... yet my mind split the screen again and again ... betrayals and ultimatums ... a poolside tumble and years of lying mistaken for a cousin's love ... marriage. Michele moaned, and I thrust with abandon, stabbing at the moment and at the moment's notions of love, foolishly hoping something in my labors would shut down the stock room's projectors once and for all.

6/16

A Pictorial History of the Great War, gold printing on a blue leather cover, a book as heavy as a trio of Chappies. As a child, I had been terrified by this book of my uncle's, page after glossy page of shrapnel-mangled corpses, muddy trenches, severed limbs snared on barbed wire (now *that's* finality!). Rising to Bobby's pre-accident dares—for Bobby had been the one who was always egging me on, an instigator, the hatcher of fantastic plots, the leader of tomato-patch raids into Mr. L's yard—I would return to the bloodiest photos, forcing myself to stare, a count to ten without blinking, until the images burned into my mind, guaranteed visitors to my nightmares, and now, all these years later, I find myself returning again, the pages turned in the strange hush that falls over the house after Bobby goes to work. Crushing, man's self-importance when balanced by his fragility, his flesh no match for the world of cool equations. Pages of truncated legs, absent chins and noses. Men missing things I thought they couldn't survive without. Here, in these horrible photos, lies life's perplexing dichotomy, the men's wounds arguing that no network of caring is possible in this world, their stitched-up survival whispering a hesitant rebuttal of hope.

6/17

Late again to another wedding, and Michele and I waded into the church vestibule amid the last minute fussings of the day's supporting cast. Whispering excuses and best wishes, we slipped past a bridesmaid pinning a boutonniere on an usher and claimed an empty space near the back. A mellow-toned organ played. A lost bee barnstormed above. Uncles and aunts dutifully checked their cameras. Sunlit stained glass. Sweet smells of flowers and perfume. Pews sticky with humidity. Michele and I have been caught up in a wedding deluge this past year, her friends mostly, and my eyes have become attuned to the days' accents, the flowers and the lace, the ushers' cufflinks and the bridesmaids' ruffles. Given the backdrop of Michele's ultimatum, the details grew even sharper for now I'd been thrust squarely into their not so cool equations—the imprecise variables of cake flavors, the interpretive variations of a florist's phonebook-thick wedding planner, the age-old dilemma of DJ or live band—each detail a Lilliputian rope that lashes down this bewildered Gulliver.

The pews rippled with blown noses and snuck glances. The parents were seated, and next came the satiny dresses and black tuxedoes of the wedding party, the priest alongside the groom who made the plank walk with sweaty composure. The bridal march trilled on the organ. As one, the congregation stood and turned. Pretty, radiant, cooed the crowd at the first sight of the bride, a frightened, beaming smile meshed by delicate lace, the wisps of baby's breath in her hair, the trailing hiss of her long, white train. Cameras flashed and clicked, the moment captured from a dozen different perspectives. As the bride passed, I noticed the happy tears on her cheek, and I wondered if a finality willingly surrendered to qualified as its own strain of freedom. Already the tissues were being broken out in the front aisles.

Prayer, and Michele knelt. I was one of the few who didn't, easy to pick us out, the arthritic, the unbelievers, the children who stared about, pleased with their suddenly clear perspective. Stained glass hues highlighted Michele's hair, and I marveled at how willingly she planted herself in her faith, envious once again at the immutable convictions that formed the solid core of her somewhat ragged edges. I studied the silent bride and groom, and I was struck by the power of the ritual, the celebration of connectedness and shared beliefs. A charge sizzled through the warm, perfumed air, the amiable static of belonging raising the hair on my neck. I sat up straight, a human lightning rod, straining above the sea of bowed heads, and if the path to a world of connectedness and belief led through a florist's silly book, then perhaps it was time to crack the cover. Chances are it can't be much more gruesome than *A Pictorial History of the Great War*.

And later, a country club reception, ice-sculpture swans whose dripping wings became prisms of captured light. An open bar and commemorative match packs. At the piano, old favorites played for a dollar stuffed into a silver tip jar. From my claimed spot at the bar, I slipped a Xanax onto my tongue and washed it down with the day's first vodka. I needed a buffer before joining our table full of Michele's teacher friends, a group I found extremely kind but also disturbingly perky, and as I waited for the first inklings of my buzz to find me, I entertained myself by watching the wedding photographer at work.

Beneath a white trestle twined with artificial bluebells, the photographer arranged family shots, look-alike sisters and brothers, growth-spurt teens fidgeting beneath the confines of last year's Sunday clothes, wandering aunts in dated bonnets coaxed to get closer … closer. The photographer concerned himself with the big picture, but I zoomed in for the undercurrent of telling details, the woman's wrinkled fingers picking lint from her husband's lapel, the hip checks given by prankster cousins trying to hold their composure until the flash, a bashful child kneading the soothing material of her mother's dress.

And I imagined my parents in the same picture … my father's nervous hands straightening his tailored shirt, patting his gelled-stiff hair, but never straying beyond himself … my mother ghost-like, a vaporized substance, already half-absent. In my bomb of a nuclear family, caring occurred not in touches or words but in gaudy flashes, elaborate spectacles. Come see! Come see! the ringmaster of the moment would announce, the purchase of a sought after gift (a ten-speed! a regulation football! a used car! more!) allowing the giver to turn the limelight back on themselves. Come see (me)! (Come see) me!

Michele's met my father, and she's heard a selective history of my mother, but she hasn't met the ugly chimera that is THEM. Perhaps I should arrange a pre-wedding get together. Then it would be Michele's turn for second thoughts.

6/22

I dropped Bobby off for an evening of softball and general mayhem with his group home crew. My mood wasn't stellar. How many times was it possible to ask the same question—*the pool, Stan, the pool*—a line of interrogation that somehow morphed into an obsession of finding his old baseball glove, and before I knew it, we were both on our hands and knees in the grimy depths of his closet, a closed space where Bobby ripped what I believe to be one of the world's top-ten foulest farts. Cap the dinner hour with a call from Elaine, her tone in turns hopeful, hurt, angry, and after I hung up on her in mid-tirade, I wondered if I really had led her on, if I'd made immediately forgotten promises just to oil the machinery of seduction. God, I can be an asshole.

The glove, the glove, Bobby moaned, twisting strands of his uncombed and slightly thinning hair, his thoughtless efforts producing a curl that corkscrewed sadly from his skull. I sat back, and for a moment, I simply gave up, elbows on my knees and head bowed, the pose of a pummeled boxer dreading the next round's bell, and yes, I'd undoubtedly met my match. It was Bobby's utterly empty look, slack jawed and dazed, that beat me down, the unblinking search for comprehension that dulled his once mischievous eyes. Impossible to predict what Bobby would latch onto—his glove, the pool, a TV show he needed to watch, a breakfast cereal he couldn't start the day without—and once snared, he wouldn't—or couldn't—let go, his thoughts locked on with the single-minded determination of a snapping turtle while the more human characteristic of seeing beyond the moment was erased long ago.

I knew the way to the home, but Bobby insisted on playing

co-pilot. Confused by left and right, he guided us using finger points and vague landmarks, the yard with the black dog and the house that had a painted mailbox, the intersection where a pair of laced sneakers dangled from the overhead powerline. Every other weekend Bobby packs up his gym bag and stays at the group home, two house parents and a gaggle of retarded adults, Saturday get-togethers with their sister house, the home of the mysterious Jane, a name Bobby can't say without blushing. Finally, we arrived, and from outside, the house appeared normal enough— a pair of pink rose bushes bordering the porch stairs, a just washed and still dripping minivan, a river of suds slowly flowing down the driveway and into the gutter—but then I imagined the multiples of Bobby's antics that waited behind the shut screen door, the tantrums, the foolishness and forgetfulness, the loopy transgressions and masturbation talks. Even before the car was fully stopped, Bobby had the door opened, and if he heard the buzzing safety alarm, he didn't let on.

Bob-BEE! Bob-BEE! exclaimed a helium voice. The screen door flew open and out emerged a shirtless, rib-protruding stickman. He scampered toward us, tugging on the khaki pants that slide from his bony waist. He shook with nervous twitches that caused him to pogo up and down on bare toes.

I got out of the car and was introduced to Nate the stickman and all the other sad stories who came pouring out of the house to greet Bobby. A final guest joined us, this one with a ponytail, the keener gaze of higher intelligence, and a hulking white cast that entombed his right arm from wrist to armpit. Randy, one half of the husband-and-wife team who ran the home, invited me in, but I declined, unnerved suddenly by the gawking stares of Bobby's friends.

I said good-bye, reminding Bobby I'd be back for him in a few hours, but on my way to the car, Bobby ran out to me, his left sneaker dragging over the sidewalk, and for a moment, I feared he'd resurrect the glove debacle. Instead he locked me in a wordless, sweaty hug, and then ambled back. Halfway through my U-turn, I glanced back at the house. Already Bobby had plunked himself squarely in the middle of the driveway basketball game. He slapped a two-handed dribble, heaved an errant shot. He laughed and smacked a meaty high-five with another man-child in coke-bottle glasses.

6/23

Posted throughout the house are laminated index cards, reminders my aunt and uncle have made for Bobby. DID YOU TURN OFF THE WATER? outside the bathroom. MILK GOES BACK IN THE FRIDGE in the kitchen. LOCK THE PATIO DOOR and DON'T FORGET YOUR KEY at the front entrance. I am now so familiar with the cards that when I pass one, I hear the words spoken in my aunt and uncle's voices, muted urgings to their forgetful son.

6/23—later—

I'm the restless one in a house of peaceful souls, Bobby snoring behind his bedroom door, his nightly jerk-off behind him, Michele asleep in the bed I've just abandoned, my pinned arm tenderly pulled from beneath her snuggled-close body, my only companion my swirling thoughts, my beer and just-gulped pill, and Mr. L's ever-yipping Chappie.

An arm's length—I thought of that distance just now as I inched my hand from beneath Michele's ribs. An arm's length—since that night over sixteen years ago it has been the measuring stick of my life. I've noticed most people aren't in tune with that distance—all I have to do is watch how they lurch at the heavy bag or muff a ground ball, the groping way they reach for a sugar bowl on a diner counter. But Bobby's accident has brutally tattooed that arm's length distance on my brain, giving me an intimate, personal knowledge that has served me well in the gym and on the infield, but not in the haunted moments of quiet thought. Despite the whitewash of years and pills and booze and Freudian repression, I can't escape the faint image of my hands pressed into my cousin's broad back as we scrambled a moonlit escape from our raid into Mr. L's tomato patch, a scene that plays ghost-like beneath every other on my split screen. An arm's length— how close! how far!

6/26

A solo afternoon, Bobby at work, Michele at school writing curriculum. Cloudless sunshine outside the patio doors, acrobatic squirrel play in the swaying willow branches, a hosta-nibbling rabbit crouched in the deck's rectangle of shade. Sporting a wide-brimmed straw hat, Mr. L tied his tomato plants to their stakes with knotted cloth strips. Chappie sniffed a broccoli plant's wide leaves while balancing his front paws on the sagging rabbit fence.

I stepped back from the glass door and reconsidered the tyranny of the empty calendar. Trapped in my MELCO cubicle, these were the hours I'd dreamed of, my face projected into stock footage scenes of "gentleman of leisure." I saw myself opening *Anna*

Karenina and all the other books I'd told Michele I'd read. I'd take up jogging, restring my ancient tennis racket and hit the courts, and with each page, stride and serve, I'd narrow the gap between the man I was and the man I wanted to be ... but showing on my split screen was this summer's reality, the guest star strangely agitated, tense, the empty hours illuminating an even deeper emptiness that I fill with afternoon naps, a lunchtime beer or two, a gradual immersion in the numbing netherworld of cable TV.

I cut half the lawn, then rested in the willow's shade. Chappie continued his frenzied barking, bouncing and turning whiplash circles on Mr. L's porch, his radar-dish ears strained to attention. Some nights Chappie's staccato barks so thoroughly invade my skull that I slam the windows shut, preferring to sweat rather than endure one second more. And on nights too hot to close the window, when even the fans' highest settings can't mask the yapping onslaught, I fantasize about kidnapping the mutt, a silver band of duct tape wound over its snout, a bundle deposited on a farm road miles from town. Mr. L appeared at the door, and for a thankful moment, the racket stopped ... but then promptly resumed when the old man retreated to the air-conditioned insulation of his retirement.

Chappie bark-bark-barked, yet despite the assault and my dog-killing daydreams, there was a brief spark of tenderness in my heart because I understood the runt's hysterics were a fault of memory. Once a door shuts, a dog fears he will always be alone. How empty a feeling it must be, the panicked belief that the sorrow of the present might be with you forever triggering barks and sobbing phone calls from jilted girlfriends, pharmaceutical binges and endless questions about a lost glove. Yap, yap, yap, I sometimes wonder if this is the sound of the world, all of us scared, all of us longing for the happiness we believe waits on the other side of a shut door. Yap, yap, yap.

6/28

Bobby came home from work, and the second he saw me, he burst into tears. I imagine him stewing on the bus ride, each passed stop torturing, his news that he would soon be placed temporarily on second shift eating him up inside. I was weeding the garden, and he plunked right next to me, flanked by his mother's cauliflower and string beans. You're OK, you're OK, I soothed, patting his back and reassuring him that he'd like his new boss despite what he'd heard, that he'd find a friend to eat with, that I'd pick him up each night if the busses didn't run that late. Gradually, his goose-honking sobs abated, and the tears that ran in black-soot rivulets down his cheeks dried.

We walked to the house but Bobby stopped short. *The pool, Stan,* he said softly, *what about the pool?*

For a few moments, we simply stood by the diving board, Bobby staring at the leaf-speckled surface, his bloodshot eyes unflinching. No room for split screens here, and here was a focus that would have made Chappie proud, the here-and-now promise of swimming all that mattered, and everything else—his shift change, his absent parents, his nightly jerk-offs and his crush on Jane—forgotten behind the shut door.

6/29

Another confession—or perhaps a bit of remembered truth, one aspect of a darker whole—the fact that before the accident, Bobby was somewhat of a bully ... or maybe he was simply an oversized child who knew bruising shoulder punches and hulking intimidation provided the surest avenue to getting his way. He was a starting-line tripper in schoolyard foot races, a fastball pitcher who didn't hesitate to plunk the batter who'd just hit a home run off of him. I still have a chipped tooth from one of our backyard wrestling matches. We played for the same little league team, and during our games, my aunt and uncle rooted for both of us. I knew their encouragement, while genuine, was also meant to atone for my absent parents, and thus—at least in my little, fevered head—their cheers came across a bit awkward, forced, a guest star's canned applause, not as sincere as the hoots and whistles they showered upon a son who didn't secretly yearn for their love and approval the way I did.

Once, when I was going through one of my low points, Michele asked if I'd like to go to Mass with her, but I stopped believing long ago. And it wasn't because of what had happened to Bobby—but because of His failure to punish me. In the weeks after the accident, I prayed with a child's miracle-believing persistence for Bobby to rise from his white-sheeted bed, to rip off the tubes and wires that grew from him like sterile vines. I prayed my cousin would once again pull down my shorts in front of the neighborhood girls or clamp me in a breath-stealing headlock until I cried 'Uncle' or whatever his word of the day was. Months passed, and as he remained in a coma, and my story that Bobby had simply tripped became accepted fact, I grew impatient with God, my choirboy's faith soured by His lack of action. If God wasn't going to heal Bobby and He couldn't deliver the retribution I deserved, then I vowed to supply it myself. I pried the reflectors off my bike and pedaled furiously along unlit stretches of road, my eyes squeezed shut with each approaching car, my lips trembling with whimpering goodbyes. I became the neighborhood daredevil, the climber of roofs, the holder of fuse-dwindling firecrackers, the teaser of ill-tempered dogs, the boy unafraid to pick a fight with the older kids in denim jackets who smoked cigarettes in the alley behind school. Still, I survived; in fact, I seemed to be rewarded, popular at school, talented in sports, reasonably smart, the girls willing to be near me. I accepted these gifts with outward nonchalance, yet the desire to atone for my sins still oozes within me, a black, internal current that's steered me toward car accidents and sleazy affairs, booze and pills. Perhaps a good round of cancer will make me see the light. Halleluiah!

7/1

And after much delay and endless inquiries, the backyard pool is officially open! Ta-da! My uncle has called nightly from the hinterlands of America, patiently talking me through the steps—the filter backwashed and reinstalled and run for five days straight, the pump and catch baskets cleaned, the lights' breaker flicked, the leaves skimmed, the water shocked with chlorine, the pH and alkalinity levels checked and rechecked, Chappie yip-yip-yipping as I hosed down the pebbled apron. Michele lovingly gripped my hand as Bobby christened the season with a board-twanging dive into the deep end, and there I was, my split screen a triptych of lies and irony and clownish good intentions, Bobby and Michele and the pool all brought together. I excused myself, and inside, my hands shook so badly I spilled my pills all over the kitchen floor.

7/2

I finally made good on a promise made months ago to take Bobby miniature golfing. Oh, the humanity—Bobby's whacked ball often bouncing from our holes' confines, his retrievals plodding through other players' shots, their concentration foiled, the group behind us sighing audibly as Bobby lined up one do-over after another on the windmill hole. Oh, the butchered math of our scorecard as I fudged the tally to make him the winner by a single stroke.

The flat ping of aluminum baseball bats echoed from the nearby batting cages, and Bobby's obsessions discovered a new itch. *Let's hit some balls, Stan,* he said, once, twice, a dozen times.

A high chain-link fence ran the length of the cages, netting above and between, Perhaps the mechanical *tick-tick-tick-thwap* of the pitching machines spooked him, for despite my coaxing, Bobby shied away from going in. *You, Stan,* he said. *I want to watch you.* So I selected a bat, stretched, took a few practice cuts. Twilight now, a rosy-gray tint for the horizon, the first glimmer of stars above. The floodlights clicked on.

Years had passed since I'd tapped my bat on home, but the feel, like the arm's-length reach itself, has been branded in my brain. For years, baseball was my greatest desire, and I played not just for myself, but also, secretly, for Bobby, for the ghostly image of the player my cousin could have become. School teams, summer leagues, Babe Ruth, Ponies, all-star traveling teams, sandlot games after the season had run its course—ball kept me out of the house, my mind occupied in such a fixed focus that there was no room for split screens. On the morning before my crash, I was named starting shortstop on the all-state team, and when I received the congratulatory call, the bottom dropped out of my world. It was as though, through years of weight lifting and hundred-degree practices, of playing through the pain of broken fingers and spiked, twisted ankles, I'd climbed a giant mountain, and when I gazed down from the peak, I felt utterly alone, heartsick, foolish for pursuing such a limited, meaningless endeavor.

I dug in as best I could with my worn sneakers. The pitching machine seemed farther than it did before, the cage a tunnel-vision chamber, the mesh of fences and nets, the pitches whizzing by on either side of me. *Tick-tick-tick* chugged the machine, and as the ball barreled in, I bailed out of the box with a half-hearted, protective swing.

Strike one! Bobby laughed.

Squinting, I stared down the length of the cage, but unlike the easy concentration of my youth, tonight my thoughts wandered. My depressions and funks, I've learned, are deep-focus ailments. Senses of worthlessness and guilt, of inescapable sorrow and folly, of my incongruity with the locked march-step of my species— these demons, instead of lingering on the edge of my periphery, begin to loom large and the shadows they cast plunge deep into my heart, the darkness so spreading and vast that it eclipses all notions of joy and belonging, my should-be-happy childhood memories transformed into a brand of harsh, personal mythology that set the fates against me long ago…

Strike two! Bobby called after I didn't even bother lifting the bat from my shoulder.

Seventy-five read the radar gun at the back of the cage. *Tick-*

tick-tick and when the next ball was released, time slowed. Bewitching, the ball's white flight, the hiss of split air and the cool equations at work—force, speed, velocity. And I thought of my old car, my foot heavy on the gas and the frantic windshield view. I remembered the warp of images and time, going so fast that I became speed itself, the windows rolled down and the rush of farmland manure drying my wet eyes...

I swung, level and smooth, plugging myself into another cool equation, the violent collision unabashedly pleasing, the meaty reverberation resonating in my mended bones. Nine more pitches barreled in, and I hammered each one, the overhead net rippling, and one by one, my split screens shut down. Here was the artificial peace of sports, the ambiguously confusing world whittled down to simple rules. *Home run!* Bobby yelled after each hit.

My dog of a car was running hot again on the ride home, and each red light brought a nervous inspection of the thermostat's climbing needle. I examined the hood's outline for escaping steam while Bobby peeled off his shoes and rank, wet socks. His thick fingers harvested the lint between toes mangled from years of minor factory mishaps. Absorbed in his task, Bobby inspected each gray ball before flicking it out the window, all the while droning a list of his favorite swimming strokes, the crawl and breast stroke, the side stroke and butterfly...

I know your favorite, Stan. The doggie paddle!

That's right, bud.

Mom always said, 'Look out for Stan in the pool. He can't swim good the way you can.'

That's right, bud. That's right.

7/4

A rainy Fourth of July, the fireworks and group home activities cancelled. Boo! My aunt and uncle called around dinner time, Michele's answering bringing an initial queasy reflex that maybe it was another poisonous call from Elaine. My aunt and uncle are spending the night at a Midwest campground with a suspicious sounding Indian name—Anawanna-something—all set for tomorrow's eight-hour drive to the Badlands. *Yes, yes,* Bobby droned, *Sure,* he was taking his seizure meds, *Uh-huh,* he was listening to me. He handed the phone to me and gazed forlornly out the patio doors at the rain-percolating pool.

And again, my aunt and uncle thanked me—for housesitting, for opening the pool for Bobby, for making sure things run smoothly during his second-shift stint. *Love you,* my aunt said. And I love you, too.

Mindful of my vow to find Bobby's glove before his next practice, I agreed to a post-dinner attic expedition. Michele took the lead, the first to scale the attic's pull-down ladder, then Bobby, me in the rear, a nervous spotting of my cousin's unsteady climb. Hot in the attic, stuffy, the echo of raindrops pinging on the sloped roof inches above our bowed heads, the uncirculated air thick with mothballs and dust, midnight dark until I located the light cord. Here was another variety of stock room, the fodder for a hundred split screens, boxes and trunks, items forgotten yet, for one reason or another, saved from the junk heap, baby clothes, a disassembled crib, record albums and scrapbooks, a manual typewriter, drinking glasses mummified in yellowed newspaper.

Michele discovered the baseball mitt in an unmarked box. Sweat stung my eyes, the taste of salt on my lips, but I still lingered, picking through the box's other items—old report cards and elementary school photos, a tarnished trophy topped by a bat-swinging baseball player. *Havertown Little League. Home Run Champion—Bobby Smith.*

Look! Bobby called from the across the starkly lit attic, his face hidden by the grimy game box he held up for Michele and me. *Mousetrap!*

Downstairs, we sat around the kitchen table. The *Mousetrap* directions were lost, and none of us seemed to remember the rules. Using only his right hand, his left wedged into a glove so small it resembled a child's winter mitten, Bobby arranged the game's plastic parts—ramps and chutes, a bucket kicked by a red plastic shoe, a diver perched on a springboard. So familiar, the pieces, but I couldn't decide whether the memory belonged to me in the first-person or a TV commercial.

Ready? Bobby asked when his structure was complete. A gleam shone in his eyes. Easy to see he heard the whisper of another time, an unimportant memory that for some reason burned bright enough to cut through the permanent twilight of his thoughts. He released the silver ball, and we watched it travel down, falling here, caught in a funnel there, rattling through a twisting tube before triggering the boot that kicked a bucket. It was an orchestration of linked chaos, and in a flash-moment, I considered the propensity of unconnected incidents to build to a critical mass, the overflow of circumstances whose only connections were accidents of time and geography … a belt loop tug … a frustrated push on poolside concrete…

With a shudder, a domed cage descended upon a helpless plastic rodent.

Mousetrap! Bobby cried.

7/6

Chappie sniffed his way into my aunt's garden again, a tail-wagging inspection of leafy watermelon vines. I stood poolside, my beckoning chores a weak sister to my powers of daydreaming. A white butterfly flitted between the staked sunflowers, and Chappie gave chase, bouncing on springy legs, little jaws snapping vainly at the teasing wings. When Chappie's barks betrayed his whereabouts, Mr. L migrated onto our lawn. With each arthritic stride, Mr. L's bony knees jabbed at the loose material of his khaki pants. He stooped and gathered his dog. The white butterfly landed unnoticed on his straw hat, and the three of them slowly made their way back to his yard.

The skimmer's net stirred faint currents in the pool. I snagged a leaf, a gum wrapper, one of Bobby's rubber flip-flops. Every day, save the Fourth's rainout, Bobby's made the plunge, careless springs from the twanging board. Last night, each leap was accompanied by a shout of *Mousetrap!* his mid-air proclamations followed by prolonged submersions, his warped, hulking frame gliding from the deep end to shallow in one, bubble-trailing breath.

Sitting on a patio chair, I applauded the shower-producing dives Bobby insisted I watch, politely waving off his offers to join the fun. Most nights he swims until the twilight grows thick, the day's heat fading and the fireflies mimicking the starry show above. Water drips from his suit, his triangle of chest hair matted, the night's first breezes causing him to shiver, goose bumps across his back, but when I suggest going inside, Bobby pleads for one more dive … then one more … another… Hard for me to say no, to deny his simple joys. A can opener, a cannonball, a headfirst spring, a stinging, tidal wave belly flop … each pose marred by his reluctant left leg, a defect perhaps unnoticeable to most but glaring to me.

One of the few positives I salvaged from my otherwise deadly freshman psych class was a deeper appreciation of the human brain. Amazing, the brain's delicate balance, its textured gray-white landscape of living tissue, its dizzying nexus of dendrons and axons, a chemical soup of proteins, firewalls of fatty substances. If man is the king of all species, then surely the brain is his crown. To prove it, look no further than the acquisition of language, the mysteries of emotion, the ability to understand a shut door is simply a shut door. A poolside push years ago, an action which, whether deliberate or not, has forever mangled Bobby's crown. Now the poor kid has to wear it everywhere, oblivious of its dents, its missing jewels.

I captured a floating moth in the skimmer net, but my own species crown was far away, snared in thoughts of Bobby's affliction, the hard facts verified in laboratories, observed in clinics and tested in special classrooms, yet the true inner workings of the mind, the knowledge beyond IQ tests and electric pulses, the knowledge of a man's own awareness, remains as much a mystery to me as it does to Bobby. Bring me one of my aunt's marigolds, and I can recite the formula for photosynthesis. I can pinpoint its wavelength and describe which parts of the visible spectrum it absorbs and which it reflects. I can quite simply say, "This is a yellow flower," but that particular hue, known so directly and intimately to me, is impossible to communicate to another, leaving me powerless to share my yellow-vision despite its intense reality.

And what happens when this incommunicable awareness turns even deeper inward? What happens when a man becomes achingly aware of his every breath, and in the place where he should find a sense of knowing and belief, he finds only emptiness? If a person can never describe what yellow is, how can he hope to understand the workings of his heart? And if a man can never know his own heart, then isn't the only thing that separates Bobby from me the ability to balance a checkbook or understand a pun? Then why not abandon the illusions of the heart and surrender to the only elements in this life that are certain, the physicists' world of cool, cool equations? Mousetrap, indeed.

7/8

Elaine's sporadic calls have only heightened my empty-calendar agitation. Pure Pavlov, the icy jerks that accompany each ring, the curses she spits onto recording machine tape exploding like flares over the no-man's-land of my vacant hours. Sometimes she pleads when I pick up, mostly she rants, and while I hear her out, the receiver held far from my ear, I think of her in a way I hadn't before, not so much the rounded flesh of her but the role she occupied, the most recent foil to my obsession to balance my life over the flimsiest and most unpredictable of fulcrums. *Yes, I used you*, I wish he had the courage to say when she starts her sobbing, *but now I see that you used me too, your vague hopes for happiness pinned on me. I'm sorry I didn't see that before. I'm so sorry.*

7/10

If I were a smart man, I would have tasted the fear that lingers in the suburban air of my aunt and uncle's neighborhood and gone into the home security business. Last week there was another home invasion three blocks away, a brutal assault of pistol whippings and broken bones. Today I counted three vans parked on our street alone, deadbolts drilled, alarm systems rigged, motion detector lights installed.

But Bobby's too preoccupied to be afraid—his focus set and unbudging—and when he barrels in the front door, he's already thinking about the pool, his path marked by discarded clothes, his greasy shirt and crumpled jeans, the skunk-stink sneakers he wears to and from the factory. On my way upstairs to ask how his day was, I pick up the frantic trail, but more often than not, Bobby, now clad in his orange swim trunks, passes me on the stairs, too busy to engage in my notions of small talk. The slapping parade of his feet over the kitchen linoleum halts only to snack on whatever goodies have been left on the counter, then it's out the patio doors.

Funny how water changes him. A different medium, a different person, his clumsiness shed like another pair of old sneakers. He dives in with fearless aplomb and emerges, geyser-spouting water, on the other side of the buoyed deep-end rope. Back down he goes, disappearing and resurfacing, the biologist's checklist leaning more toward amphibian than mammal. He would forgot to eat if I didn't call him, and when we settle in, Bobby shovels his food with water-shriveled fingers, the sharp scent of chlorine radiating from his skin. *Come on, I'll teach you*, he says, but I've never been much of a swimmer, low body fat and a long memory of the water I swallowed the night I jumped in after Bobby. Ever since, I've remained a shallow-ender, afraid to journey beyond the buoyed rope.

7/16

OK, you want a confession, a real, honest assessment from the Badlands of my heart? How's this—I'm an asshole. With a capital fucking A. Here I am, the survivor of another pill and booze binge, my issues on display once again for the world to see. And the funny thing is, this round started with an attempt to do something decent. I can handle life being indifferent, even cruel, but is malignant irony really necessary?

Looking back, maybe it was the scent of the oil I'd been rubbing into Bobby's mitt that got things started. I'd wanted to get his glove in shape before his softball practice, and on the drive to the park, Michele at my side and Bobby obsessing about Jane, that smell started getting to me—it was the nostalgic flavor of another era, a time when my life seemed a bit more certain, a shade more cohesive.

By the time we arrived at the park, the others had already claimed the baseball diamond. Bobby dutifully identified his teammates as the three of us crossed the dandelion-speckled field. Beanpole Nate. Gus with the mailbox physique, the low evening sun aglow on his glass's thick lenses. Fred, the near mute, and the dwarfish, chocolate-skinned Chris. Randy, the houseparent, with one arm in a tie-dye sling, the other circling the ample waist of his redheaded wife, Lisa. Joining them were the women from their sister house. Her glove in the dirt by her feet, Tina squatted on second base and chewed the tip of her long black pigtail. Moonshine-pale Carrie tickled Chris's balding head with a yellow buttercup.

Bobby brought his glove to his face, his chin and lips masked by the webbing. *That's Jane,* he said. *In the blue shirt.*

Sitting on the wooden bleachers behind the backstop, Jane reached into a red cooler and fished out a piece of ice. She shook the water from her hand, glanced around before licking her wet fingers. Her jaw danced as she shifted the ice across her closed mouth. She jogged onto the field and the outline of her solid, stocky calves bulged beneath her knee-high gym socks. Near third base, she made an abrupt about-face and ran back to the bleachers for her cap and another chunk of ice.

Michele and I watched for a bit, and I wondered if the scene on the field owed more to Abner Doubleday or Hieronymus Bosch. Chris motored his stumpy legs in a fruitless chase to tickle Carrie with a leafy twig. Jane stared blankly as Bobby showed off his glove, opening and closing it with such delicacy that it soon resembled a living thing gasping its last breaths. Tina was still camped out on second, only now she was chewing the tips of both pigtails at the same time. Nate stood alone in center field, his finger in his nose, his glove draping his head like a leathery babushka. Gus had taken it upon himself to gather the softballs. The white spheres filled his beefy arms, two balls spilling out for every one he tried to pick up.

We sat for a bit of batting practice, Randy attempting left-handed pitches and Gus taking murderous, breeze-wafting swings, his stocky body corkscrewing in his futile efforts, and the sight must have triggered some do-goody, latent trait for I found myself approaching Randy and offering some help. My first thought— partner everyone up for a little throw and catch. I chose Bobby, Michele picked Jane, and after some confusion and searching for misplaced gloves, the rest paired up. Bobby took blinking stabs at my easy throws, most often snaring it, the ball pulled from his glove with a *Mousetrap* smile; sometimes not, his attention often wandering across the diamond where Michele lobbed soft, underhand throws to a cowering Jane. With each miss, Bobby set off, chasing his rolling prize and muttering *Crap!* under his breath, his sluggish jog abandoned before the ball came to a rest in the ankle-high grass. I used these breaks to judge the rest of my talent pool. The other pairs were plagued with shot-putting form, horrendous aim, gloves held out not to catch but to shield and protect, the bouncing balls avoided as if they carried explosive charges. Screams and cries rose from our ranks, and the strange calls drew the attention of the distant tennis players, the half-naked hardbodies frolicking on the sandy volleyball court, and the small band of picnickers whose hibachi sent up hazy smoke signals just outside the deep left-field line.

Pop fly, Bobby called. Rearing back, nearly tipping himself off balance, he launched the ball toward the clouds. I followed its lazy trajectory into my glove, and with the cradled smack of leather, I thought of the two of us years ago in Bobby's backyard. Every third game, Bobby rotated from first base to the pitcher's mound. We practiced his two-pitch repertoire—fastball and a frighteningly erratic curve—on the sloped yard beyond the pool, me with the catcher's mitt our coach had lent us, Bobby taking aim forty-six feet away, the distance verified by his father's tape measure and marked with a piece of scrap wood nailed into the turf with ten-penny nails. I cowered behind my glove, a wincing pose I now recognized all around me, fearing a heater that carried more hiss and pop than any I would face until high school, my hand numb and beet-red by the time we were through.

Sure, Bobby said when I asked if he wanted a pop fly in return, but the moment I sent the ball skyward, I realized I'd made a mistake. Bobby looked up, and with his perspective skewed, he began to fidget, his feet pattering confused half steps beneath his bulk. He let out a little yelp and covered his head with his mitt, his back turned from the ball as it landed with a plop three feet from him.

My fault, I said.

Sure was. Sink out this time, Stan. Way out.

I backpedaled, but for every step I took, Bobby took two forward, a foot-dragging, javelin-thrower's stride. With a breathy grunt, he launched the ball. Only problem was he'd muffed his cool equations, substituting distance for height, and the ball whistled in a line drive high over my head.

I gave chase down the left-field line. Ahead of me, the picnickers, the smoke of grilling sausages a greasy haze as I approached. The first one I noticed was a girl with lacquer-teased blond hair and pimpled chin, pale arms sticking out from a black, sleeveless *Led Zeppelin* T-shirt. An open baggie of pot rested in her lap, and in her pink-nailed fingers, she rolled a joint, a task that seemed to consume every atom of her concentration. A rope-muscled, ponytailed man with a shoulder full of red and blue tattoos tended to the smoking hibachi, spatula in one hand, beer can in the other. The last one was a stocky bulldog of a man, Fu Manchu mustache and wide sideburns, slicked-back hair styled in what just might be the last of the pompadours. The ball rolled to a stop near the pointed tips of his scuffed leather boots, but he didn't make an effort to get it, his hands occupied with the chewing tobacco he shoveled into his cheek. Here, I thought, was a refugee straight out of high school metal shop and detention hall, the delinquent details honed right down to the dangling wallet chain and cigarette pack rolled into his T-shirt sleeve.

Sometimes those retards don't know their own strength, do they? he said as I picked up the ball. Ponytail laughed, spatula-swiping at the mosquitoes lingering near the colored landscape of his tattoos.

Come on, Stan! Bobby called, his beckoning saving me from an exchange of words that could only lead to trouble.

Back on the infield, I gathered the troops, dug deep into my smartass's vocabulary until I found some suitable words of praise, my offerings humbled by Randy and Lisa's Sunday school brand of encouragement. A host of dim, grinning faces waited their next set of instructions, and my suggestion we work on hitting and base running was met with cheers.

Randy and Lisa walked the crew across the diamond, patiently shepherding them into their positions. Separated from one another, their blabbering waned, and most assumed awkward, shuffling poses, tugging on shirts or caps or various body parts as I shouted out instructions. I was going to hit the ball to a selected infielder who would try to throw out a designated runner at first. Fred, who'd ignored Randy's calls to join them in the field, became my first runner by default. *Hooray!* shouted Nate as he wandered from shortstop to shallow center field. Gus pounded his fist into his glove and yelled *Batter up!*

I pitched the softball into the air and struck it as softly as possible toward third where Jane straddled the line. The infield grass stole what little momentum I'd offered, the ball barely rolling by the time it reached her. Charging forward, eyes set in a burning, almost frightening desire, Jane overran the ball. Her left foot slid from underneath her as she tried to stop, and her pudgy legs shot out in an improbable split. On hands and knees, she crawled after the ball that had stopped just short of the bag.

Michele joined Fred and me at home. She trotted off, motioning for Fred to join her. After a moment of hesitation, Fred lit out, passing her halfway down the basepath, a dirt-kicking burst of speed that sent him well past the bag and into the emptiness of right field. Finally, Jane located the ball, and from a sitting position, flung a throw that barely cleared the pitcher's mound.

I tried again. And again. I did my best to maintain order, to stop the fielders from roaming, to keep the basepath runners moving in the proper direction. *Safe!* Gus bellowed repeatedly, even on the infrequent occasions a fielded ball beat a runner to the bag. Nate overthrew first base, and when the ball disappeared into a thicket behind the backstop, he sprinted after it. Fearing stickers or poison ivy, I stopped him before he could wade in, promising I'd get it later. Heckling laughter and a faint hint of pot smoke drifted from the picnickers down the left-field line.

The calamity I'd been fearing struck when Gus's throw to third pegged Tina, who'd wandered onto the infield grass to pick dandelions. At first she was shocked, hand raised to her temple, and then came the tears, a drawn-out sob that rose and ebbed like an air raid siren. Lisa and Michele ran to her and tenderly guided her off the field. On the bleachers they dug into the cooler for a cold soda she could press against the already rising welt. Nate clamped his hands over his ears and muttered silently to himself. Bobby yelled at Gus for not paying attention. Gus hurled down his glove, and with fists clenched, he steamed toward Bobby.

Randy hustled between them, his paltry frame sandwiched by their mountains of perspiring bulk. Calmly but forcefully, he delivered a speech he'd obviously practiced on them before, how punching solved nothing and how there were no winners in a fight, only losers. Gus and Bobby bowed their heads, mumbled *I'm sorry* to each other before separating. Gus jogged to Tina, kissed her cheek, and returned to the infield.

Wary of basepath injuries and waning attention spans, I decided to switch to hitting practice. I set the plastic T-ball stand on home plate and gave the most simple directions I could. Everyone got five swings, and on the last one, they'd run the bases. The idea was met with cheers, even by Tina, who was now dry-eyed and sipping from the soda can that had been icing her bump.

First up was Carrie. I kept a firm, cautionary grip on the bat until I'd placed the ball on the tee and then stepped safely back. With a grunting swing, she launched a decent fly into shallow left. The ball arced over the heads of Bobby and Gus, who had seemingly forgotten their differences and were now inspecting the red plastic *Mousetrap* rodent Bobby had produced from his shorts pocket. With her fifth hit, I jogged alongside Carrie as she toured the bases, her hand connecting solid high-fives with the others in the field. Her run ended with a double-footed trouncing of home plate.

Round and round they went. Amazing how their spirits soared, their fielding disasters forgotten. Cheers greeted each metallic ping. Bobby and Gus proved to be the big bombers, grounders that scattered the infielders like frightened ducks, high flies that sailed deep into the outfield. When Fred finally got his turn, he stepped back for a running start, a samurai charge that missed the ball but sent the tee helicopter-whirling past second base.

After Fred's victory lap, everyone gathered on the bleachers. The players exchanged back slaps and hugs, wild gesturing tales of how far balls were hit. There was a giddy anticipation of the next practice and of the victories that surely awaited them at the summer's-end softball tournament. Michele's lips grazed my ear, a whisper that she was proud and that our own little victory celebration would commence later. Yummy.

Tina smiled despite her temple's goose egg, her magic-markered sneakers tapping a nervous drumbeat on the wooden plank. Without so much as a warning, she raised her soda can and poured a tepid, backwash stream over my head. Lisa scolded her, and again, the tears, this time Tina explaining that's what she'd seen players do to their coaches on TV. It's OK, I assured all, mopping the sticky liquid from my neck.

Randy and Lisa announced it was time to go. I admired how deftly they corralled wandering interests, soothed little disappointments. I spotted Nate wading into the nearby thicket, and I remembered the lost ball. In the next moment, he screamed, and his stooped form straightened as if seized by an electric shock. Bamboo-thin fingers swatted the air around his head. He staggered back on stiff, unbending legs, managed to yell *Bees!* before launching into a looping, pell-mell sprint.

Dropping my bat and glove, I jumped from the bleachers and ran off after him. Nate's strides were giant, windmilling motions, bounding steps punctuated by swift, screaming turns, jack rabbit starts and stops. My legs shaking from the chase, I finally caught up to him near the left-field foul line picnickers. I grabbed his shoulders, told him everything was cool, everything was going to be OK, my messages of calm repeated until Nate's banshee cries dwindled into incoherent whimpers. Startling, how frail he felt in my arms, more ragdoll than man, the sunken chest, the bony ribs that protruded with each panicked breath. I held tight, squeezing Nate's arms to stop him from clawing at the already swelling stings on his neck and cheek. Metal Shop and Ponytail howled, while an uncomprehending haze seemed to have settled over the pimple-chinned girl, and my hatred for them boiled down to a hard, bitter stone that rattled in the cage of my jackhammering heart. Just as I opened my mouth to curse them, a bee, no doubt lured by the soda's sugrary scent, stung me.

The exact exchange between me and the picnickers now eludes me, its details blurred by the self-serving nature of memory,

Ponytail and Metal Shop making initial comments a better man would have ignored, my equally unkind responses fanning the flames. I let Nate go and stepped to the Metal Shop's strutting approach.

Let me say this in my defense—Metal Shop was the first to lay on hands, a hard, jarring shove to my chest. In quick succession, my split screens shut down, and in my head, the blissful batting cage focus. I sized him up, the distance between us and how quickly I could close it calculated, the vulnerable points highlighted—throat, groin, eyes. Some men lose control when they get into a fight, the haymaker-throwers, the ones who exhaust themselves in the time it takes to pick three songs on the jukebox. Other men choke, their will like a dried up flower, their limbs as limp as dead stalks. I, however, sink to a new level of sub-zero, physics-driven cool. I become detached, analytical, no different than a surgeon or butcher, my opponent tabled meat. A paradox, the peace I find in the whole affair, the peace of finality, the freedom of abandoning the ambiguous world of words.

Wheezing mightily, Bobby was the first to reach us, and again, the hazy nature of facts, but these two things were certain—Metal Shop uttering the word *retard* and me christening the proceedings with a reach-back, coil-spring blow, a clean shot to Metal Shop's square, hairy chin. Metal Shop staggered back, choking on his swallowed wad of chew. The jolt rode up my arm, and I thought here was a real, telling connection that would make MELCO proud of their prodigal son. Nate squealed, and before Metal Shop could raise his mitts in defense, I was on him. Pleasing, the flesh-thudding connections, the visceral grounding to this fleeting speck of life. Perhaps I wasn't much of a wedding reception dancer, but here I transcended into a regular Fred Aistaire, sidestepping Metal

Shop's takedown attempts and lurching, grunt-fueled punches, making him pay with quick, snapping strikes to the ear, the ribs, kidneys.

I pulled back for a moment. *Never pick a fight with a man in tune with the distance of his arms,* I said coolly.

Wha—? Metal Shop said, his words cut short by a right cross to the nose.

Stop it! called Michele, but her voice was distant, unconnected to my narrowed world, population two, me and a man who was a stranger only moments before.

Metal Shop was cowering now, stunned and hurt, every peek above his raised hands met by a stiff jab or body-torquing uppercut. *Ahh!* he mumbled, his ugly wolfman's face buried in his grease-stained hands. Blood oozed between his fingers, and then I noticed its presence everywhere—the front of our shirts, my hands, even specks on the dandelions—the two of us linked by hatred and a common stain, linked by the blank human spaces on our hierarchical checklists.

Only when my next swing cut harmlessly through the air did I realize that Bobby had grabbed me from behind and lifted me off the grass. With a Coke belch deposited directly in my ear, my hulking cousin lugged me away. I cursed incoherently, my eyes welling with tears, my cold focus broken as I Chappie-twisted in Bobby's arms.

Calm down, Stan, Bobby said softly, panting for breath. *Calm down, OK. No one wins a fight.* He set me down on infield dirt, outstretched arms pinning me back as I tried to bull rush past him. With the help of the stoned blond, Metal Shop staggered to the parking lot, his footsteps marked by a dripping blood trail.

The others gathered around me, but not as close as they had

before. Gone was their urge to high-five or pour a congratulatory soda over my head, and in its place stood a new distance, a space wary and fitful and distrusting. Even the tennis players and volleyballers had abandoned their games to watch. My cut, blood-smeared hands quivered at my sides. I tried to speak, but the words to say I was sorry, to say Randy was right, no one won a fight, were lost somewhere deep within me.

And then … late night. Alone. Fuzzy with pills, a green, beer-bottle forest on the kitchen table. A summer's quiet, Michele pissed off and at her place, Bobby snoring, his nightly, Jane-dreaming jerk off behind him. The kitchen dark save the muted TV, the Phillies on a west coast swing. Deep shadows and snowy gray light bathed the refrigerator, the stove. I stood on shaky legs and knocked over the trashcan. Papers and empty cereal boxes cascaded over the linoleum, a watermelon rind I inadvertently kicked beneath a counter. Blue and pink pills dotted the countertop. I wet my finger, dabbed it into the toxic spill, and brought my pharmaceutical catch to my numb lips. A new beer in hand, I slid back the patio door, and the effort drained what little strength I had.

A dry breeze and the stars sparkled. A neighbor was using a clothes dryer, the air wafting with the wet, linty smell. Fireflies but no crickets yet. A cool night, the drone of air conditioners absent. Mr. L's tomatoes past knee-high. Unsteady, my path, a puppet on unthinking strings, a weaving that led me to the pool where the diving board struck me as sensible furniture. The seductiveness of chemical weight, a moat around my aching soul, and in my protected kingdom, the questions and doubts that screamed daily in my skull crumbled into a murmur, a song that harmonized with the nonsensical lapping of pool water.

I sank onto my knees, and with great difficulty, lowered my cloudy body across the pool apron. One hand reached over the edge, the deep-end water cool on my fingertips. I gazed up to the stars and thought of the flickering promises of distant worlds. Then my eyes shifted focus, snapped into the figure-ground that beheld the infinite blue spaces between these worlds, and once I saw the sky this way, the stars, with all their glimmering allure, went dark, and all that remained was the icy blue, the vastness drowning me, pulling me in…

7/17

Beautiful, a sky of painted explosions, arcing blossoms of green and yellow, blue and red. The reflected bursts splintered across the calm river waters, and on the open boats, children waved starshine sparklers. A free summer concert in the park, and who cared if the Fourth's festivities were rained out because the Fourth was as good as the fifth or the sixth or the twenty-seventh when one was operating on an empty calendar. A John Phillips Sousa soundtrack oom-pahed from a nearby costumed band. The conductor glanced uneasily up to the sky, trying to synchronize his baton beats with the heavenly eruptions. The rainbow colors melted over Michele's tanned cheeks. Good to see her smile, and I hoped this image would replace my playground memory, her pretty face shock-frozen, pulling away with a reflex that originated in brainstem and spine, as if recognizing for the first time the ugliness of my heart. These past two days I've reverted to my slapstick persona in an attempt to make amends—flowers and foot massages, a conscious reduction in my drinking, my pills locked away, my willingness to tolerate the city crowds for something as corn dog and banal as a fireworks display.

Boom! and the brilliant white tore into the dark. Boom! and I admired the fiery patterns, their precision and execution, the premeditated elegance that struck a chord with all the elegant miracles of man, his aqueducts and ruffled potato chips, his symphonies and artificial hearts, and Boom! the stock footage flip side, the trenches of Flanders so graphically detailed in my uncle's book, the waiting photos of finality and flesh cowering in the trenches below, just another example of man's inclination to spear his wondrous species crown through his rival's heart, the dark intent that made it easier to punch a stranger than to reach out and catch a tumbling cousin. Boom-boom! and as I did the other drugged night by the pool, I let my eyes become lost in the eternal backdrop of a murky night sky, ignoring the brief and resplendent flares that had the other blanket-sitters oohing and ahhing.

Back home and with the boom-boom of explosions singing in my chest, Michele and I unbuttoned and unzipped, a shedding that revealed Michele's pretty bands of winter white, my hideous network of scars. Shameful, the sight of my fight-scraped knuckles against her skin, a private production of beauty and the beast so wrenching I had to shut my eyes.

and later...

Hate second shift, Bobby said as I drove him home from work. The intermittent streetlights ebbed into my car, and they offered brief glimpses of my uncharacteristically sullen passenger, the metal lunch pail gripped tightly on his lap, his hair's yellowing chlorine streaks. On a city corner, a gang of shirtless boys lit Chinese firecrackers. The boys held the twisting, dwindling strings until the silver-white bursts neared their fingers. The dry, flinty smoke of gunpowder drifted toward my car. I tried to get Bobby to talk, but he just turned and gazed out the window, saying nothing until we got home, and then only a thoughtless *Goodnight* outside his bedroom door.

Peaceful, peaceful, Michele's slack-muscled form. Her long legs scissored across the bed, my pillow clutched tightly to her side. In sleep, I care for her even more, her body unmoving, like a painting or statue, her inertia allowing me to appreciate the details blurred by motion. I pulled the padded stool from my aunt's makeup table, and sitting by her side, held my fingers near her mouth and felt the current of her warm breath. She stirred, and I hoped that at some subconscious level she understood I was near. Slivers of moonlight crossed her nipples, the hollowed nook at the base of her throat. Here was everything I could want—sex and acceptance, the trappings of love—and another flip side for here was also everything I'm certain I don't deserve. Nothing, I now realize, unnerves me more than my own happiness.

The soft cry of bedsprings, lip-nibbling moans from Bobby's room. Leaving Michele, I paused by my cousin's door, then went down and opened a beer. A milky reflection played on one of the butterfly cases my uncle had rescued from his biology classroom, short-lived beauty preserved and motionless in a death sleep. Fleeting, a man's time, his fireworks days of rainbow colors. Inconsequential, the waves born of his desperate flounderings. Outside, Chappie bark-bark-barked.

7/18

A blazing mid-afternoon sun, the weeds surrounding the factory lot where Bobby works standing at a perfect, breezeless attention. Drooping willow branches teased the sign at the employee lot entrance. With the grinding of gears and tooting airbrakes, long flatbeds slid into the loading bays. Familiar, the smell here, the arid grit of the adjacent foundry, the scent of Bobby's work clothes. A whistle blew, and through the rows of opened windows, I was greeted by the long sighs of shut-down machines. Bobby and I waited by the front door. Inside, the first-shifters formed a shuffling, chatty line by the punch out.

There's Phil, Bobby said.

A dust cloud trailed a jacked-up yellow Nova across the gravel lot. The cloud billowed, the dust mingling with the slack willow leaves before settling in a grimy mist over the parked cars (and on my split screen, stock footage of Coliseum charioteers, Rommel's charging desert tanks). One last chorus of cranking heavy metal heart-pounded from the Nova's stereo before the driver killed the engine. With a readjusting tug on his oversized belt buckle, Phil—Bobby's second-shift foreman—climbed out and hip-checked his door shut. Shoulder length, kinky black hair escaped the rear of his Pirates cap. He took one last, cherry-burning drag on his cigarette, and with a casual flick, launched the butt a good twenty feet, and I wondered if the world was populated by more Metal Shop refugees than I'd imagined.

I stopped him before he could barrel right past us. Miss Manners would have been proud of the way I introduced myself, my explanation that I was Bobby's cousin, and would I be able to hang out with him for a shift to see if I could help him with his new routine? *Trained monkey could do his goddamn job*, Phil said as he punched in. The anger flash caught in my belly, Phil's ignorance like spilled gasoline, and I knew I'd find all the spark I needed if I kept looking into the asshole's beady eyes.

With a Chappie-like determination, I followed Phil into the dank changing room. *Not running a charity ward here*, Phil said as he swung open a battleship-gray locker door. Bobby, sitting further down the pine bench that ran between the lockers, eavesdropped indiscreetly. Finally, my persistence paid off, and Phil slapped a hardhat into my hands, warning that he better not see me without it and that if I got hurt, our little conversation never took place. *Fucking bullshit*, he huffed on his way out.

Maze-like, the factory floor; a regular mousetrap land of twists and turns. The assaults of clattering, whirring machinery had me sticking close to Bobby's side. A haze of harsh fluorescent light filtered down from the girdered ceiling in Bobby's shop, and I wondered if the long, flickering tubes were the source of the prickly buzz that itched beneath my scalp. A grinder spit orange and silver sparks. Looping strands of oiled metal tangled in the bin beneath a giant lathe. The din and echo forced Bobby and me to yell to each other. Beside us, a man astronaut-bundled in rubber apron and gloves, a welder's mask. Bobby handed me a pair of safety goggles and the hard plastic pressed its raccoonish pattern over my face. A myriad of wheeled contraptions zipped across the concrete floor, forklifts, scaled-down boxcars and flatbeds pushed along with the groan of metal wheels. What? I found myself saying again and again, suddenly understanding the origins of the first index card hanging in my aunt and uncle's vestibule— HOME VOICE, NOT WORK VOICE!

Bobby explained his tasks, and, yes, in all deference to his asshole boss, a trained monkey could probably do it. Shovel blades and rakes, these were his specialties, and the first thing Bobby showed me was the wheelabrator, a turning drum loaded with metal slugs. After Bobby tossed in the heads of shovels and rakes, the cylinder spun, and the rattling slugs knocked off the dull foundry coating. Five loads filled a boxcar, and off Bobby went to a far corner of the shop for rustproofing. He hung the pieces from T-bars attached to a conveyor belt. With a button click, the belt jerked to life, a ride that dipped them in a chemical goo before ushering them back. Structure, that was what the boy needed, because for Bobby, an evening of unmarked time was an abstract notion, as consuming and unfathomable as staring into a starry sky. He needed some sort of discipline, a framework in which to operate. For a few moments, I observed his disheveled hustling until an idea began to form. I set Bobby's wristwatch to beep every half hour, a signal for him to patrol the shop for items waiting to be shipped out. On the same trips, we checked the receiving area and distributed the filled crates and boxcars to their stations. While waiting for his wheelabrator loads, Bobby pushed a stiff-bristled broom over the concrete floors. It was a dance—one, two, three, four; one, two—and soon, I began to detect a hint of grace rising into Bobby's plodding drills. I stayed until his dinner break, and when I gave Phil his hardhat back, he mumbled sourly under his breath.

Dark on the way to pick up Bobby. The evening's humid air circulated through my car, and my lengthening hair tussled this way and that. I cranked the radio. *We can be heroes, just for one day*, and here I was, the knight in rusting armor, only I'd traded my steed for an overheating car, abandoned my lance for a bag of Chappie shit, a little present for Phil, my weapon of choice trunk-locked but still potent.

Eerie, the industrial district at night. The pinkish tint of halogen-lit streets. The dreamy steam clouds. The blocks-long echo zones of factory shops. Potholes and train crossings shook my car. The blare of a shift whistle a wild animal call. How artificial it all seemed tonight, the business of production and consumption, the stock images that substituted for meaning in a man's life. Pointless, sometimes, the fruit of our species crown, the window dressing accouterments (blue jeans! perfume! self-propelled lawn mowers! more!) that have become the one, true global currency. A toss-up as to what pains me more – my inane, pointless life or its setting in an even larger, more pointless inanity.

The lush green smells of weeds twined with the lot's foundry dust. A hidden cat mewed, a sense tapestry that lent a bristling texture to the dark. In the shadows by Phil's yellow nightmare of a car—a vehicle made even more ridiculous when I spotted the black shag dash, the chrome gearshift knob in the shape of a fist with raised middle finger—I left a putrid trail of Chappie shit leading to the driver's side door.

The shift whistle blew. In twos and threes, the workers exited. Moths swarmed beneath the single, harsh light that hung above the door. No one accompanied Bobby. Lunch pail in hand, he shuffled sadly toward the car. His nostrils flared as he shut the door. *You step in dog-doo, Stan?*

On the ride, I told him to let me know if Phil gave him any more trouble, but to my surprise, Bobby stuck up for the jerk. *He's under a lot of pressure, Stan. At least that's what the other guys say.*

And later—the deck outside my summer bedroom. Chappie barked, and I thought of Phil's puzzled look, the contortions of his dullard's mug as he snorted his way home, wondering where on earth the stink was coming from. But the scene's comic promise was tempered by Bobby's defense of him. With a mug contortion of my own, I toked on one of Michele's joints. The smoke was mild and sweet, the warmth a pleasant tickle in my chest. Leaning back, I blew a fragrant current skyward, another parcel of haze to gather around an already hazy moon.

From beneath me came the opening vibration of the patio's sliding door followed by the slap of flip-flops. Through the deck slats, I spied on the shadowy figure, a substantial form that could have easily been mistaken for a lost bear or a fearsome burglar. Bobby fiddled with his trunks, the pullstring that required adjustment due to the pounds he'd shed since we'd opened the pool. Barely making a splash, he slipped into the shallow end.

I stabbed out the joint and called his name. He was startled at first, then he laughed and disappeared beneath the water only to surface alongside the diving board. *Why don't you come in?* he invited. *It's nice.*

Maybe it was the weed, maybe the relentless humidity, maybe it was the urge to wash away the shit stink that had embedded itself in my nostrils and thoughts. Whatever it was, I was soon poolside in my uncle's baggy trunks. Light orbs shimmered like mellow sapphires beneath the lovely, lovely blue. The laws of refraction warped Bobby's body, a giant's head on a Toulouse-Lautrec frame.

Why're you laughing? he asked.

I'm laughing?

The pebbled concrete tickled my feet, and the sensation triggered memories of the way Bobby used to dunk me when his parents weren't looking, the underwater, oxygen-starving holds I struggled vainly to escape. Bobby pushed back his wet hair, exposing the tip of the scar that formed the most obvious and arbitrary tally on our checklist of differences.

I'll look out for you, Bobby said. *Mom always told me to look out for you in the pool.*

It was no daredevil's deep-end cannonball, but with a lungful of drawn air, I took the plunge. Cool, cool, the water, a mild shock I quickly overcame. Bobby laughed, then submerged. He moved with arms tucked close to his sides, his pressed-together legs flailing like a single appendage, only the dolphin-twisting of his body propelling him beneath the buoyed rope. For nearly a half hour we swam. I was the king of the doggie paddle, the fretful crawl, never straying beyond the shallow end, while Bobby approached the realm of perpetual motion. He popped up here and there, laughing and calling my name, always surprising me with the distances he'd covered since his last breath. It was only beneath the water that I could keep track of him. Shrouded in bubbles, Bobby approached me. For a moment, we were both weightless, immersed. Bobby's hair rose like seaweed strands, bubbles escaping the corners of his grinning lips. *Hey Stan!* he mouthed, tapping my shoulder before shooting back to the deep end.

7/19

Ironic, Bobby's line of questions on the ride home tonight—he has no idea of Michele's wedding ultimatum, yet he talked endlessly about why we're not married, and if we were, would she then be Aunt Michele? I nudged up the radio's volume, an auditory diversion from both his endless queries and from the approaching lights of Elaine's apartment.

Perhaps I can simply drive by Elaine's for the rest of my life, screen my calls, opt for an unlisted number, just ignore her and the months will flow into years, and when the inevitable public reunion takes place, the tension and secretive glances will have dwindled into a less obvious brand of embarrassment. It would be escape, finality, and freedom all rolled into one low-maintenance battle plan (or was it more a siege, or perhaps simply a coward's willy-nilly retreat), but that kind of wait-until-it-blows-over slacker's luxury isn't an option with Michele. Breakups—it's been my experience that there are two distinct varieties. There's Type-A, the ones full of venom-spitting, punch-slapping scenes, raging hellfire assaults that have me scrambling for cover, but at least once the smoke clears, I'm left safely on my side of no man's land. Perhaps Type-A's over-the-top charges lead to bruises, a smashed windshield, clothes thrown into the river, but I prefer them over Type-B any day. B-girls are the masters of the unblinking stare-off, the look that leaves me feeling naked despite the pat-down assurance that I am indeed wearing clothes. While A's try to crush me in the avalanche of their fuming barrages, B-girls let fly with the harpoon words, remarks carefully selected and honed, that can pierce the tender spots I've been foolish enough to expose. Their good-byes (usually something along the lines of *You're the coldest person I've ever known* or the ever popular *What's it like to have no soul?*) are unforgettable, the scripts for the continuous film loops that haunt my split screen. But try as I may, I can't picture Michele in either role, and the unpredictable possibilities of Type-C disturb me even more.

7/20

What have I done today?

Not much. Wielding my aunt's red teacher's pen, I circled here and there in the classifieds—programmer and tech assistant, systems analyst. Momentarily appealing, the ads' parade of abbreviated promises, but their fireworks shine quickly faded into the dead-end image of a MELCO-like cubicle. Where's that gun when I need it? Michele's gone for the week, a trip out west with her sister, a package deal of nature trails and mountain biking, rappelling and campfire songs, kayaking on pristine glacial lakes. *Check, check, check* on our tally sheet of differences, so many marks that I imagine the page looking like the trail of one of the exotic birds Michele and her nature-loving guide may well be tracking at this very moment.

7/21

Here is the rhythm of our days—Bobby up before me, a knock on my door and questions about breakfast. Over cereal, I read him the sports page, the Phillies latest woes, and after we've loaded the dishwasher, he slides back the patio doors and heads to the pool. He's in for an hour, two, three … Now and then he pulls himself out to catch his breath, the water cascading from the sloping mass of his body, his thick middle heaving until he's rested enough to slide back in.

Bobby, it's time for lunch—

Come on, Stan, one more lap, just one.

I lure him inside for a bachelor's feast of peanut butter and jelly or leftover pizza, our non-pool time spent chasing down Chappie for Mr. L or with me hounding Bobby to finish the chores that spill like water from his thoughts—pick up his clothes, run the vacuum, bring in the trash cans. From lunch until the time he leaves, my role is reduced to that of a human clock, a tolling of how many hours or minutes he has left to get out the door and catch his bus to work. Only the mailman's arrival brings a halt to our unproductive bustle. Upon hearing the metallic clank of the mailbox lid, Bobby scampers to the door and sifts through the magazines and catalogues and bills, searching for the postcards that arrive at least three times a week. *What a wonderful view* they read, or *Just as beautiful as we thought* or *Drove ten hours today*, and each ending with a reminder to Bobby of their love and that I am boss while they're gone. Bobby and I have started a collage of sorts, the postcard pictures of canyons and deserts, waterfalls and other roadside wonders taped to the kitchen wall, a panorama of panoramic views. Upon their return, I imagine my aunt and uncle pausing here from time to time, their dream vacation kept a bit more fresh in their memories, butterfly-preserved and forever vibrant.

Typical, Bobby's departure today, a door slam and his lunch box swinging; perfunctory, automatic waves to the neighbors, and suddenly, like it has every other day since he's gone on second shift, the unbearable silence descended upon the house. Here was the dark side of my open calendar, the emptiness thick with a secret weight … or was it simply the weight of my secrets? Perhaps the key to happiness may lie in constant distraction. Perhaps what I need is a surface existence, a catamaran skimming, a swim trunks and suntan lifestyle, a Chappie focus that doesn't stray beyond closed doors.

7/23

At first, I wasn't sure of the date—just the Bobby-proven fact that it's the weekend, the church bells proclaiming *Sunday! Sunday! Sunday!*

This morning I opened my sleep-heavy eyes, the bedroom awash in summer light and the clock radio pushing quadruple digits. I squinted Michele into focus. Her skin was flushed from her post-jog shower, and how productive her day had already been, early Mass followed by an up-tempo three-mile run. A flowery scent radiated from her hair. I rubbed her silky arm, and my little Rocky stirred. In my gut, a butterfly swarm, the rising urge to confess about Elaine ... yet I didn't, for within me burns not only the fear of Type-C but also the starshine flicker of another world, this one right here on earth, a world populated by the vague image of my better self.

Michele unwound her towel turban. Leaning forward, she worked a brush through her long hair. Sunlight lent the strands a richer spectrum. All these years and still there were surprises, an unnoticed color in her hair, her new lover's nickname (piglet—in honor of my wallowing abilities). Stupid, my hatred of the world's banality yet spurning the least banal person I know. Mesmerizing, the rhythms of her brushing, the dangling length of her hair. I fingered her robe's terrycloth belt loop and gave it a tug. Through contact, through the proximity of shared hours and wrestled-over blankets, was it possible to absorb a bit of her goodness? A germ mutation on my DNA, that's what I need, a rewiring to turn the notion of my better self into flesh-and-blood reality.

Michele threw her head back, flashed her teasing grin as she began the upright phase of her brushing ritual. Impossible to take my eyes off her, and I wished I could cocoon myself in this moment, drown in her smile for one, her invitation into a limited and exclusive network of caring. I could stay here all day, the beckoning sunlight and splash of pool water be damned, draw the curtains and together invent a new brand of love, a hermit's love, a biodome love, a Skylab-for-two love … but even Chappie's kiwi-big brain understands shut doors usually open, a fact proven by Bobby's doorknob jiggle, his asking of what's for breakfast.

I fished the sports page from a tree-killing mass of Sunday paper and read Bobby the news of the Phillies' split doubleheader. Then we all huddled over the movie section. Our plan—a Sunday matinee at the new multiplex and then, if all went well, a swing by an open house in an older section of town. *I drove by it the other day,* Michele explained. *It's a little thing. A starter, in the parlance.* I reminded her Realtors probably have their own circle of hell waiting for them, one I hope they're forced to share with radio talk show hosts and self-righteous hippies, but my sarcasm couldn't dim her enthusiasm.

Off we went, Bobby absently claiming the front seat after I'd opened the door for Michele, her smirk captured in the rearview for the ride as I endured Bobby's stories of Jane, Jane, Jane... A labyrinth of carpet-hushed hallways awaited us inside the multiplex, the dialogue of competing soundtracks choked off behind closed doors, the air conditioning goose-bump frigid. Small lit signs advertised the movies above individual entrances. After a short search, we found our theater and settled down before the lights dimmed. Bobby belched and took another a lip-smacking slurp of his soda. *Want some, Stan?*

For a moment, utter darkness. I smelled the chlorine residue from Bobby's skin, listened to the rasping of his breath and the gurgle-suck of his straw. Michele's hand sought out mine.

Coming attractions assaulted us, fistfights and car chases and mattress tumbles set to blaring music. *Wow,* Bobby called in his factory voice, *that car's really moving!* A popcorn morsel flew from his mouth. And a minute later, *Did you see that, Stan? That guy punches just like you.* I held a finger to my lips. *Just like you,* Bobby repeated, softer but still heads turned.

The movie was my choice (second choice really, but I couldn't imagine Bobby in an R-rated show, the chorus of howls that would have greeted every scene of nakedness or foul language), a supposedly true story of arctic exploration. Wide-screen vistas of wind-sculptured ice, mountainous bergs and enough snow shots to exhaust any Eskimo's vocabulary. The action was limited and grim. Bundled men dashed off on dogsleds never to be seen again. Starvation set in, the pace gradually slowing as if it too were in danger of icing over.

Must be really cold there, Bobby said, forgetting my whispered pleas. *Freezing.*

I nodded, not wanting to encourage him.

No swimming for those guys, huh? he asked with a laugh.

Shh! scolded a woman in the next aisle.

Bobby pointed to his chest, mouthed *Me?* and I nodded again.

Impossible though for him to stay quiet. The plot was beyond him, and during a teary death scene, he was yakking again, laughing at all the wrong times, his child's sense of justice easily upset (*That's wrong, isn't it, Stan?* he blurted when the gaunt-faced survivors decided to eat their dogs). *Shh!* hissed the woman again, this time joined by others.

With a popcorn shower raining from his lap, Bobby stood. *Got to pee, Stan.*

About time, a voice called as Bobby wobbled up the aisle.

Peace at last, and I tried my best to assemble the shards of my comprehension. The wheels of fate and chance churned across the screen, crushing one character only to deliver another. Brutal and strangely lovely, the expanses of snow and ice, and tiny, the images of a lost man's tracks across the wasteland, but as the minutes passed, I began to worry about Bobby. Too long, his pee break, and what was transpiring in the movie couldn't compete with my split screen—Bobby embroiled in a situation at the candy counter or, god forbid, the bathroom.

I scooched past Michele, only half-kidding as I told her to come if she heard screaming, and as I trudged up the aisle, I glanced back to see my parkaed twin on the screen, both of us setting out on our daunting and thankless journeys.

The imitation art deco concourse was quiet. Only bored teens in red vests behind the candy counter, the bathroom thankfully empty, but still I pushed open each stall door. My search led from theater to theater. With a splash of light, I entered the midnight spaces and stood in the rear until my eyes adjusted. Fragments of disjointed stories tangled in my brain—a college campus comedy, a courtroom drama, a World War II battlefield, more—so many plot lines and dialogue snippets that I soon started to second-guess my path and wondered if I was backtracking.

Finally, I discovered him in the place where I should have looked first. Easy to spot his hulking silhouette in the rows full of children. Easy to pick out his amused gut-rumbling among the shrill laughs. The screen was an animated explosion, deafening, frenetic, the stuff of sugar highs and induced seizures.

I like this movie better, Bobby said with an earlobe tug when I settled in beside him. *Anyway I forgot where you guys were.*

Cartoon light shone in his unblinking eyes. My tongue probed
the crown of the chipped molar Bobby gave me when we weren't
much older than the kids surrounding us. Two grown men lost in
a sea of children. Two grown men hopelessly awkward around
their fellow man, the only difference between us a matter of
placement, Bobby's awkwardness painfully public while mine
was painfully private...

A kiddie riot erupted. I'd lost track of the movie, but the
children screamed, threw popcorn. On the screen, the heroes had
prevailed and evil had been defeated. Bobby's meaty hands
thunder-clapped, and his airy, imperfect whistling provided an
odd harmony to the crowd's pixie shrieks.

Michele filled me in on how our movie ended on the way to
the open house. Balloons painted in colors knowable to me alone
adorned the FOR SALE sign that featured a woman's photo a
plump face and beauty shop hair, a smile that assured me she was
the graduate of one too many workshops on positive thinking.

You look just like that picture out front, Bobby said when we
met Camille at the door. He studied her with a forward-leaning
intentness. *Look Stan, she's even got on the same orange jacket.*

Poor Camille, there was probably nothing in her motivational
sales seminars that could have prepared her for the likes of Bobby.
I snuck a glimpse at her clipboard of selling points, *SMILE!!!*
written in bold red at the top.

On with the tour, and we were shown the breakfast nook (*Cozy,*
Camille said, checking her clipboard), the kitchen (*Modern*), the
den (*Roomy*). Impressive, Camille's Realtor's vocabulary of
'natural light' and 'addition possibilities' and 'organic form,' her
ridiculously rouged cheeks balling with self-pleased smiles that
had a habit of falling short of full blossom when she caught Bobby

peeking into drawers, shoving his hand behind couch cushions, or turning faucets.

Look at the view, Stan. Michele stood by an upstairs window, the sunlight in her hair, but I was now in no mood to search for new colors.

I lagged behind as the cavalcade headed to the laundry room. If I were to snatch the clipboard from Camille's manicured hands and write *HOME* on her list of selling points, I'd guarantee Michele's and my Rorschach responses would be equally strong and polar opposite. I've spent Christmas with her family, a house of happy, boisterous dinner tables, conversations void of subtextual attacks … a setting so near stock footage that I often catch myself slipping into guest star mode. Not hard for me to imagine Michele inhabiting this house of character and nooks. I could see her crashed on the couch after work, exhausted after a day of Lilliputian attacks and little blown noses, her shoes kicked off and school clothes wrinkled around her motionless body, her winter jacket pulled over her curled up legs. I could see the basement transformed into a mayhem comprehensible to her alone—her cluttered workbench and half-finished boxes, the smells of shellac and glue gun, the shoebox files of fabric swatches and magazine clippings, the old postcards she bought at the auction house. Imagine … imagine … and soon enough, through the wonderful coming attractions made possible by my species crown, the rooms became filled with her, her presence as natural as the hairline plaster fissures, the corner cobwebs, the closets' faint mothball odor. I could even see her in the future perfect tense, a faithful wife and loving mother … but the reception of my future vision grew dim when I tried to fine tune myself into the picture.

Back downstairs, I waited in the stuffy, windowless foyer while Michele took Camille's business card. How distant, our bedroom morning, poisoned by my misadventures in the outside world. There was a crack in the foyer mirror, my face slashed, eyes unaligned. The chitchat and shuffling goodbyes were making me ill, and I needed desperately to breathe, to change the scene, to have something else to look at beside Bobby, the one I'd hurt in one fell swoop, and Michele, the one I was torturing with a hundred stealthy injustices ... and give me half a minute, and I was sure I'd think up something to bring down poor, witless Camille, too.

And then, the altercation, only this time Metal Shop's bad-guy black hat was worn by me—Bobby filling his pockets with candy dish mints, me grabbing his wrist and squeezing a bit too hard when he wouldn't put them back, my grip pinching his skin, the surge of his pulse on my fingertips. A frightened look in his eyes, uncomprehending because Camille had said he could have some. A pastel lime hunk of sugar bounced across the hardwood. *That's all right*, Camille interjected, her face twisted into an expression I'd previously imagined for a Chappie-doo sniffing Phil.

Stan! Michele said.

Bobby's expression, teary and frightened, pissed me off even more. With a yank, he jerked his arm away, a flailing which knocked a vase of silk flowers from a shelf. Painted shards scattered across the hardwood in a pattern worthy of a fireworks display. We stood silently, each studying the spot where the vase had fallen. Camille broke the spell, a gentle and sincere reassuring, a reaching out to touch Bobby's trembling hand. *Are you OK, honey?*

Outside, and while Bobby poked at the sign balloons, Michele and I squared off, the spitfire anger glowing in her eyes and the piercing accusations flying from her lips, me sputtering in a hapless defense. Was this a preview of Type-C?

And when all the words were said, the two of us framed in a summer sunshine accented by unknowable greens and rose reds, we stared at each other, just another layer of unknowing heaped upon a thousand more. I heard the whisper of dropped veils, the naked truth of my ugly heart exposed, the negation of my better self. How intent, her gaze, a searching that left me lost within the tundra beneath my own skin.

8/4

How much can change in a week. In a day. In a heartbeat moment. *Start at the beginning*, my analyst encouraged, a somewhat redundant and obvious request, but fitting, and this story starts with a farewell that mimicked the departing of the Luxury Land Cruiser (Ta-da?), only this time it was me at the helm, my just-out-of-the-shop car our road trip vessel.

Reaching between Michele and me, Bobby adjusted the rearview to run his fingers through his hair. He spoke excitedly, first about Jane, then about the latest break-in in our neighborhood. *It was Rich's house*, Bobby said. *Rich on our baseball team. Second base, and he had that red bike. They put his dad in the hospital. And they took their new TV. All sorts of other stuff, too. That's what Mr. L says.*

Second base, red bike. The projector was broken in Bobby's private theater, the film frozen in a single, fading frame. Twenty-eight and forever going on ten. Perhaps somewhere in his twilight he understood that Richard (Huston, DDS) had traded in that banana-seat Schwinn for a silver Lexus, but the core of Bobby's memories were locked in that stalled frame of bikes and Little League, secret night swims, raids on a neighbor's garden.

Ahead of us, Lisa and Randy's van, the seats packed with Carrie and Gus, Fred and Chris and Jane and Tina. Palm prints smeared the windows. Nate turned back at every stop, and when he saw our car, a look of relief passed over his drawn face, and he offered a timid wave.

Humid this morning, and my air conditioning struggled to keep the elements at bay. The distant sky thickened with clouds, but there was no turning back this caravan, and with a toot-toot, we merged onto the dizzying exodus of I-95 South. Our destination— Baltimore's Camden Yards, an Orioles Saturday afternoon game, the excitement feverish back at the group home, Gus and Bobby clutching their gloves and dreaming of caught foul balls, Nate rapt in the counting and recounting his change purse coins, Randy and Lisa running down their checklist with the sober attention of arctic explorers—first-aid kit and sunscreen, medications, the emergency collection of 'just in case' clothes and underwear.

On the highway, Lisa camped out in the right-hand lane and dutifully respected the speed limit. Cars zipped by, eyeblinks of color, Doppler whistles born of cool equations. With each passing semi, the van crew pumped their clenched fists, imploring the drivers to blow their horns. Bobby joined in too, the van's excitement contagious despite the fact no truck driver could see him, and with each complying toot, Bobby bounced with a car-rocking glee.

The rain began as we crossed the Maryland border, an initial splattering that within the course of a mile deteriorated into a monsoon. Puddles formed, hydroplaning skips, cascading fountains from load-rattling trucks. My slapping wipers couldn't keep pace. Lightning in the near distance, a sky-splintering strike, thunder, the radio's reception momentarily fried. In the van's windows, Nate clamped his hands over his ears and rocked furiously in his seat. By Havre de Grace the torrent had eased into a steadier fall that pestered us all the way to the ballpark.

In the lot, Randy and Lisa broke out the ponchos. Raindrops stirred the parking lot puddles. Not a single, promising sliver shone amid the clouds. The game was already officially delayed and the radio's forecast offered little hope. Gus angrily pounded his fist into his glove. Bobby, his anticipating face framed in the drawstring oval of his poncho hood, stared dejectedly at Michele and me.

A quick huddle with Michele and Randy and Lisa, and we came up with a plan B, a walk to the Inner Harbor's aquarium. Disappointment greeted the news, questions if their baseball gloves could be brought to the aquarium. Gus kicked the van's back tire, threw his Oriole's cap into a puddle, but after a short walk and some of Michele's subtle salesmanship, even he was nearly sold on the notion of sharks and whales and stingrays. Curbside at a six-lane intersection, we choked on the diesel spew of a boarding bus. A speeding taxi splashed Tina, her jeans soaked from knees to cuffs. When the WALK sign flashed, Chris's doll-sized hand latched onto mine and didn't let go. Carrie's shoulder clipped a light pole, her gaze drifting between the skyscrapers and the harbor's covered boats. Seagulls circled down from the gray clouds, gathered in pecking groups beneath the empty sidewalk cafe tables. The rain beat straight and steady on umbrella canopies and poncho hoods. The head count on the aquarium steps came up one short. Scanning the harbor's brick promenade, we spotted Nate emptying the contents of his change purse into a panhandler's palm. Beaming, Nate ran to rejoin us, explaining to Randy, *He said he needed some money.*

Echoes filled the dim world beyond the aquarium doors. Poncho hoods were peeled back. Carrie leaned over the edge of the ground-floor tank, shrieking each time a shark or fin-flapping stingray swam near. Tina twirled her pigtail and stood transfixed beneath the whale skeleton suspended alongside the escalator. Chris bolted to the gift shop and returned with an unpaid-for pencil. Lisa, her red hair frizzed into afro proportions, walked him back to the cashier, patiently explaining that it wasn't right to take things without paying.

OK, let's buddy up, Randy said.

Buddy up, buddy up, Nate chirped.

A shuffling dance as they searched for partners. Fingers twisting and twining, Bobby asked Jane to be his buddy, and Jane accepted with an indifferent shrug. Pencil receipt sticking out of his shirt pocket, Chris latched onto my hand. Chris didn't speak or glance up toward me, and his little body swayed as we rode the escalator, his misshapen head peering over the moving handrail.

Amazing, the life forms we encountered on our sneaker-squeaking climb from floor to floor, the evolutionary twists both bizarre and beautiful. Electric eels and sleek gars. The boneless grace of octopi and jellyfish. The hornfish's poisonous spikes, the prehistoric stonefish. Vivid blue frogs as small as quarters. Scampering monkeys in the tropical rain forest. Chris yanked me from tank to tank. Raised on tiptoes, he spied into the artificial worlds, his already bulging eyes opened wider, his forehead touching the glass until I tenderly nudged him back. Whatever shyness Chris had soon disappeared, and in his craggy falsetto, he repeatedly asked me if I liked this or that fish, and with each of my positive remarks, Chris chimed, *Oh, yeah, he's a good one.*

On our way down, we took the slowly descending carpeted ramp that curved along a stacked series of enormous tanks. The water's bluish tint illuminated the dusky walkway, our group reduced to distinctive silhouettes that paraded before the glass. Schools of brightly colored fish swam by, identical packs that twisted and scattered as if wired to a single brain. The sharks performed their solitary glides, the tiny cigar, the mighty hammerhead. Nate shrieked and ran ahead, momentarily tripping on the sloping grade when he spotted a bubble-producing diver. I, too, stopped to gawk, the scene turned inside-out when I pictured the moment from this stranger's bubble-obscured view, his lonely world of beauty and peril, the crushing silence broken only by the internal workings of heart and lungs.

Bobby and Jane lagged behind. They held hands, paused, pointed and whispered. In his free hand, Bobby carried his poncho and Jane's, his damp baseball mitt. Chris waved to the diver, his Munchkin laughter drawing the attention of strangers. I momentarily pried myself from Chris's clammy grip and stepped back to eavesdrop on Bobby and Jane. *You think this is what God feels like when he looks down on us?* Jane asked

There was a tug on my shorts. I turned sharply, my fists balling, my initial urge to come out swinging snuffed when I caught Chris sliding his gift shop pencil into my pocket. Chris grinned, clutched my hand, and forcefully led me toward the next fishy wonder.

Back at the park, we crammed into the van, eating peanut butter and jelly sandwiches and sipping juice cartons. Randy returned from the ticket booth with the news that the game was officially off. The rain continued to fall, steady but softer.

No baseball? Chris's voice was nearly swallowed by roof-drumming raindrops and the trapped slurping and chewing of his van-mates. In between ponytail nibbles, Tina said she was glad because in baseball someone always got hurt. Nate rubbed his neck and agreed.

The van loaded up, and we said our good-byes, our caravan discontinued because Michele had picked out a scenic route home. Bobby slapped a high-five with Gus. Nate raised his hand too, but the smack of flesh caused him to yelp and shake out his stinging fingers. Jane waved, her mouth fish-puckered around a juice straw. With a horn toot, the van sloshed through the parking lot puddles and melted into the city traffic. At our car, I shook out Bobby's poncho.

Looks like you two did lots of hand holding, I said.

Bobby stared down at his palm. *Yeah, we did.*

A roadmap unfolded across her lap, Michele guided us onto route 40. Blooming daylilies had sprouted alongside signs for Gunpowder Falls Park and Joppa, Magnolia, Aberdeen Proving Grounds. We played games of Highway Bingo and I Spy, Michele's usually competitive rules diluted to assure Bobby's participation. Michele and Bobby begged and begged until I finally stopped at a roadside stand selling the twin temptations of fireworks and sweet corn. As Michele paid for our things, Bobby peeked into a wooden bushel basket of red crabs, and I grabbed his hand before he could reach into the shifting pile. A hundred yards beyond the stand lay the Chesapeake's stretching waters. Pulses of uncresting waves, their gray mimicking the clouds above, rippled toward the shore. Scrub grass ran to the water's edge, and the briny smell of open estuary water swelled in my lungs in a way that made me think of breathing in a new light. In the distance, cawing gulls circled an anchored fishing boat, and I imagined the aquarium's tidewater tanks, the crustaceans and fish, the wondrous layers of life lurking beneath the surface.

Across the Susquehanna's muddy mouth, we stopped for dinner in a lapstrake bar. Sand filled the cracks in the parking lot macadam. Rain-washed fishermen's traps formed a high, teetering pile by the kitchen entrance. A handful of mismatched tables inside, a seven-seat bar, the walls decorated with beer signs and sagging nets, a pair of crossed, weathered oars. A pleasant smell here, cooking fish and beer, the sea smell that survived the air conditioner's filter. Our round-figured, motherly waitress introduced herself as Dolly, and she took an immediate shine to Bobby, called him 'sweetheart' and helped him tie on his plastic bib when our crabs arrived. She draped newspaper sections over the table, gave us mallets, even demonstrated proper technique. Soon I discovered myself in the midst of a crab massacre, the succulent taste washed down with cold beer. Bobby surprised us all with his deft hammer strikes, a force a breath short of pulverizing, the shell split without the spraying of meat.

Dolly asked if everything was OK. Her hand rested on Bobby's shoulder, then a realigning tug for his bib. Pushing aside the spent shells, she lit the table's dimpled glass lantern. Specks of crab meat stuck to Bobby's lip, his butter-glistening chin. With a push, I had made him forever innocent, the darling of kind waitresses, a man-boy who found a deeper sense of wonder in aquarium fish or walking beside his girlfriend than I ever would.

Bobby's hand-covers couldn't contain his belches. Seated at

the bar, Dolly exhaled cigarette smoke and laughed. *You keep enjoying yourself there, sweetheart,* she said. I watched him and wondered what the two of us would be like if I could go back and whitewash the arm's-length tragedy from our lives. Surely Bobby would have matured beyond his bullying, his no-nonsense mother would have seen to that. The incense aroma of his altar boy robes may have lured him to the priesthood . . . his schoolyard copying of homework could have held the seed of a tax cheat. He might have had a crack at pro ball, or he could have become a good-old-boy gym teacher or an overbearing little league coach. His scheming ways may have been a precursor to an adulthood as a philandering husband or local politician. Perhaps he would have become a quiet man uncomfortable with the big-boned mass of his body, a recluse who retreated every night to the sawdust and machine buzz of his basement woodshop ... and when I considered this infinite spectrum of possibilities, I understood that I didn't steal just one life from Bobby but many.

Outside, Bobby lingered in the restaurant door, saying good-bye to Dolly, the plastic bib still knotted around his thick neck. Oily rainbows rose from the rain-soaked macadam, Bobby deliberately stomping through every puddle on his way to the car. In the car, the green, silky aroma of the sweet corn we'd bought earlier. A quick map consultation before I turned the key ... but the car's only response was a single click, a sickeningly empty sound I tried to mask with gas pedal pumps and more ignition turns. Michele nibbled her lower lip, offered me a wincing, shrinking look.

The drop-dappled windshield blurred the outside world, and was this an inkling of how those artic explorers felt when they first realized their plight? I popped the hood, tried my limited tricks, testing spark plug wires and radiator hoses, the mystery of internal combustion just another subject beyond my comprehension. I ordered Michele to try again, hoping I'd unknowingly worked some miracle. Nothing. When I emerged from beneath the hood, I discovered Bobby huddled alongside Dolly beneath a black umbrella.

Dolly guessed it was my starter. She said her son could fix it, but he was out on his boat. She untied the breeze-fluttering bib from Bobby's neck and pointed to a lit motel sign about a quarter mile down the flat road. Her sister-in-law ran the motel, nothing fancy, Dolly said, but it was clean. My options limited, I handed her the keys. Oddly liberating, that leap, my fortune placed in the hands of a woman I trusted for no other reason than her affection for Bobby, her air of motherly assurance.

Dolly hurried inside and returned with two brown paper bags stuffed with hush puppies, shrimp poppers, chocolate chip cookies, and a two bottles of beer. She insisted we take the umbrella, saying she'd call ahead and get us a room with a fridge.

At the edge of the parking lot, Bobby turned to wave goodbye. With me picking up the rear, the three of us shuffled a hobo's walk along the stone-sandy shoulder. Cars passed, a pickup with muddy motorcycles strapped in its bed, and the truck's windy currents teased the umbrella Bobby held over Michele's head. I kept a watchful eye on Bobby, calling for him to get further onto the shoulder with each approaching car. THE BLUE NOTE beckoned the motel sign, aqua neon curlicues straining against the gloaming. Three cars in the parking lot, Maryland plates and rusting bumpers, the motel white-painted cinder block, two stories, pink doors and green metal railings. A film-topped pool dominated the parking lot's center. In the cramped office, Bobby spun a creaking metal rack of postcards. He picked out a card, laughing at the photo of a fisherman holding two giant crabs, and asked if he could have it to mail to his parents. Sure, buddy, no problem.

Surrounded by green shag and imitation wood paneling, Bobby and I watched TV as Michele showered. The air conditioner whirred like a crippled jet engine, and no matter how I yanked, I couldn't shut the thick curtains completely. I opened one of Dolly's beers. Bobby flicked through the TV's offerings, a carousel of tidy images, an absurd Mobius strip that led us nowhere but where we'd already been. An arctic explorer had to learn to trust his compass because the wasteland distorted his perception. Without guidance, his path would form a giant circle, the unappreciated urgings of his dominant leg looping him back to his desolate origins. With his finger kept down, Bobby sped the procession, laughing as the pictures melted into a blur. Sitcoms and cartoons, Godzilla and the poorly dubbed citizens of Tokyo, kinetic music videos, a game show where a contestant grabbed wildly at a green and white rainstorm of bills. Around and around he went, his finger pinning the button, and soon I was laughing too, each fleeting image tickling me even more. How ridiculous, our pursuits and desires, the seriousness we invest in production-consumption … and how absurd to think of killing myself, as if one more meaningless act would breathe a speck of difference into the world—

Morning, and dawn's stretching rays glowed around the thick window curtains. With its mechanical drone, the air conditioner spewed its arctic blasts, and I woke with the tip of my nose chilled. I studied the room's other bed, then turned to the body next to me, then another double-take to set myself straight. Sometime during the night Bobby must have crawled in next to me, a move which forced Michele to migrate to his abandoned bed. Funny, imagining that particular expedition, the round-and-round of sleepy bodies while I lay unaware. Bobby snorted, gasped, phlegm-choked hacks, a range of sounds vast enough to compose its own guttural symphony.

Making as little noise as possible, I rose to get a shower. The mirror fogged, dew on the shower's green and black tiles, a mist roiling beneath the single ceiling light. I nudged the hot, and the splashing water loosened my stiff back. Soaping down my network of scars, I contemplated the nature of redemption. In movies and books, in religious TV shows and extra-inning ballgames, redemption came swiftly, a single defining act that severed a man from his shameful past. How wonderful, to jettison the weight of regret and guilt, to emerge forgiven from the shadows of one's disgrace. I turned off the water. My feet wetting the cool tile, I wiped a clear streak from the mirror above the sink, exposing my morning-bloodshot eyes.

The frigid AC instantly numbed my exposed skin when I opened the bathroom door. To my surprise, Michele and Bobby were already up. Michele had picked up coffee in the hotel office. Bobby crinkled back the plastic wrapping from an icing-lathered breakfast pastry. Other news—Dolly's sister had told Michele my car would be ready in a few hours, and to top things off, Michele had learned of a nature trail just across the road, a morning leg-stretch that would serve the dual purpose of killing some time and keeping Bobby occupied.

With Michele in the lead, we crossed the two-lane highway. The coffee's warmth and potency made me pleasurably light headed. No cars waited in the gravel trailhead lot. Spiderwebs hung from the wooden sign pointing the way to the trail. Bobby had commandeered my sunglasses, and behind their dark lenses, he appeared almost threatening, bodyguard-large, a stubbled, square chin and thick arms that tested the stitching of his T-shirt sleeves. The trail ran flat and single-file narrow. The sandy dirt churned harshly beneath our feet. The trees thinned out, and the trail grew wider. A sweeping flatland of wavering, waist-tall grasses greeted us, and further out, the perspective-filling sheen of the bay. Michele's hands were already filled, smooth pebbles, a papery snakeskin, a long white feather, her unique vision at play again, gems for her future boxes.

Look Stan! Bobby said.

Ahead of us, a butterfly storm. Currents of yellow and white flecks tumbled and rose, hundreds of wings capturing radiant moments of sunshine. Michele walked ahead, joining Bobby, who'd already jogged into the butterfly cloud. Beside me, an unhatched chrysalis dangled from a slender pussy willow. The shell was hardened, whatever life there was now trapped inside. Inside I was breaking, but I couldn't say how or why.

I walked toward them. Butterflies landed on my shirt and shorts, the sensation tickling and light, weirdly negligible yet persistent. The three of us were similarly adorned, Bobby with a wing-fanning butterfly perched in his hair. Wonderful, our laughter, the unlikely images of ourselves covered in patches of flitting, nervous color. I thought of shower steam and redemption, of the power of a single act to steal a hundred futures or whitewash the past—

Yes, I said.

Michele shooed a yellow butterfly from her nose. *What's that?*

Yes, I repeated, and with that uttered syllable, a crumbling began within me, my locked-away heart no match for her smile and the assault of butterflies. Yes, Michele, if you hadn't come to your senses yet, if you hadn't stopped believing in the better me I had yet to meet, then yes, let's get married.

I told you, Stan! Bobby pointed wildly from me to Michele, his waving arm stirring the butterfly cloud. *Aunt Michele!*

By noon we were on the road, and twenty miles ahead awaited Elkton, the border town of quickie marriages. I gripped Michele's hand as I drove. If the measuring stick of my life had been the length of an arm, a reach not made, then maybe I could close the distance now. Wildflowers strained from the roadside ditches, horses and cows in the flat-land meadows, the scenery speeding past, our car hurtling us toward finality or freedom or perhaps, I hoped, some Type-C future I couldn't even begin to comprehend.

WEDDINGS proclaimed the sign at the first chapel we spotted. White clapboard, a tiny steeple above an arched door. Swallows darted around us, daredevil swoops from the entrance-shading sycamores. Michele called one of her sisters on her cell phone, talking softly as she dabbed her watery eyes. A second wedding for her, and she'd always said she wanted it simple, the ritual and artifice of the first too much to relive, and what could be simpler than this, a modest, weathered exterior, a vestibule where the holy water fountain had been replaced by a placard of prices.

The man who introduced himself as the on-duty reverend pulled his fountain pen and pad from his vest pocket and jotted down our requests—taped organ music, video, a rice packet— *The works,* as Bobby so aptly chimed in.

With a button push, the altar's boombox played the wedding march. Our unnamed reverend slapped a tape in a camera perched atop a tripod, and after a bit of framing, pressed the record button. Bobby waved at the blinking red eye. A three-legged golden retriever sniffed his way into the room and curled up beneath a pew. I turned to Bobby only to find him kneeling on the floor, his hand extended so the dog could slurp his fingers. I shut my eyes, a temporary blindness that echoed a much great blindness, my blindness to the future, my ignorance of what made a happy marriage. I felt myself swaying, the reverend's lips moving but his words unclear. Steady, steady, for this was the guest star's big scene, and I hoped my face didn't betray the fear I had of my own weakness, the fear that I would never again get the chance to whitewash my past, never again get the chance to be struck by lightning, to plant myself in a network of caring—

Michele nudged my arm. *Stan?*

I do?

And weary, our return home, our afternoon spent stopping in roadside towns, antique barns and used book stores, a deserted parking lot where we let Bobby light a few of the fireworks he'd been pestering us about since the wedding. Something within me relaxed at the sight of the wide lawns and curving streets of my aunt and uncle's neighborhood, the twilight hiss of sprinklers, the only betrayal of stock image bliss coming when Bobby leaned out the window and bellowed, *I'm the best man!* to a perplexed group of neighbors.

We pulled into the driveway to a yapping welcome from Chappie. An insistent hubbub of cicadas, fireflies that blinked like Christmas lights around the house. The stuff of happy endings that this oft-wished-for set was the place where I returned tonight. Someday, when Michele and I came here for a barbecue or Thanksgiving turkey, perhaps I'd feel as though I was truly coming home, our newlywed nights and Bobby's summer swims forming ties stronger than any I could now imagine.

Inside, Bobby scuttled ahead to the bathroom. I stacked our corn in the refrigerator, hid the fireworks amid Michele's wheat germ and vitamins on the top pantry shelf. I didn't think of the answering machine until I spotted Michele pressing its playback button. After the warbled spin of tape, I was relieved to hear any voice but Elaine's.

Hi, everybody, my aunt said. *Guess we missed you. Hope you're well. Be good, Bobby. Love to all.*

I thought of the videotape, the tears they would no doubt shed when they watched it. Having changed into his trunks, Bobby brushed past us. *Going swimming, Stan.*

A beep from the answering machine, then a deep, unfamiliar voice: *Mr. Watson, this is Sergeant Phillips from the Lincoln barracks of the Nebraska State Police.* A pause. *There's been an accident involving a Susan and Mark Smith...*

The message played on, Michele hurriedly jotting down phone numbers and names, me staring blankly out the patio doors. Bobby leapt from the diving board, a cannonball splash into the pool.

These were the sensations I had yet to shake—the fleshy union of my palms and Bobby's shoulders, a thud's solid call when I'd expected a splash, the sight of a still body haloed by bobbing tomatoes. The resurrection of these images never failed to jerk me from a near sleep, my heart drumming, a breathy gasp escaping my lips. Now I understood a new unshakable had my scent, the squeamish sensation that at a basic, sub-atomic level, the world was suddenly a less solid place. I shuffled through my aunt and uncle's house, a steadying hand resting on walls and porcelain sinks, but even the most solid substances had acquired a rubbery element of give, my every step no better than a barely avoided tumble.

I called the police, the hospital, two confirmations of the worst news imaginable, a late-night wreck, the Luxury Land Cruiser (ta-da?) enveloped in flames, no chance for survival. I couldn't tell Bobby, not yet, so we let him swim until he grew tired, the sky dark by the time he left a sloshing footstep trail back to his room.

After he went to bed, Michele and I cleaned the house. We vacuumed and dusted, scrubbed linoleum and tile, one job leading to another, our brushes uprooting grime from the tiniest nooks. Wordless, our work, no music or TV, no buffers against the silence. It seemed important to have the place clean, important to claim a bit of dominance over the world, to wipe out its dirt and shape it, ever so slightly, to my will. Down on my knees in the bathroom, woozy with fumes, I tried to practice the words I'd use to tell Bobby, but the thought of delivering them made me tremble, an attack of nerves so shaking I vomited, once, twice, again—then dry heave spasms that hurt as much as any knockdown pitch, my gags smothered in a chlorine-scented towel.

In the small hours of the night, when there was nothing left to clean, Michele and I stirred whiskey into our coffee and fucked on the couch. I couldn't call it 'making love' or even 'consummation'—it was more of a grunting self-affirmation, an emphatic placing of ourselves among the living. Dazed by Jim Beam and scrubbing bubbles, knocked senseless once again by the haymaker of cool equations, I lay beside Michele, my hand placed over her beating heart, and slipped into a shallow, hallucinatory sleep.

When I woke, I made the necessary calls—my father, who thankfully agreed to set the arrangements in motion, a disbelieving chorus of aunts and uncles and cousins, the principal from Lower

Merion—enough contacts until I felt a phone chain had been set in motion, a network of tears and stunned grief. Michele set out to tell a few neighbors, while I stood for many long minutes studying the Ken Griffey poster on Bobby's door, my hand on the knob, my thoughts lost in the thesaurus's thicket of 'death.'

8/7

A pair of long, black Hearses sat outside the church. Sweltering inside, the pews crowded with somberly dressed, fan-waving neighbors and relatives, Lower Merion faculty, two generations of ex-students, and civic group members. Having claimed the back pew, Randy used his one good hand to readjust Nate's clip-on tie. Next to them, decked out in their consignment shop best, Chris and Gus and Fred, while an already crying Lisa anchored the pew's end. Up front, Michele rubbed my neck, and beside her, last night's arrival, my father.

I watched my father framed against an arch of stained glass, and realized my old man was now really an old man, the corner past middle age turned, his scrupulous grooming and tailored suits unable to detract from his new crop of wrinkles. Yet he was still handsome in a country club sort of way, a hell of a snapshot poser, racquetball-toned body and tanning booth skin. Characteristically polite, his grief, a mourning that consisted of long sighs, his gray eyes dabbed with a monogrammed handkerchief. Bobby sat on my left, and his squeezing palm engulfed the Mousetrap rat I didn't have the heart to take.

I lowered my gaze when the sight of the deeply stained twin caskets became too much, my focus shifted to the scuffed shoes my father would no doubt give me hell for later. I sneezed, blew my nose, a reaction to an altar thick with hothouse flowers. I tried to sink into myself, become lost in the world of split screens, but there was only one feature showing today. *God's will is unfathomable*, the priest said with a snowy-headed nod toward our pew. Unfathomable, the word echoed in my mind. Unfathomable, my heart and its haunting keepsakes of unpurgable guilt and the infinite spectrum of questions beyond the realm of cool equations; unfathomable, the simple yellow hues of this world. The priest's words tangled into a knot of meaningless syllables, and I clutched Michele's hand, perhaps too hard, fearful to let go, to drift alone in an unfathomable world.

Cushiony soft, the graveside grass, and bright the sun that lit the well-kept flowers and their butterfly guardians, the greensward of swelling lawn. Sycamores lined the cemetery's twisting lane, and hidden in their leafy branches, the chickadees called—*hee-ho, hee-ho*. Squirrels rummaged among the polished headstones—signs of life everywhere!—but I couldn't deny the seed of the inevitable in my belly, the fade to black that escaped no checklist, its roots of pre-pre-pre-cancerous destruction, a violent blooming, a silent time bomb, the body's ultimate card that trumped all of mankind's vain notions, his dreams and follies, the fallacy of production and consumption. Dizzying, this ledge, the joy-erasing knowledge of the shaded pit I couldn't stop staring into.

Good Lord, my father whispered. *Are my eyes playing tricks on me?*

I followed my father's disbelieving gaze. Approaching our gathering was my mother, a bit lurching in her high heels on the sloped grass. Black hat and black sunglasses, a hint of gold around her throat. It was a scene straight out of a bad rerun, the dated sense of class I hadn't witnessed since *Dynasty* was canceled.

Hi, Aunt Alice, Bobby said with a finger-fanning wave. He nudged my arm, whispered. *It's your mom, Stan.*

The planets of my personal universe were swinging into alignment, and already dazed, I spun helplessly, trapped in their competing orbits—Michele and Bobby, my parents, the lifeless bodies of my aunt and uncle—and a mad, internal friction kindled in my belly. I was angry at this outcome of a long-dreamed-of vacation. Angry at the stale answers in the reverend's words, angry at the hollow finality that lingered in the humid air, a finality with no inkling of freedom. I baked beneath my dark suit. Sweat bathed my chest and back. *Oh,* Bobby said, his palms turned toward the heavens, and down came the sunshower. Teary beads on the coffins' beveled edges, the sun even more brilliant, the water in the air transformed into a thousand fleeting prisms.

I stared into the identical graves. From Mesopotamia to Verdun to this very moment, this has been the last stop in every man's crusade, this was the trap lowered upon him by the clattering haphazardness of circumstance. No tent shielded the mourners from the unpredicted shower, and in my mind, the gurgle of puddling rain deep in the hole overtook the reverend's words.

I was breaking again. All my projectors shutting down, the screens blank, and while I'd always thought death might bring the peace I desired, I was now left alone in the moment's harsh reality and the sight of the deep, gurgling holes. The breaking intensified, and I marveled at the fact I was still standing, my legs ignoring the crumbling I felt was betrayed by my watering eyes, my quivering lips. Like a jar of spilled ink, the black thoughts spread beyond my control. *Heaven,* the reverend said, a single, pointed reference piercing my ink-dark mind ... Heaven, the species crown's greatest hoax, and the one I wished I could believe ... a dirt hole, a fade to black, the period of our breathing moments … the rain ended, a mist beneath the distant trees and the sunshine brilliant, brilliant … a flower laid on each casket and the squeak of a turning crank … the caskets lowered, lowered … Mousetrap, I whispered.

I went to my mother. Michele cried softly, taking the supporting arm my father offered. Bobby wandered off to talk with his group home friends. A gauntlet of condolences followed me, gentle words and handshakes that rolled off like water beads on polished wood, my attention limited to my mother's waiting gaze. She lowered her sunglasses, revealing puffy eyes. Dreamlike, my teetering walk, the deep focus centered on a woman I feared I was more alike than I'd ever admit. If death was as close as this, a miscalculation, a faulty brake, an inhaled microbe, then what really mattered? The steps I was taking now could just as easily walk me off a rooftop, a plunge into the cool equations that had once again flexed their muscles and proven their stranglehold upon the world.

I'm so sorry, darling, my mother said, air kissing my cheek.

Afterwards, a gathering at the house. Family and neighbors, co-workers, a network of bloodshot eyes. Drinks were served, my father the default bartender, the first rounds gulped with all the grace of parched marathon runners, and the ensuing buzz lightened the mood. Bobby, seemingly uninterested in playing the role of devastated son, entertained his Pittsburgh cousins with factory-voiced stories of butterfly clouds and being a best man, and unfortunately for me, Bobby wasn't the only one slipping back into character.

How easy it was for my parents to remember their uglier selves, the trading of snipes; my mother telling my cousin that she had retaken her maiden name, the information broadcast in a tone guaranteed to be heard by my father. The only thing they agreed upon was their indignation over not being invited to my wedding. Too familiar, the heated exchanges in whispered tones, another absurd Mobius strip of accusations and barbs, a rehashing of arguments begun decades ago. Desperate to escape, I slid back the patio door and stepped outside. From the street came the calls of bike-riding children, voices fading as they pedaled off. Next door, barely visible over the straggle-topped hedges I should cut, Chappie barked at Mr. L's shut back door.

Tears, a sucker gush, my breaking no longer internal. Tears that burned hot, that left me gasping like the floundering swimmer I was. I stormed from the shaded patio and into the wilting sunshine. Blinding, the glittering sunplay on pool water. Bark, bark, bark, the endless soundtrack of my summer (along with Bobby's *Stan! Stan, what're you doing?*). The nearest thing I found to fill my hand was a gleaming section of the skimmer rod, and reaching back with my best shortstop's form, I launched it with a curse toward the joke of a dog. The rod cut silver, whooshing arcs through the sky, and landed with a tumble on Mr. L's porch stairs. Chappie took a brief respite, sniffed the rod's rubber end, and resumed his barking.

Swim trunks and towel in hand, Bobby slid back the patio door. His bare feet protruded from the cuffs of his dark slacks. His plan—to change in the shed, his bedroom claimed by a napping infant. I squeezed Bobby's solid arm. I wanted to scream, to tell him his parents were fucking dead, didn't he understand? I wanted to shake him until a hint of comprehension lit his vapid eyes, but instead, my tears came even harder.

Oh, Stan. Bobby hugged me, squeezing the breath from my lungs. *Everything's going to be OK.*

8/10

Breakfast the next morning, and my parents were already delving into their dramatics, each seizing their opportunity to pull me aside and detail the barbarities they'd suffered at the hands of the other during the last twenty-four hours. At the breakfast table, Bobby spooned cereal to his never-closed mouth, while Michele had turned her back to the proceedings, water rushing as she rinsed the breakfast dishes. My mother stood at the opened patio door, her body inside save the hand holding a long menthol cigarette, her exhales—usually a smoke signal form of emphatic punctuation—blown out into the early morning heat. My father's hand clawed through the smoke that wafted into the kitchen.

Amazing, this genetic soup beneath my skin, the alleles from two warring camps that filled my Punnett squares. On and on they bickered, her smoking and his grooming, their polar-opposite politics, both of them blind to their similarities, their flare for grand, hollow gestures, their strange hybrid mix of being simultaneously over-sensitive and blindly callous.

We were a group of five who took three separate cars to the lawyer's office for the reading of the will, a dramatic scene culled from the lexicon of movie clichés, the proceedings made necessary by my failure to return my aunt's phone call last spring and provide a solid *yes* to her request to be executor. Upon hearing the news, my father shook his head in shamed disappointment. Fidgety, Bobby's lacing fingers, a chubby, fumbling dance, and the leather chair squeaked beneath his shifting bulk. Beside him, Michele nodded politely as the lawyer droned through the will's particulars of heirlooms and financial holdings, silver settings and coin collections, the trust arrangements and placement options for

Bobby, his power of attorney split between my father and me. Next to me, my perfect-postured father in his razor-creased Armani suit, not a misplaced strand in his gelled-back salt-and-pepper hair, and next to him, my mother, whose gaze through the sun-streaked window hinted at her own plans for escape, and in my eyes, she was already deteriorating into static, her features vague and snowy.

On the lawyer's desk, an autographed baseball encased in plastic. Bobby leaned forward, nudged the ball's stand. I guided Bobby's inquisitive fingers away from the ball. Leaning over, I whispered a promise we'd have a catch when we got home. And then, another sucker punch, one that caught me flush and hard and knocked my last, microscopic hopes for heavenly retribution on their collective asses. I was now the owner of my aunt and uncle's house.

After asking the lawyer to repeat his last sentence, I sank back in my seat. On he went, citing insurance policies, a scholarship fund for their old high school, a donation to Bobby's group home. They even left thousand-dollar chunks to public TV! the SPCA! Head Start! the Adopt-A-Highway program! Their will wasn't just a document, it was a fucking masterpiece of finality. Before we left, I deliberately wedged my wallet in my chair's cushions, its retrieval an excuse to return solo to the office, where I asked a pair of awkward, stammering questions about the legalities of annulments. Smooth.

In the brutally sunny parking lot, we parted ways. Bobby's sloppy hug ruined my mother's air kiss, her ruby red mark smeared on his cheek. *Be good, honey*, she said to me as she climbed into her bug-like yellow sports car, and in a tire-chirping instant, she disappeared again, the Lone Ranger of my abandonment. My father left, too, his silver BMW's alarm beeping with a button push, an already delayed business trip to Hartford cited before he sealed himself behind his smoke-black windows. On the ride home, Bobby went on about the baseball, its signatures and faded leather. Does he really understand what's happening?

Pulling into the driveway, I heard my aunt and uncle's bon voyage voices, words thin and whispery ... or was it the rustle of leaves? My aunt's blooming garden seemed brighter this morning, the brickwork of my uncle's front walkway more intricate. And now, after a childhood of wishing this was my home ... it was ... but the emotional payoff I'd expected had been gutted by cool equations, the guest star unsure of his motivation, knowing he should be thankful but only feeling a charlatan's shame, an intruder's sense of unwelcome.

8/11

One last call from Elaine, this one to say sorry—sorry about my aunt and uncle, sorry about her harassing calls, sorry, sorry, sorry for everything. I told her about marrying Michele, and after a moment, she offered best wishes. She said she wanted to love me, or rather, she wanted to be loved in return. She said happiness seemed so far away sometimes, like something that only happens on TV, but sometimes, when we were together, she thought she was happy ... or at least she could fool herself into thinking she was.

All I could do was echo her words—sorry, sorry, sorry.

8/14

I sat alone on the deck outside my (my!) bedroom. Bobby asleep, back on first shift, thank God, yet my opinion of Phil had softened again, this time due to the barely legible condolence card he and the other second-shifters sent. Lovely, this view, the pool lights off and a deep-shadow night, the scents of honeysuckle and the damp leaves waiting to be cleared from the gutters. How fluid it all seemed, the rich details of this life rushing past me … and the bigger details in flux too, my aunt and uncle, my parents, my apartment-hopping bachelor days, all gone, each in their own way. Yet this scene remains fixed, its reality and solidness assured by its endless play on my split screens, and below me, the ghosts crouch in the bushes…

Chappie barked, a restless silhouette beneath Mr. L's back porch light, and if I couldn't admit my secrets to a therapist or the woman I loved, let me at least come clean to myself. Back then, back then … I was afraid of Mr. L, afraid and fascinated in much the same way little boys are fascinated by train tracks and junkyards and gory pictures. *He's just widowed*, my aunt would say, but what did that mean to a pair of ten-year-olds who only wanted their errant baseball returned from its unlucky, foul-ball flight into Mr. L's prized tomatoes? We were too young or too selfish or too stupid to understand how our screams and pool splashes made his widower's house seem emptier still. Raiding his garden was Bobby's idea, a fitting retribution for our kidnapped ball, our harvest of his cherry tomatoes the perfect, splattering projectiles we'd use to decorate his car and shed. On a humid sleepover night, Bobby and I crept out beneath a hazy crescent moon and picked our ripening ammunition, the tiny red spheres piled to overspilling in our baseball caps.

Mr. L's porch light came on, and we froze, jungle-hidden among the sunflowers and staked vines. Cricket calls vibrated through the dark. My chest tightened, fearing capture, or worse, banishment from my aunt and uncle's. Bobby bolted without warning, and I scrambled after him. Tomatoes rained from our hats, and the pulpy squishing beneath my bare feet made me slip more than once. Still, I was faster, and I passed Bobby as we neared the pool, but with a ripping yank of my T-shirt, Bobby—never one for fair play—pulled me back long enough to charge ahead.

Who's there? Mr. L called. A flashlight beam passed over his birdbath and clay-potted geraniums, his brick barbecue pit and empty clothesline. Bobby laughed, the winner once again headed for the safety of his unappreciated starring role, headed for the house with a pool and full bookshelves, a sanctuary where there was always a mother to bring him juice and clean towels, where there was a father who knew the names of constellations and who never forgot to pick up his boy after practice. I accelerated, a shortstop's base-stealing sprint. Tears blurred my vision, and my heart thudded with rage, my gut twisted in ugly knots, the whole sorry escapade Bobby's idea, but now I was certain to be the one caught. The pool lights were dark, the sky starless, Mr. L's flashlight shine snared in the tangles of his yard, yet I had no trouble seeing my hands reaching out to shove Bobby's back, a scene painted in the night's muted palette, silvers and blues, grays and blacks. And even more haunting, the imagined view from the deck where I now stood, Bobby's mother many years before her fiery death rushing out in her nightclothes and spotting the two shadowy figures below, the larger one floating, unmoving limbs outstretched, the other, an obvious non-swimmer, floundering beneath the diving board. The boy splashed, swallowed choking mouthfuls of chlorinated water between screams—

Michele stepped out to join me. She was in true summer mode

now, her latent California girl look, white tank top and khaki shorts, tanned feet in her dollar-store, pink flip-flops. How pretty she looked, but when she joined me at the deck's railing, my scarred knees turned watery, and the next words that left my mouth escaped before I could even contemplate their impact, their utterance just the latest unthinking act in a lifetime bursting with thoughtlessness.

The phone calls, I said, my voice arid and thin, they've been from a woman I was sleeping with.

And there it was, the unpretty truth for a pretty woman, a fact I coughed up with all the grace of a bone dislodged from a choking victim's throat. We stared at each other, each dumbfounded and dazed. How was I even standing? How was she still standing? And why, exactly, was I coming forward now? Maybe I wanted her to open her eyes and finally recognize the man I saw in the mirror every morning. Perhaps the dungeon of my thoughts already had its own 800-pound gorilla and it didn't need any company. Perhaps I told her the sordid truth because it would make me feel better, the ultimate, trumping proof of my selfish nature.

The poor girl slumped onto a chair. Once again, I had beaten down an opponent. Quiet ... crickets ... the rattling hum of Mr. L's air conditioner, Chappie's bark-bark-bark. There I stood, in a setting of past horrors and covetous desires and present-tense pain. Here was the virgin territory of Type-C, the last solid thing in my life about to be swept away on a foolish tide I had created. Gradually, she came around, and I answered her questions, sparing no details but the most shameful and graphic. I told her it meant nothing, and she scoffed, asking how could I risk her happiness and trust for nothing. To which I could only say my now sickeningly familiar puppet-man's refrain—sorry, sorry, sorry. I tried to put my arm around her, but she wriggled free, and now, in a heartbreaking closeup, she fixed her watery blue eyes on me. In my head, no words to close the distance, no dramatic encounters to emulate on my split screen, only the spinning hiss of unthreaded projectors, the wasteland hues of projected white. I followed her through the house, just wanting to be near her, to be there in case she cared enough to lash out at me with the reassuring venom of Type-A. Without a good-bye, she left, the front door slammed, her car bucking angrily out of the driveway, the headlights sweeping over me. Back inside, the silent shouts of index cards bombarded me, words spoken in voices I'd never hear again.

A long-awaited reunion, the easy fit of the Lilliputian key in the lock of my uncle's trunk. Too much, the banality of cool equations, the thought of hurting Michele and betraying the mysterious gems she saw in me, and here in my hand, cast in cool, sleek metal, lay the sentence-ending period to my pointless, rambling days.

Downstairs, I gulped sips of my uncle's bourbon, my hand shaking as I raised the glass to my lips and used the bitter liquid to swallow back pill after pill. I slid the World War I picture book off the shelf. Nightmarish, the gore, the intersection of tender flesh and the killing products of man's species crown. In the midst of the carnage along the Marne, I saw the twisted hull of the Luxury Land Cruiser … in the hell of Ypres, I pictured Bobby's pool-sprawled form among the heap of bloated, gray bodies.

I rose and traced my finger over the mosaic of postcards. Each of them a piece of a realized dream, each containing the thrill of escape but also the subtle desire to return home. I peeled one off. *You can't imagine how truly immense Hoover Dam really is until you've stood upon it. TV doesn't do it justice. Listen to Stan, Bobby,* *and be good. Love to all.* I yanked down another card, then another, and with angry swipes, down tumbled whole swathes, the pretty scenes fluttering to the floor.

I slumped down to the kitchen table and took a greedy, shuddering bottle swig. Another reunion, the gun in my palm, the puzzle's final piece, the guest star's climatic scene. Even the love of a good woman couldn't halt the inward lure that kept dragging me back to the lies and hurt I'd authored. I laid the barrel against my fevered cheek and thought perhaps this was the true feeling of finality, hard-edged and cool, solid and blunt and unapologetic. I teetered, graveside-woozy, the barrel pressed against the bridge of my nose, my hands shaky and wet. Dark, yet the gun's chrome found the faintest of lights. I thought of a walk across cemetery grass and a step off a bridge, a push in the back, a highway accident—the slim margins of life, the razor edges which cut so deeply—and here I was again, unsure of my lines in a scene that made all the difference.

A scratching came from the patio door, and my already revving pulse torqued higher. I thought of glasscutters and violent break-ins, neighbors bound and beaten, Bobby sleeping in his bed. The scraping continued, a mystery on the other side of the drawn curtains.

Rare, this opportunity to hear my own breathing, the scuba diver sounds. The gun's barrel danced a jittery step. I aimed toward the handle, a belly shot. The scratching distant now, as if I'd plugged my ears with cotton.

I lowered the barrel. Knee-high, enough to wound, but not kill. Thin, thin, the curtains, the slim margin between two lives. With a magnificent, unexpected blast, the gun fired. My hand jerked back, the front legs of my kitchen chair rocking off the floor. A spill of glass. The curtain breathed in and out of the jagged break, and moments later, the sound still filled the room, a fireworks-loud echo beneath my ribs. A mistake, so quick I was just now recognizing it as such, a slip, a sweat-drenched spasm.

Stan? Bobby called groggily.

The gun locked in my grip, my elbow braced against my heaving belly, I pulled back the curtain. Sprawled on a twinkling glass bed lay a motionless Chappie, the blood midnight dark on the concrete, his tiny rodent mouth opened as if he'd died trying to squeak out one last closed-door bark.

Stan! I'm scared!

I called up the steps that all was well, I'd dropped something and he should go back to sleep.

Three times I misdialed, my fingers crippled by nerves and surging chemicals. I crouched in the open patio door, my shoulder leaning against the door jamb. A police siren wailed in the distance. Michele answered at her apartment, and I hurriedly talked her out of hanging up with a quick confession of shooting Chappie. I knelt on the glass, stroked the poor thing's side and began telling another story, the one of how I'd pushed Bobby all those years ago.

8/17

A tinted sunglasses world, the chlorine scratchy in my throat. Magnificent sunshine freckled the blue pool surface. A buoyant lounge chair for the shallow-ender and a holder for his beer. I let my hand hang, and soothing, the cool water on knuckles raw once again, this time from scrubbing patio concrete, labors that couldn't totally erase the puddle of Chappie blood. The glass man had come and gone, Michele and Mr. L off to the pound to find Chappie 2. I haven't left the house in days, but the dog pound was Michele's second excursion of the afternoon, her first to the pawn shop, my uncle's gun now officially in hock. With Bobby back on first shift, I figured I had at least another hour of hermit peace.

An unanchored perspective, the minutes sliding past. The rope that separated the shallow end from the deep lay coiled upon the pool's apron. A yellow butterfly inspected a nearby patch of honeysuckle. Beside the honeysuckle, the garbage cans waiting to be hauled away, bags weighted by glass and bloody rags.

The sun's warmth sank into my chest, my network of white scars. Foolish, the belief that one act could whitewash a man's past. Marriage could no more save me than a handful of pills, and my confession to Michele that I had pushed Bobby hadn't unburdened my soul the way I'd hoped it would. I drifted to the center of the pool, a slow spin, a summer's panorama, trees and green hedges, house and garage and shed, and everything I saw, this setting I'd once yearned for so greatly, was now mine.

My hands doggie paddling, I swung the raft toward the house. With a toegrab, I grasped the diving board and anchored my drifting. Michele's potted impatiens bloomed above on the deck. We've spent many hours on the deck these past few nights. We sip beer, pass a joint (but after discovering me bleary and mush mouthed the night of the shooting, she flushed the last of my pills), and beneath the star tapestry we talk about fidelity and commitment, secrets and lies and forgiveness. Wholeness, Michele contends, comes from accepting one's circumstances, not resisting them, and that often within the very things we fight awaits our salvation.

With barely a splash, I slid off the raft. A dead man's float, arms and legs outstretched, and I stared down through the chlorinated blue. Loud, my heartbeat, the mechanical rhythm of my days, the biologist's bottom line. I studied the submerged portions of the raft, the shiny, wavering image of the deep-end ladder, and I wondered if I was man enough to accept my circumstances. A slow trail of exhaled bubbles tickled my cheek, the last pockets of oxygen purged from my lungs, and less buoyed, I felt the pull of the bottom.

A massive splash engulfed me. In an instant, my world turned tumultuous, a blizzard of bubbles; vague, grasping shapes; swallowed water and a shallow ender's panicked clawing. I was turned around, and when my face resurfaced, I sucked in gulps of warm summer air, only now I was being choked, an arm under my chin as I was tugged across the pool. When we reached the shallows, I found my footing and wriggled free.

Stan! Bobby gasped. *Are you OK?* He stood in soaking wet work clothes, his tin lunch pail bobbing in the diving board shadow.

I tried to respond, but all I could do was cough, spit water through my nose and mouth. Bobby pounded my shoulder with a series of bone-rattling slaps. *Mom always said you shouldn't go in the deep end, Stan. See what happens when you don't listen?*

8/21

A half-struck set, Bobby's bedroom, boxes on the floor and in the one nearest my feet, Bobby's collection of Little League trophies, the silver and gold statues poking out to examine their chaotic surroundings. Over the course of the next week or two, Bobby will relocate to the group home, a move he seems uncharacteristically excited about, and tonight, I was going with him, a shared room, a summer sleepover, *Just the way we did when we were kids*, Bobby said. He was keyed up, jumpy, finger-twisting and drag-foot pacing, his wet hair just beginning to curl after his post-work swim.

Michele entered the room. A flowered bikini top, the frayed white ends of her cutoffs tickling her thighs. Tense, some moments between the two of us, the mistrust and the shame . . . yet she'd somehow managed to see beyond all that, and her belief in the better me had inspired me to start believing as well. Bobby zipped up his bag, patted its bulging side. *I've got a surprise for Stan tonight,* he said, a factory-whisper aside to Michele.

Dinner at the group home. Music on the stereo, oldies, loud enough to be heard from the porch, and framed in the kitchen doorway, Nate crooned into a spatula microphone, *Baby love, my baby love.* A pull on my hand no longer caused me to flinch, and I looked down to find I'd been claimed once again by Chris, who led me into the dining room. *Bob-BEE!* Nate shrieked into the spatula. *We're having pork chops!*

Lisa and Randy orchestrated the dining room bustle. Fred waved a meek hello as he set the plates. Chris lurched around the table on stunted legs, counting out silverware and napkins. Nate chopped tomatoes, and Bobby tossed the salad, while Randy supervised Gus's cooking of pork chops and French fries.

And somehow, it all came together. His tongue clamped in the corner of his mouth, black-framed glasses sliding down his flat nose, Gus set the pork chop tray beside the vase of cut flowers from Lisa's garden. Nate followed with the French fries, Bobby with the salad. *Right here, Stan,* Bobby said, slapping the seat beside him. As I picked up my napkin, Bobby nudged me. Looking up, I realized mine were the only hands not clasped in prayer.

It was Fred's turn to say grace, and his eyes squeezed shut in an expression of excruciating concentration. There was a long pause, a silence punctuated by Gus's nasal rasping. *Thank you, God, for our food and our house…*

I scanned the faces, the bowed heads, the intentness on the moment and the focus of child-like faith.

… and thank you, God, for our guests, and thank you for our food—

You already said food, Nate interrupted.

OK, Fred said. *Amen, then.*

Amen, the table echoed.

After dinner, dish brigade, a bit of TV-watching followed by driveway basketball. No need for rules here, the double-palm slaps, the underhanded heaves that ricocheted wildly off the backboard. Notions of team distinctions quickly faded, and soon it was all for one, one for all, putting the ball in the hoop our common goal, and on the rare occasions it happened, there were cheers from everyone. Lisa and Randy sat on the back porch, talking to one of their supervisors, while I oversaw the athletics and tried my best to keep order. I encouraged Nate and Gus despite their lack of aim, passed the ball to Fred and Chris, who'd retreated shyly from the beneath-the-basket fray.

After the game, the evening wind-down began. Showers were taken, medicines handed out, pajamas plucked warm from the dryer. The announcement of ten p.m. bedtime was met with groans when the ball game was turned off in mid-inning, the protest followed by a gridlock of toothbrushing at the bathroom sink. In the hallway, calls of *Goodnight*, Nate's hyper exclamations, Gus's deep baritone. Bobby's room was the small one at the end of the hall. I laid a sleeping bag across the floor and prayed Bobby wouldn't stomp on me during a half-asleep bathroom trip. A lamp whose shade featured images of cowboys atop bucking broncos sat on the nightstand.

Ready for the surprise? Bobby asked. He grinned and pulled *Mousetrap* out of the bag. We played . . . or rather, we built, me assuming the role of an operating room nurse handing over the parts Bobby requested. When we were done, he held up the ball. *Ready?*

With a clunk, the ball dropped, a silvery path down the chutes, the triggered chain of barely related actions, a kicked bucket, a sprung high diver ... but tonight, the chaos came to an unclimatic halt. A break in the chain, a miscalculation, the mouse left untrapped.

So what was left for us to do but to try, try again, and piece by plastic piece, we disassembled our creation. And as we worked, I remembered a promise I'd made to Bobby's mother at summer's start, and with a throat-clearing hack, I launched into my masturbation talk. I thought I'd latched onto a good simile when I compared it to *Mousetrap*. Sure, Bobby said with a wide smile, he'd like to play *Mousetrap* every night for the rest of his life.

No you wouldn't, I reasoned, you'd get tired of it if you played every night. It wouldn't be special anymore. I scoured for an outlet for his Batman night-light as he put on his boxers. *Turn around, Stan*, he said. He stomped his foot when I balked. The light on the bedside table jiggled.

I turned, but in the dresser mirror, I spied on my cousin. Digging deep into his gym bag, Bobby produced his mother's apron, the one patterned with dancing cartoon cows. Oh, the wonderful, heartbreaking, perplexing absurdity of this life! For a moment, he touched the material against his chin before stuffing it into his pillowcase.

With a ruffle of sheets, Bobby nestled into the bed. A faint white and black swatch of apron peeked out of the pillowcase. A click and the lamp died, the night-light an annoying beacon that shone in my eyes. Through the floor, I felt the vibration of feet, the rattle of water pipes. How distant the ceiling appeared from here. Long shadows cast by the night-light crept up the walls.

The empty space above me pressed upon my chest like a crushing weight, and for the first time, I spoke to Bobby about the night of his accident, filling in the gaps he'd never remember, how I'd pushed him, yes, but I never wanted to hurt him, and if I could, I'd go back and gladly take his pain and suffering upon myself.

He was silent for a moment, then said, *It's OK, Stan.* And after a bit, he started to laugh, guffawing snorts that made his bed shake.

What's so funny? I asked

Bobby leaned over the edge of the bed. In the night-light shine, monster shadows crossed his grinning face. *I was thinking about how you looked the other day when I saved you in the pool. I'm going to have to talk with Michele.* He settled back into bed. *Somebody's going to have to teach you how to swim some day.*

8/26

Summer's countdown of Saturdays continues toward its inevitable end. Today was the group home softball tournament in Fairmont Park. A cloudless day, the sun unbothered and bright, and before the first pitch, I sped off to a nearby convenience store and bought cheap sunglasses which I handed out to Bobby and the others. Four teams had claimed the cluster of fields along the river, four parallel universes of chaos and childish tears, of quick tempers and even swifter forgiveness. The various group home leaders urged their charges to drink water, and between innings, they lathered on tubefuls of coconut-scented sunscreen. Bobby's team sported carnation-red T-shirts, ELM STREET PHILS silk-screened on the front, Michele's creation, a labor that had kept her up half the night.

The games began with handshakes and ended with hugs. Sandwiched between were innings of tantrums and accomplishments, slapstick comedy and heart-rending drama. Nate failed to score the winning run in the first game when he backtracked from third to retrieve his dropped sunglasses. Chris wandered off from left field to watch the scullers' long boats row down the river. Tina, who'd abandoned her ponytail to chew the damp, stretched neck of her T-shirt, snared a line drive, tagged a runner on his way to second, and then, smiling as Randy and I yelled deliriously, stepped onto the bag to complete an unassisted triple play. Bobby hammered a home run so far it was accidentally put into play on an adjoining field. Final tally, one loss and two wins, and a double trophy presentation for most improved team and the tournament's most coveted prize, best sportsmanship.

Afterward, the team returned to our house. *Pool par-TEE!* Nate piped. The trophies, each glimmering in the late day sun, were displayed on the picnic table alongside the chips and pretzels. Barbecue smoke stung my eyes, burgers and dogs and the smell of charcoal, and me, the grilling man of the house. A nibble on my shoelace, and I gazed down on Sparky, Mr. Lehman's new shin-high mutt. The dog could chew all the laces he wanted because he'd proven himself a non-barker, my prayers of sleepless nights answered.

The pool party ruckus escalated. Bobby showed off with board-twanging dives that rocketed geysers high into the air, a rainstorm over the pool apron and poor Sparky, even a few sizzling drops for the grill. Between splashing, unsure strokes, Nate stopped to pull up the Hawaiian trunks that slid down his bony hips. Carrie latched onto a kickboard with white-knuckled determination. In her bathing cap and goggles, Jane resembled a WWI flying ace. Chris and Fred sat silently poolside, their dangling feet kicking in the water, smiling and shaking their heads when Lisa tried to coax them in. The whole gang cheered when Sparky leapt from the diving board. Hooray!

And add one more accomplishment to an afternoon of victories—my very un-MELCO-like job offer to be the new recreational coordinator for the region's group homes. Go figure! Ahead wait the rewards of shitty pay and hopeful fulfillment as I organize seasons of flag football, street hockey, and basketball. The sports world may never be the same. Michele says she couldn't be prouder.

In the pool Bobby cradled Chris's tiny brown frame. Turning gently, his torso stirring ripples, Bobby guided his housemate across the water's surface. *You're doing good!* Bobby yelled. Chris, his eyes squeezed shut, mimicked the mechanics of swimming, his stunted feet kicking wildly.

Bobby climbed out, and through the barbecue's haze of smoke and rising heat, I watched Michele drape a towel over his wet shoulders. I still ache with the hurt I've brought them both, a pain more stubborn than Chappie blood, its mark indelible and dark. No way to erase the past, and what else can I do but coat it with the faint whitewash of everyday kindness, hoping some day I can blot it out completely?

Gus and Bobby pushed through the border rhododendrons with Mr. L's picnic table. Whoops sprung from the house windows as the guests toweled off and changed into dry clothes. Places were taken, legs squeezed beneath the table, a round of poking and nudging and giggling before grace. Corn on the cob was served, Mr. L's red potato salad, everyone wearing the sunglasses I'd bought earlier, the picnic table scene mirrored in their green lenses. Tiki lanterns flickered, the bugs kept at bay. Twice, I caught Jane breaking off bits of hot dog and secretly slipping them to Sparky, who'd camped himself by her side.

After dinner, a little show on the patio beneath the bedroom deck. Lisa strummed a guitar, and by the applause and airy whistles, I guessed the tune was a group home favorite. It was one of those rambling songs, a story of a traveling hobo, plenty of audience improvisation that ensured each verse ran longer than the one before. Bobby disappeared for a moment before returning with a broken mop handle and one of his mother's old housekeeping babushkas.

Help me tie this, OK Stan? he asked.

Bobby laid out the red cloth and filled it with the treasures from his pockets—loose change, a movie ticket stub, a stick of gum, tissues both used and clean. I knotted the corners and through the power of a simple prop, Bobby was transformed into a regular vagabond. With the mop handle shouldered like a rifle, he paraded around the pool, a pied piper who quickly had the others in tow, Jane and Gus, Nate and Chris and Tina, the guitar strumming Lisa and silent Fred, Randy with his burdensome cast, even Mr. L and his toenail-clacking Sparky.

Come on, Michele said, pulling me from the table. *This is the kind of thing recreational coordinators live for.*

We joined the line's rear, and yes, I even forced myself to clap and sing along. The lock-step amusement of the mob eluded me, but I still tried, my claps timed with theirs, my lips mouthing the words. Near the deep end, I paused and fished out the babushka that had fallen unnoticed from Bobby's pole. The change gathered near the drain, the tissues and ticket stubs floating along, the gum temporarily suspended in-between on its slow ride to the bottom. Lonely sometimes, the trails I've chosen, and heavy, the load I've carried, and perhaps the best way to make the journey manageable was to fill my bundle with good things—a sense of hope, a desire to understand. Perhaps these were the true jewels of the species crown. With a twist, I wrung out the babushka and hurry-stepped to rejoin the dancing line.

about the author

CURTIS SMITH is the author of the novel *An Unadorned Life* and two collections of short-short stories from March Street Press, *Placing Ourselves Among the Living* and *In the Jukebox Light*. His stories and essays have appeared in over fifty literary journals and anthologies including *American Literary Review, Mid-American Review, Cutbank, Bellingham Review, Passages North, Hobart, Lake Effect, South Dakota Review, Greensboro Review, Mississippi Review, North Dakota Quarterly,* and *West Branch*. His work has been cited by *The Best American Short Stories, The Best American Mystery Stories* and *The Best American Spiritual Writing*. He received an MFA in Fiction from Vermont College in 1996. He lives and works in Pennsylvania with his wife, Michele, and son, Evan. Visit Curtis online at www.curtisjsmith.com.

about the cover artist

MICHELE SMITH has created collages and greeting cards. She is currently working with textile designs. Her work can be seen at www.smithandsmedley.com.

www.ingramcontent.com/pod-product-compliance
Lightning Source LLC
Chambersburg PA
CBHW031226020726
47499CB00002B/661